DAUGHTER OF THE RED DAWN

The Lost Kingdom of Fallada Book 1

ALICIA MICHAELS

Snowy
Wings
PUBLISHING

DAUGHTER OF THE RED DAWN: The Lost Kingdom of Fallada Book 1, 2nd
Edition
Copyright 2012, 2020 Alicia Michaels

Published by Snowy Wings Publishing
P.O. Box 1035
Turner, OR 97392, USA
www.snowywingspublishing.com

Cover design by Kate Cowan, Broken Arrow Designs
Edited by Melissa Ringsted, There For You Editing

ISBN: 978-1-948661-95-9

Dedicated to:
_____

Mary Ann Stephens, for introducing me to the wonderful world of fantasy fiction by sending me a box set of The Chronicles of Narnia when I was a kid. Because of your encouragement regarding reading and education, I became a lover of books and the written word. When most aunts gave their nieces toys as gifts, you always gave me books and I will always remember you for that.

Prologue

These are dark times in the land of Fallada, and I fear they will only continue to grow darker. When we erected the wall between our realm and the world of man, we could never have foreseen this. Had I known, I would have destroyed the evil that is Eranna when I had the chance. But alas, dear friend, she has grown too powerful and now only the return of those we have lost will even the score.

Forgive me for allowing my thoughts to run away with me when we've only just met. My name is Adrah and I am queen of the Fae folk of Fallada. I have lived for thousands of years, and during that time I watched our world fall into utter ruin.

We lived in harmony with man once; it was such a wonderful and peaceful time. Endroth, our great high king, was the perfect ruler. Having spent much time with humans as well as his own people, he understood both worlds well. All he ever wanted was for both lands to exist together in peace, and for a time they did. However, this could not last, as the world of men began to change and evolve. Their greed and violent nature turned them into our enemies instead of our friends, and we soon found ourselves in the midst of an unwanted war.

King Endroth's heart was heavy at the thought of obliterating the world of men. While it was certainly within the power of the people of Goldun, the northern region of Fallada where Faeries dwell, we were in agreement with Endroth that it went against our morals to do such a thing. We are a peaceful people, and wanted nothing to do with the destructive and corrupted legacy of mankind.

And so, it was with a heavy heart that King Endroth charged me with a most monumental task. Instead of going to war with man, we settled on separating ourselves from them forever. For months we stood on the border between our world and theirs, our arms outstretched as we used our magic to create the enchanted wall that now bars them from entering, or even seeing, Fallada. As if that had not been hard enough, we were forced to strike our history from their memory, ensuring that contact between us could never again be achieved. This occurred in the year of 1868.

My friend, I would love to tell you that this is the end of my story. I would love to tell you that Fallada continued on in peace, and that our troubles were no more, but it is not so. Not long after the wall was erected, the stirrings of evil echoed through the west. Queen Eranna of the icy region of Mollac was its cause.

Eranna has ever been discontent with her lot in life. Being queen of Mollac was never enough for her, and she fancied herself above those who ruled the other three corners of Fallada, including myself.

She is, I'll admit, the most beautiful woman in all of Fallada, and well she knows it. Her vanity and discontent are, I believe, what drove her to an interest in black magic. It began innocently enough, for she only wanted to learn how to keep her youth and beauty. While the royals of Fallada are not immortal, as the Fae are, they have long life reaching at least five to six hundred years. This was not enough for Eranna, and so began a life of covetousness. Once youth and beauty were attained, Eranna began dabbling in spells and witchcraft. She also spent years learning to manipulate and bring others under her will.

She was not yet strong enough to overcome the mind of King Endroth, who she had always wished would take her for a wife after her own husband died of suspicious causes. The great kingd mourned the loss of his first wife and had vowed not to take another. In her conceit, Eranna thought her beauty would be enough to turn the king's head, but alas it was not. By then Eranna's goal was clear; she wanted ultimate power and control. She wanted to be queen of all Fallada.

Forgive me, I am running away from the point once again, aren't I? We Fae tend to take our time with things, as we are immortal and have all the time in the world to spare. But you have not, have you? You wish to know what this darkness is that I spoke of in the great land I call home. Very well, I shall tell you.

Eranna wanted the high throne, and she wanted the adoration and worship of every man, woman, and child in Fallada as well as the human world. Her mind became more and more deluded every year she spent practicing the dark arts, until eventually she was flung completely into madness. She would not rest until Fallada, and Earth, were hers.

When Endroth gathered the kings and queens of every region of Fallada to his council, Eranna was the most vocal against the building of the enchanted wall.

"We need only to demonstrate our superiority over them!" she'd exclaimed. "We are strong enough to rule them, to make them our eternal slaves!"

King Endroth would hear none of it, though, and the wall was erected.

Eranna retreated into the west quietly, seemingly defeated. I am ashamed to say I did not see her next move coming. All my strength and power were so focused upon building the wall, that I did not keep a watchful eye on her corner of the kingdom, which is one of my many duties as the Fae queen. What I did not see was that Eranna had taken Witches and Sorcerers unto her and was gathering power. The vain woman wanted no barrier between herself and her ambitions; she would not tolerate any perceived threat to her greatness.

Not long after the wall had been constructed, Eranna gathered all of Fallada's princesses—there are seven in all—and sent them away into the world of men. Two there were from her own home of Mollac, one of them birthed from her own womb. Two more each were taken from the southern desert region, Damu, and the eastern underwater kingdom of Zenun. The seventh was the only daughter of King Endroth and heir to the throne of Fallada. Not only were these children a threat to Eranna because of their youth and beauty; they were a threat to her coveted power as well.

Never has such a tragedy befallen Fallada; seven young princesses, lost to us forever. King Endroth fell into a state of mourning so severe, I fear he will never come out of it. The four regions have become distrustful of one another, each blaming the other for the loss of the royal daughters. Endroth could put an end to all if he would only make the effort, but you must understand that his sadness is great. It has fallen to me to see to the welfare of Fallada. The other rulers turn to me for guidance and counsel; alas, there is only so much I can do.

It is because of this that I have turned to the scribes known as the Brothers Grimm. Perhaps you've heard of them and their fantastic tales? Of course I am acquainted with them. Before the walls were built, they spent almost all their time in Fallada, scribbling down tales of their encounters within our borders. It was their choice to remain in our land when the walls were built. King Endroth allowed this because he had quite a soft spot in his heart for the brothers, and knew their souls truly thrived within the boundaries of our great kingdom.

What have they to do with what's happening now, you ask? Well, I am just getting to that. When the princesses went missing and the eastern, western, and southern corners of Fallada fell into chaos, I took it upon myself to bring Jacob and Wilhelm to Goldun. Within the realm of the Faeries, they were each given a drink of the Elixir of Life, bestowing upon them immortality until such time as I supply them with the antidote. The men were old and feeble and I needed them alive and fresh. They alone hold the knowledge that is key to finding the girls.

You see, when we created the wall, we also created a time gap that ensured even more separation between us and the human world. While the girls were taken from Fallada in the year 1868, I have estimated that they arrived in the world of men sometime in the 1990s. The girls, in infancy when taken, range anywhere in age from sixteen to twenty-one by now, and will be hard to find.

The Brothers Grimm are as dedicated to this cause as I am. They love Fallada, and will not rest until it is returned to its former glory. For this to happen, they know as well as I, the seven lost princesses must be found and returned to their homes, and Eranna must be destroyed.

In the years since the disappearance of the girls, Eranna has grown in strength and power and has now captured King Endroth, whom she holds captive with her dark spells. She has erected a fortress impenetrable by Faeries and Fae magic and has partnered with her Witches and Sorcerers to create an army worthy of her vanity and conceit.

Now, in our darkest hour, haste is needed. I have entrusted Jacob and Wilhelm with the task of finding the lost girls.

How, you ask?

Ah, we Fae are wise, perhaps because of the amount of time we have lived. While King Endroth did not ask it of me, I took it upon myself to install a portal within the wall. It is small and impenetrable to anyone that does not have the key. I myself wear this key upon my person at all times and have not let it from my sight all of these years.

Today is the first day that I will be making use of the portal, to send the brothers on their way. As they embark upon their journey I can only hope that all my faith isn't for naught. The land of Goldun will never fall—the Fae are too powerful—but it would grieve me beyond all imagining if the rest of Fallada were lost to Eranna's evil.

And so, dear friend, we embark upon the dawn of our mission. Seven missing girls and not a clue to where any of them have been all this time. I can only keep my energies on shielding our comings and goings from the far-seeing eye of Eranna, and pray for an end to the blackness that is spreading out, even unto the far reaches of Fallada.

Chapter One

Twin Oaks, Texas

B lades of tall grass swayed in the gentle Texas spring breeze. Wildflowers in shades of yellow, red, and orange blanketed the grassy field and bluebonnets covered the landscape in patches of deep lavender. The sun blazed in a cloudless sky, and the only movement besides the swaying grass was the figure of a lone girl wading through the foliage.

Selena McKinley's coppery red hair blew around her heart-shaped face. Her whiskey brown eyes, narrowed against the sun, gleamed from behind long bangs as she moved across the abandoned field she walked through every day on her way home from school. Selena always enjoyed her walks home because they were the only time she ever had to herself. Once at home she would have to endure her grandmother's questions about school and Selena just didn't feel like talking about that. Not today, or any other day for that matter.

At school she was often alone, but not in the way she would like. The eyes of the other kids were always on her and their whispers always just loud enough for Selena to hear. It didn't matter that she kept to herself and never bothered anybody. It didn't matter that she hardly ever raised her hand in class, or called attention to herself by appearing too smart or too dumb. Her grades might be high but she didn't flaunt her intelligence, and she didn't strive to be popular.

None of that mattered, because as long as Selena could remember she'd been different from everyone else. She'd never found a place to fit in. While all the other kids seemed to fit pretty nicely into some category or other, Selena had never really found her place.

The only thing that had ever brought her solace was her spot on the track team. She was the fastest girl on the team and was always chosen to run third leg in the relay. But even her athletic abilities hadn't earned her very many friends, and Selena still found herself sitting alone at lunchtime and without dates to school dances. There was Zoe, her best friend since Kindergarten, but no one else really. Evenher teammates were standoffish around her.

It was as if they knew, just like Selena did, that something was wrong with her.

Screw them, she thought to herself as she adjusted the one strap of her messenger-style backpack and walked on. *Only a few more weeks of school and I'm done with ole Dirtpatch, USA.*

Living in such a small town only made Selena more aware of just how awkward and different she was. In a town where the kids drove tractors, wore Levi's, and listened to Trace Adkins, a girl who preferred Converse's over Cowboy boots stood out like a sore thumb.

She couldn't wait to graduate, just one week before her eighteenth birthday. Selena's earnings from her part-time job at Dairy Queen had been going into her savings account for years, and now she had more than enough to move away from Twin Oaks. She was hoping to start over in a place like Dallas or Houston, somewhere big enough for a girl like her to get lost in the crowd. With so many people around it would be difficult to feel out of place or abnormal.

A sleek apartment, a car of her own, a steady job, and the freedom to do what she wanted would be more than enough for her.

Although, she thought as she paused at the center of the field, *I will miss one thing about Twin Oaks: wide, open spaces.*

She glanced around her one last time to ensure no one was watching before taking off at a run. The grass bent beneath her sneakers and the wind whipped at her hair and filled her expanding lungs. She pumped her arms and willed her legs to go faster, barely cognizant of the blur that was Twin Oaks whizzing past her.

A flock of birds sensed her approach and scattered, frantically beating their wings to escape the whirlwind breezing through the field. When she finally skidded to a stop, Selena felt as she always did after a good run—cleansed and free. She couldn't even cut loose like that on the track, afraid that someone would know just how fast she could run and turn her into a science experiment. She wasn't foolish enough to think showing people what she could do would make them like her more. If anything, it would brand her a freak for the rest of her life.

Unless Professor X and the other X-Men decided to make an appearance and offer her a place in their crew, Selena was on her own and probably the only person in the world with such a bizarre talent. Even her grandmother, who'd raised her from infancy, didn't know the truth.

As Selena contemplated taking another lap around the field, she turned and found the lone figure of a boy standing at the edge of the meadow, which was ringed by cedar trees. Her eyes widened as she took him in from head to toe: impossibly black hair falling into his eyes, stony features, long legs, and a slender frame. In his skinny jeans, Converse sneakers, black t-shirt, and sleek sunglasses, he was unlike any other guy she'd ever seen in Twin Oaks, where Wranglers and large belt buckles were the dress code.

He raised his chin slightly in acknowledgement and Selena stood rooted to the spot, unable to move or even utter a sound as the boy stepped into the tall grass. The sun glinted off of his black hair, giving it a bluish tinge, and his dark sunglasses mirrored her reflection to her as he closed the distance between them. The grass seemed to part to make way for him, and Selena couldn't make her legs function as he approached.

He's strange, she thought as he stopped in front of her with his hands in his pockets. But strange was good. It meant that she was now one of two people that didn't belong in Twin Oaks.

"Hey," he said.

One word, but Selena couldn't help but notice the silky smooth tone of his voice. He smiled, showcasing a row of perfectly straight, white teeth. The canines were a bit on the long side, but she liked them. She also liked his pale blue eyes, which he revealed by pushing his glasses up into his hair.

"Hi," she answered back breathlessly. She tried to smile, but her lips wouldn't move. She fiddled with the strap of her backpack instead.

"I'm Titus," he said, rocking back and forth on the balls of his feet.

"Selena," she answered.

"Pretty name," he replied.

"Thanks. I like your glasses."

I like your eyes. I like your hair. I like your skin.

Selena bit back the words, embarrassed by her almost instant crush on the cute stranger.

"Are you new in town?" she asked, trying her best not to gawk at him and failing miserably. "I don't think I've ever seen you before."

"Not that new," he said with a shrug. "I've seen you around a lot, at school, on the track field, at the Dairy Queen."

Selena's eyes widened in surprise. "You have?"

He nodded, a sly smile spreading across his face. "Oh yeah. When I saw you today walking through this field I thought, 'now's the perfect chance to get to meet the prettiest girl in Twin Oaks'."

Selena couldn't help but laugh at that one. Prettiest girl in Twin Oaks? Hadn't he laid eyes on Allyson, the cheerleader with the biggest boobs a teenage girl had a right to have? Or Janelle, who's long, perfectly shaped legs had earned her the honor of being captain of the dance squad? Or what about Trisha, whose hair was that perfect shade of blonde that most girls had to buy a box of hair color to achieve?

This guy obviously didn't get out much.

Selena snorted. "Yeah right."

"It's true," he said, taking another step toward her. Selena felt her hands shaking as he reached up to stroke a lock of her straight, red hair. "Besides, you're different, and I like different."

"You must be the only guy in town that does."

He laughed. "Would you believe me if I told you that we were two of a kind? That I'm as different as you are?"

Selena frowned. "What do you mean?"

He leaned even closer, his nose nearly touching hers as his grin widened. His white teeth flashed in the sunlight, the sharp canines displayed proudly.

"I saw you," he whispered. "Running."

Selena clutched her stomach as she felt nausea welling up in her. From the expression on his face, it was obvious he didn't mean to say he'd seen her on the track at school. How could she have been so stupid? She hardly ever allowed herself the freedom to run uninhibited in broad daylight. She had thought herself alone, completely oblivious to the watching eyes of a boy named Titus.

What to do?

Titus' smile was blinding, a flash of white teeth that left her stunned while she tried to find words ... any words ... even 'please don't tell my secret and make me end up on the six o'clock news, or on a lab table with a bunch of tubes coming out of my body'.

Her mouth opened, but nothing came out. As panic gripped her, Selena could think of only one thing to do.

Run!

"HI, SWEET PEA."

"Hey, Gram."

Selena quickly breezed past her grandmother and into her bedroom. She slammed the door and leaned against it, sinking down to the floor and covering her face with her hands. Her heart pumped rapidly, sending a rush of blood through her veins that created a pulsing sound in her ears.

"Holy shit," she murmured as she fought for air.

The run from the field to the small, two-bedroom house she shared with her grandmother had taken less than thirty seconds. It had to have been the fastest she'd ever run in her life. Fear had been nipping at her heels, and for some reason did not dissipate as she'd hoped it would once she put some distance between her and Titus. His icy blue eyes stayed with her, lingering in her mind with a dangerous gleam. What had he meant to accomplish by revealing that he knew her secret? To make fun of her, ask her how she did it, take her to the nearest lab facility?

Whatever it was, it couldn't have been good. Something in the way he'd smiled at her; the gleam in his eyes told her his intentions couldn't be honorable. She couldn't explain it. Aside from super speed worthy of the pages of a comic book, she also had a sharp intuition. She didn't know how to describe it other than just saying that she could 'feel things'. The feelings she'd gotten from Titus were strong. Sure he was hot, but he was also dangerous and Selena had been right to run from him.

Once she'd gotten her breathing under control, Selena stood and tossed her backpack to the bed. She replaced her white peasant top with her black and red Dairy Queen t-shirt. She only had one hour to get to work, and she still had to eat something before the ten-minute walk into town.

She hated her job spooning up ice cream treats, but aside from a few mom-and-pop diners and a gas station, it was the only place in Twin Oaks where a high-school student could get a job. It paid less than minimum wage and she left every night smelling like French fries, but it was worth it. Just thinking of the freedom she'd experience after graduation because of the money she'd saved made it worthwhile. There was also the satisfaction of being able to help her grandmother put food on the table. Her deceased grandfather's pension only covered so much.

She pulled her long hair into a ponytail before looping it through the hole on the back of the black baseball cap, which matched her work shirt. She pinned on her name tag before exiting the room.

"I made you a sandwich," said Rose as Selena entered the kitchen.

She kissed her grandmother's leathery, wrinkled cheek affectionately and accepted the plate and a glass of lemonade.

"Thanks, Gram."

Rose McKinley was the only family Selena had ever known. Her parents had died in a car accident shortly after she was born and there were no siblings, cousins, aunts, or uncles. Her grandfather had died years before she was born, so she'd never known him. It was just her, Rose, and Freckles the cat. The orange tabby leaped up onto the kitchen island and arched her back, begging for attention. Selena stroked her fur before pinching a piece of lunch meat off of her sandwich and giving it to the cat. Freckles took the treat and purred happily before leaping down and curling up at Selena's feet.

"Working tonight?"

Selena nodded as she took a big bite out of the sandwich.

"You've been working so many hours during the week," Rose said with a shake of her head. She sat at one of the island's cushioned bar stools and plucked at the sleeve of her floral top.

"I was hoping you'd be off this weekend so we could go to the fair."

Selena suppressed a groan. She couldn't think of anything more boring than the Twin Oaks County Fair. Every year it was the same; local ranchers showing off their pigs for ribbons, a rodeo in which one of the McClendon boys always won the cash prize, bake sales and barbecues, and the same old carnival rides. It had been the same since Selena was a kid, and she suspected, when Rose had been as well.

She put on a smile for Rose's benefit, though. Selena knew her grandmother loved the fair. In fact, she didn't think Rose had ever been away from Twin Oaks for more than a few days at a time. She didn't seem to have any inclination to leave, either.

Selena would go to the fair. She would eat ribs and watch the rodeo and pretend to enjoy it because next year she would be gone and Rose would have to go without her.

"Sure, Gram. I think I'm off on Sunday. We could go then."

Rose smiled and lifted her glass for a sip of lemonade. "Perfect. I hear there's going to be a dance this year."

Selena rolled her eyes. "Yeah, I'll be going to that never."

Rose chuckled. "Oh come on, I bet they'll even play some of that Gaga person you all seem to be so crazy about."

Selena couldn't help but laugh, too. "Yeah, in between all the honky tonk."

"I raised you on country music, young lady. I would think you'd appreciate it by now."

"Sorry, Gram. Music about dead dogs and broken hearts doesn't interest me."

"It will, someday. Mark my words."

Selena wolfed down the last of her sandwich and downed the last of her lemonade in one gulp. She dabbed at her mouth with the napkin.

"You're probably right. I gotta go, Gram. See you tonight."

"Be careful walking home, sweet pea."

Selena waved off her warning as she always did before going to work. In Twin Oaks, everybody knew everybody. Her walks home from work were always uneventful and pleasant, and Selena enjoyed the balmy night air.

She froze, the hairs on the back of her neck standing on end as a prickling sensation worked its way up her spine.

Titus.

Just that quickly, she'd forgotten about him. Was he still out there somewhere, lurking in the field? Was she in danger of encountering him on her way home … in the dark?

"Geez relax, he's not a vampire," she murmured to herself as she put all thoughts of the strange boy out of her mind.

She'd probably overreacted earlier. Titus had seemed threatening at the time, but now that she looked back on it, she decided that she was just being silly. In fact, Titus had probably laughed all the way home at her strange behavior.

Great, add him to the never-ending list of people who think I'm weird.

❧

HE CAME in just ten minutes before closing time.

Selena paused in the middle of making a peanut butter cup Blizzard for Mark McClendon, her mouth hanging open as Titus stood framed in the doorway of the Dairy Queen, staring at her with a smug expression. She turned her attention back to the blizzard just before the ice cream overflowed in the cup.

Selena snatched the cup away from the machine and reached for a red plastic spoon. She stuck it into the ice cream and turned it upside down, once, as she always did when making a Blizzard. She always wondered at the bizarre ritual demonstrated to her during her first days of training. Was she supposed to be demonstrating the thickness of the ice cream to the customers? Did anybody really care? Every day she worked behind this counter, she was secretly hoping that she'd turn a cup over and ice cream would splat to the floor. Just once.

Mark took off with his Blizzard, eyeing Titus curiously as he left. The door slammed behind him and Selena faintly heard the chime of the bell as Titus approached the counter. Selena glanced over her shoulder, but noticed most of her co-workers had retreated to the back, probably getting ready to close up for the night. Selena glanced at the clock and turned back to Titus.

"I'm sorry, we're closing in like ten minutes. If you want something you're going to have to order quick."

"I didn't come for this swill you call food," he replied wrinkling his nose.

Selena felt the knots in her stomach tightening. "Oh, well then you should probably go. The parking lot's empty, so I'm going to lock up now."

He came forward and leaned against the counter on his elbows.

"It's late. You should let me walk you home."

"I don't think so."

"I do."

"I'm sorry, do you have a hearing problem?"

"No, but you obviously have a listening problem."

Titus raised one eyebrow at her shocked expression and grinned. Selena was green with envy. She'd always wished she could raise one eyebrow like that. She scowled.

"I'll be waiting outside," he said, his voice a warning as he backed away from the counter. "Right outside that door."

"What makes you think——"

"You know you want to, so just meet me outside when you're done, okay?"

Selena wrestled with curiosity and uncertainty. She had convinced herself earlier that she was being silly about Titus. Standing there now with a boyish grin on his face, he was like any other guy in Twin Oaks.

No, he was different. Titus was different in a wonderful way that made Selena want to know him. She didn't know why, but she felt as if they were two sides of the same coin. While one part of her wanted to run, the other part of her needed to know why.

She nodded yes, but kept the scowl on her face. He didn't have to know that she was looking forward to the walk home.

"SO, your parents let you walk home alone every night?"

Selena shrugged. "Not every night. I only work four days a week."

"That's not what I meant and you know it."

"Look, it's just me and my grandmother and we don't have a car. Besides, this place is the size of a dime. Everything's within walking distance and we all know each other around here."

Titus laughed, shoving his hands in his pockets as they walked. They were back in the field where they'd met earlier that day. She wasn't sure why, but ever since he'd shown up at Dairy Queen, her nerves had been standing on end. Once again, his presence was putting her intuition on high alert. As they walked through the tall grass, she glanced over at him and studied his profile.

He was even more stunning in the moonlight, with the pale glow of the night on his face and dark hair. His eyes almost glowed. Selena lowered her eyes as he looked up at her just in time to catch her staring.

"I take it you don't like it much."

"Seriously, I hate it here. I'm counting the days to graduation. I'm buying a car, putting all my stuff in the back of it, and getting the hell out of Ole Dirtpatch."

"Dirtpatch?"

"That's my nickname for it. Don't tell me you like Twin Oaks. I can tell you're not from around here. You've got the look of a city boy about you."

He stopped, bringing her up short beside him. He turned to face her and a wistful expression crossed his features.

"Not exactly. My home is beautiful though. There's no place like it in the whole world."

"You miss it."

He nodded. "Yes."

"What happened? Why did you have to leave?"

"It's complicated."

"You don't want to talk about it."

"Do you want to tell me what happened to your parents?"

"Point taken."

He pressed his lips together in a firm line and turned to lead her on. Selena loped along beside him, her insides burning with curiosity. Despite the nervous tension he created in her, she couldn't help but want to know more about him. What was that saying about curiosity killing the cat? Yeah, that was pretty much where she was headed.

"My parents died in a car crash when I was a baby," she blurted. "There's no other family, so Gram took me in."

"I had to leave my home because of a war," he replied "My parents are now prisoners of that war, and it is unlikely that I will ever see them again."

She'd known he had an exotic look about him. A war that had imprisoned his parents meant he was from another country. But, where?

Selena gasped, her throat clenching with emotion as she looked back up at him. His face was etched in agony, the blue eyes lowered and filled with sadness, the corners of his mouth turned down and pinched. She reached out to grab his hand. His fingers were icy against her warm ones.

"I'm so sorry."

He looked down at her, his face grown harsher in the moonlight, the glint in his eyes deadly. Selena's heart skipped a beat, but she didn't flinch as she met his narrowed gaze with her wide-eyed one.

"You shouldn't be here, with me," he said, his voice a low growl.

Selena frowned. "But you—"

"I saw you earlier Selena, running through this field. You were so ... " he trailed off, his Adam's apple bobbing as he swallowed, " ... beautiful. If only you knew the power you possessed, how important you are, and how dangerous I am to you..." he paused again, groaning in frustration and tearing his gaze away from hers. "Run, Selena."

"What are you talking about? What are you saying?"

"Run!"

His voice was animalistic this time, a roar that shook Selena to her very core. He leaned toward her, baring his teeth as another primal growl rumbled through his chest. Selena was sure that his canines lengthened, glistening behind his lips in the moonlight.

Scared to death, Selena gladly took his advice.

She turned on her heels and ran from Titus for the second time in one day.

Once home, she was grateful to find that Rose had gone to bed for the night. She checked all the doors and windows to be sure that they were locked before fleeing to her room. She closed the door and sank to the floor, Titus' words whirling through her mind like a Texas twister.

If only you knew the power you possessed ... how dangerous I am to you.

So, she hadn't been exaggerating. He'd told her with his own mouth that he was a danger to her. And to think, she'd almost ignored her intuition and allowed herself to be alone with him in an empty field at night. The situation had 'horror movie' written all over it.

But then, curiosity reared its ugly head once again. If Titus was so concerned about hurting her, why had he come to the Dairy Queen that night? Why pursue her after she'd run away from him this afternoon? How was he this cute, charming boy one minute and a menacing psychopath the next?

One thing was for sure, Selena did not have any interest in finding out.

Well, maybe just a little.

Chapter Two

Mollac, Fallada

"What news from the world of men, my queen?"

Eranna curled her blood red lips into a sneer as she turned to find Ushma, her most faithful Witch, shuffling through the door to her chambers. She wrinkled her nose at the old hag before turning back to the mirror resting against the wall in a gilded frame.

"He has not fulfilled his duty, Ushma. I fear that we may have to take extraordinary measures."

"Even more extraordinary than taking his family hostage?"

Eranna sighed and rolled her eyes in annoyance as Ushma shuffled back into her line of vision. Heavens, she hated having to look at them, but the Witches had their uses. Ushma, with her pointed nose, wart blemished chin, and leathery skin, was perhaps the ugliest of them all. However, Eranna tolerating their presence was well worth it. When she became High Queen of Fallada, she would banish the ugly creatures to some far-flung corner of the country where she would never have to look upon them again.

With that decided, Eranna turned back to the gilded mirror and ignored the ugly, gray-robed, hump-backed mass that was Ushma. She ran her hands over the ruby-red silk gown she had put on for dinner, the perfect complement to her snow-white skin and midnight-black hair. She turned to the side and felt a smirk pulling at the corners of her mouth as she eyed her perfect figure.

Two-hundred years old, and one would think she was only one-hundred.

"It would seem taking the Were-boy's parents into our custody was enough to send him into the human world, yet not enough to bring Eladria of Damu to me. I have been watching him through The Eye of Mollac. He is taken by her innocence and *beauty*."

She spat the last word like a foul curse, jealousy curling low in her belly at the thought of anyone's beauty surpassing her own. She'd seen Princess Eladria of Damu through the Eye. She'd seen the girl's discovery of her powers. Eladria was coming into her own, learning what she was really capable of. And now, those cursed Faeries were plotting against her. Oh, she knew about Adrah's plan to send the scribes Jacob and Wilhelm Grimm into the world of men to retrieve the lost princesses. Adrah continued to underestimate Eranna and did not realize that she had eyes inside of Goldun and knew her every move.

Eranna would not care about Princess Eladria's beauty or power, if not for the fact that Adrah meant to bring the girl back to Damu and see her seated on her throne. That, Eranna could not have. Restoration of the princesses would mean disaster the certain demise of her plans.

"What do you suggest, then?" Ushma asked.

Eranna lifted her gleaming silver tiara from its place of honor beside the mirror. The intricate design of intertwining branches and leaves was further enhanced by a dusting of crushed diamonds. One large, clear stone dangled between her eyebrows.

"Oh, Ushma, it's been so long since I've left this castle. It is about time I did, don't you think?"

Ushma's cackling laughter mixed with the musical sound of

Eranna's giggle. Ushma rubbed her hands—gnarled like tree branches—together and moved back toward the door.

"I will prepare your chariot, my Queen."

"I know that you will Ushma. You are so very faithful."

Ushma bowed several times before disappearing through the door. Eranna turned back to the mirror and continued perusing the hypnotic reflection staring back at her.

Perhaps I will keep the Witches around, she mused as she reached for her favorite diamond choker. *They have their uses, and at least with them around my beauty is magnified ten-fold.*

❦

TITUS SHIVERED and pulled the coarse blanket tightly around his shoulders.

He had been trying to sleep for hours, but couldn't seem to drift off. His encounter with Selena left him shaken and he couldn't get her out of his head.

How was everything going so hopelessly wrong? His assignment should have been an easy one: track down Eladria of Damu and kill her. One bite of his strong jaw at her throat would have done the job nicely, yet Titus just couldn't bring himself to do it.

He turned onto his side, facing the wall of the small, abandoned cabin he'd been living in since crossing over into the world of men. Titus felt like a fool, a failure, for allowing Eladria's pretty face to distract him from his mission. His parents and little sister were being held captive by Eranna, and all Titus needed to do to free them was end the life of one girl.

But Titus hadn't expected her to be so beautiful, and not just in a physical way. The afternoon when he'd first stalked her across the abandoned field, he had every intention of getting the job done then and there. Then, she'd started to run. With the wind in her coppery red hair and a genuine smile across her heart-shaped face, Titus saw Eladria as the pure soul that she was.

He just couldn't do it.

Titus sighed and squeezed his eyes shut, trying to tear his thoughts away from Selena. He thought about home instead. He missed Mollac and its endless stretches of pristine white snow. He missed the jagged mountains and snow-dusted pines. He missed stalking deer and hares through the peaceful forests with his pack. Most of all he missed his family.

He could picture them clearly, his father's beautiful white pelt, his mother's sleek form, and his sister's kind brown eyes. For them, he had no choice but to do what Eranna commanded. Her reach was growing, and soon all of his race would be enslaved. Titus planned to rescue his family and get the hell out of the way. When Eranna had wiped out all who opposed her, Titus did not plan for himself or his family to be among them.

He shivered again and frowned as a chill rolled up his spine. Twin Oaks had been nothing but blistering hot during the day and muggy at night since his arrival. Yet now, he felt his body temperature rapidly lowering. It felt like being home.

Titus shot up on his creaky cot, his eyes widening when he noticed his own breath, white on the night air. He trembled uncontrollably as a splintering, crackling sound filled the room. He looked down to find ice spreading across the floor and up the walls in a rapidly-moving sheet of cool blue.

Dread filled him as snow swirled around the bed, producing the form of Eranna, seated on her colossal chariot. The vehicle was made of ice and was pulled by a pair of perfectly white polar bears. The massive beasts dropped to their haunches and waited obediently for Eranna's command. Wrapped in ruby silk and diamonds, the Queen of Mollac was as striking as Titus remembered. Yet the beauty never quite reached her eyes, which resembled cold, hard bits of coal. She fixed those eyes on him now, her gaze narrow and assessing.

"Titus of Mollac," she said, her ominous voice filling the room. She stepped down from her ice carriage and stroked the head of one of her bears before approaching. "You've been a very bad dog."

She extended her hand toward him, producing a white, snowy mist from her blood red fingernails. It swirled around Titus, seemingly fragile, yet incredibly strong as it wrapped round him, pinning his arms to his sides and forcing him to his knees. Rage boiled up in him, and he felt the beginnings of transformation ripping through him. A tight squeeze from Eranna's snowy mist quickly sucked the air from his lungs and made that impossible. He settled on glaring up at her as she approached with a low chuckle.

"Now, now," she said, running her hands through his hair. Titus shivered in revulsion but remained still. "There will be none of that. You and I can speak civilly or I can kill you now, return to Mollac, and kill your family."

Titus felt his fingernails elongating and biting into his palms. His canines itched to tear free from his gums but he fought against it, knowing that one false move would ruin everything he'd been working for.

"I'm listening," he said, just a hint of a growl underlying his voice.

"Do you not care for the well-being of your family?"

"You know that I do, Eranna."

Eranna smiled. "Then why have you not carried out your assignment? Eladria of Damu is still alive and I have been watching you both through the Eye of Mollac."

Titus hung his head and sighed. "I do not understand why you wish to kill the girl. She does not even know——"

"It is not for you to understand!" Eranna bellowed, chilling him with a frigid blast of air. The very atmosphere around her seemed to darken and her eyes took on a red glow as she drew herself up to her full height until her head nearly touched the ceiling of the dilapidated cabin.

"I will not be questioned by you, you insolent puppy! All you need to know is that I want her dead. If you do not wish to find your parents and sister ripped to shreds when you return to Mollac, I suggest you do as I have commanded. I will give you one more day to see the deed done. I do not want to have to come back for you."

Titus felt her supernatural hold on him slackening and drew deep gulps of air into his lungs as he fell to his hands and knees on the floor. Eranna glided back to her chariot and took up the reins.

"Do we understand each other, Titus?"

Titus nodded once with a jerk of his head. Eranna snapped the reigns over the polar bears' heads.

"Good boy."

"OKAY, seriously Selena, have you heard a word I've been saying?"

Selena's eyes slowly focused on Zoe as she bent to tie her running shoes. The dark gray track circled the football field and gleamed in the Texas sun. Selena took a sip of water from her squeeze bottle and smiled sheepishly at her best friend.

"Sorry, Zo. I guess I zoned out for a second."

Zoe blew her dirty blonde bangs out of her face and sighed. "You've been like a zombie all day. You going to tell me what's going on, or what?"

Selena sat on the ground to begin her warm-up stretches, which conveniently gave her the chance to avoid Zoe's probing hazel gaze.

"It's nothing, really, It's just … I got a bad grade on my last English test."

It was a lame excuse, but it was all she could come up with out of thin air. Zoe rolled her eyes and joined Selena on the ground, folding one leg in while extending the other one out and bending it toward it in a stretch.

"Okay I'll take it for now, but when you're ready to talk, I'm here."

"I know, Zo."

After a few minutes of silent stretching, the two girls joined their teammates near the coach.

"All right," said Coach Kremlin as she twirled her gleaming whistle around one finger by its string, "we've got a meet this weekend against the Ellison Eagles, so this week's practices are very important. I need you all to be on time, suited up and on this field no later than three-forty-five."

Selena watched the bluish-green gum roll around the coach's mouth as she talked. Coach Kremlin stood with her muscular legs braced apart and her hands on her khaki short-covered hips.

"Coach Tomlin will take the long jumpers and Coach Lyons will take the hurdlers. I want to see the 1x400 relay team."

Zoe pushed her bangs out of her face with a headband and waved to Selena as she followed Coach Tomlin to the jumping pit. Selena moved into place with the three other girls on the relay team. The four girls eyed the coach expectantly, waiting to be informed who was going to run which leg for the meet. Selena could already feel the eyes of Alison, the team's second-fastest runner, boring into her menacingly. Alison had no love for the girl who was the fastest on the team and Selena could feel the venom in her stare.

"All right ladies, I want to see smooth passes out there," Coach Kremlin advised as she approached with a clipboard and aluminum relay batons. Running first leg, Alison Caney."

If at all possible, Alison's glare turned even deadlier as she went to take her place on the blocks. She hated running first leg.

"Second leg, Jennifer Donnelly. Third leg, Selena McKinley."

"Of course," muttered Alison as Selena walked past her to take her place.

"And on fourth leg Natasha Whitfield."

Selena ignored the stares and glares of the other girls as she took her place to await the baton. At the sound of the coach's whistle, Selena's focus moved away from staring eyes and jealousy. As she waited for the second leg to come toward her, Selena felt the familiar rush of adrenaline that came just before she ran.

When the second leg approached, Selena reached out with her arm and took off at a trot, waiting for the aluminum tube to hit her palm. When it did, she was gone with a small burst of speed— nothing too freaky, just enough to propel her around the curve and toward the fourth leg a few seconds under her usual time. Even after the fourth leg had taken the baton, Selena felt the whirl of hot air around her and wished she could just keep on running.

Wouldn't that be something, she thought; running off from that field in a blur with the dry heat of the air propelling her miles away. She stopped and rested her hands on her knees, closing her eyes, and trying to imagine the moment.

Coach Kremlin came onto the field, clapping her hands and smiling. She thrust her stopwatch toward Selena with a wide grin.

"Three seconds faster than last week, Selena. You keep it up, we might actually have a shot at district finals."

Her teammates came over to offer their congratulations, though Selena guessed correctly that Alison only came to give her more dirty looks. The brunette crossed her arms over her chest and stared at a spot over her shoulder.

"Not bad, Selena."

"Thanks."

"Who's the hottie?"

"Huh?"

Selena turned to follow Alison's gaze and felt her heart dropping down into her stomach. It landed there like a frozen stone and sent shivers up and down her spine.

Titus.

He stood with his arms propped up on the gate surrounding the field and bleachers. His dark hair was tousled and falling over his forehead, a match for his stretchy black t-shirt. He was wearing his glasses again, but Selena could feel his eyes on her. She turned away quickly and shrugged.

"What makes you think I know?"

She knew her attempt at sounding nonchalant had failed.

"Because he's been staring at you since he showed up."

Alison flipped her ponytail and shrugged one shoulder, her eyes still locked on Titus.

"Not that there's much to look at," she added before turning to join the others near the starting line.

Selena let Alison's comment slide off her back like she did every day and went to practice the 100 meter dash. She tried not to glance back, but Titus' eyes burned her skin with their intensity and she couldn't resist another peek. But when she looked back, he was gone, and Selena felt equal parts relief and disappointment unfurling in her chest.

What was he doing here? After his warning last night Selena hadn't expected to see him again. Now curiosity burned more than ever. She wanted answers, and something told her confronting Titus was the only way she was going to get them.

Resolved, Selena went through the rest of practice distractedly counting the minutes until five o'clock. When the coaches finally released them, she drew her sweats on over her running shorts and tank top and slung her backpack over her shoulder. She declined Zoe's offer to give her a ride home and headed straight for the abandoned field. Somehow she knew that she would find him there.

Sure enough, he was there, sitting on a rotting log with his back to her. His back muscles tensed as she approached and she knew that he was aware of her.

"You shouldn't be here," he said without turning around.

With a huff of annoyance, Selena walked toward the log and plopped down next to him.

"Yeah, well here I am. And I'm not going anywhere until you tell me what last night was about and why you're acting so weird. One second you're being nice to me and the next you're running me off. What's your problem?"

"Selena, I warned you …"

"Your warning didn't make any sense. You don't make any

sense! Who are you? What are you?" Her last question was a strained whisper. "What am I?"

Titus turned toward her, his dark sunglasses removed, his blue eyes penetrating. His eyebrows snapped together over them as he exhaled.

"I don't know if you really want to know what I am, but we can start with what you are."

"Okay."

Hope flared in Selena and she inched closer to him on the log. Her hands trembled as she waited, anticipation gripping her tightly. For years she'd wondered, hoped and waited for some clue, some inkling of what she was and if there were others like her.

He ran his hands though his hair and sighed.

"Damn Selena, I'm not even supposed to be telling you this. I'm supposed to …" he paused and shook his head. "I'm going to tell you anyway, because you need to know. You've felt different your whole life, haven't you? But you haven't been able to pinpoint why, to understand why you can do what you can do."

Selena nodded. That was exactly how she felt.

"That's because you're from a whole different world than this one. The kind of world filled with people that can do things a lot like what you can do. You were sent away as a baby to this world. That is why you don't feel like you belong; because you don't."

"What does that mean, another world? Like another planet? Tell me!"

He threaded his hands into his hair and pulled, grunting in frustration.

"I'm trying!"

Selena leaped to her feet, her mind racing a million miles a minute. Anxious, she paced back and forth.

"If what you're saying is true then Gram isn't even my real grandmother."

Titus continued staring at her. He looked as if he was going to be sick.

"And that means my parents are out there somewhere and probably looking for me, right?"

The hope she'd been carrying since she was a little girl sparked to life at the thought of finding out where she really came from. Maybe her father was super-fast too. Maybe he had other abilities. Maybe her mother was where she got her brown eyes and dimpled cheeks from. And then, realization hit her like a ton of bricks and she gasped.

"Gram's been lying to me my whole life. Why do you think she would do that?"

"I don't know." Titus shook his head glumly. "That's a question you'll have to ask her."

"I'm sure there's a reason. Gram wouldn't lie unless she thought she needed to protect me." She paused and turned to stare at Titus, who had finally found the courage to look her in the eye. "Would she need to protect me from anything, Titus?"

"Selena, you have no idea."

"You basically just told me that I'm some kind of alien with freakish powers from a world full of other aliens filled with freakish powers. If there's anything else, I think I can handle it and now's the time to tell me."

He came to his feet, reaching out to grab her by the arms. His grip was tight, desperate, a lot like his darting eyes.

"There is a woman, a queen from our world who is looking for you. She wants you dead."

"Me? What did I do?"

"Nothing!" he roared. He closed his eyes and shook his head, taking a deep breath in an attempt to control his emotions. "You didn't do anything. She banished you and the other six princesses from Fallada when you were only children because she knew that you were a threat to her plans. Now that there's a chance the Fae may try to bring you all back, she's sent her hunters out to find you."

"Whoa, slow down."

Selena felt as if the whole world was spinning three times faster than normal. The chaotic whirling of her thoughts made her dizzy, until all she wanted to do was sink to the ground and bury her face in her hands.

"That whole speech touched on a lot of things I've only ever read about in books. Faeries? Evil queens? You've got to be kidding me."

"I wish I was, Selena. I wish I'd never come here, but I had no choice."

He was suddenly drawing her close, hugging her tightly as if she were a life preserver in the middle of a raging sea.

"I didn't think it would be this hard. I didn't think that I would come to like you."

Foreboding gripped Selena and she stiffened in Titus' arms. The warm and fuzzy feeling that had crept over her at his embrace was now gone, and fear stroked her spine. She jerked away from him, her heart hammering like a kick drum in her chest.

"You mentioned something about hunters. You're from this world—you called it Fallada, right?—you wouldn't know anything about these hunters, would you?"

The second she'd asked the question, Selena already knew. As she took a second and then a third step away from Titus, he lowered his eyes and sighed, his shoulders and chest swelling as he inhaled.

"I'm sorry, Selena," he whispered.

His eyelids lifted and his gaze met hers, but instead of the icy blue she'd been so lost in, his eyes were a fiery, glowing red. His lips opened to reveal the sharp canines, bathed in dripping saliva. A growl vibrated through his chest as he leaned toward her, the slick canines elongating before her eyes.

Just before she turned to run, Titus dropped to the ground, his body contorting and twisting as he snarled and groaned. As her feet carried across the open field, the figure of a four-legged beast sprinted alongside her, its snowy white fur like a shot of lightning through the brown grass.

Chapter Three

S elena increased her pace as her house came into sight, running so fast that her feet left the ground several times. Her lungs were on fire, but she couldn't stop now; not when Zoe was walking up the driveway, oblivious to the danger lurking in the line of trees just across the street.

"Selena, what the hell?" Zoe screeched as Selena crashed into her.

She grabbed Zoe by the arm and pulled, yanking her friend into the house and sending the books and papers she'd been carrying flying across the driveway. Ignoring her friend's protests, Selena pulled the flailing girl into the living room where Rose was watching a re-run of *Oprah*. Freckles jumped down from his spot on the couch and darted into one of the bedrooms.

"Selena, what's going on? Is everything all right?"

"You tell me, Gram!"

Selena was very aware that her voice was raised above the limits of normal conversation, but she couldn't seem to control it. Her breathing was harsh and swift, her eyes wide as Rose shot to her feet, her eyebrows wrinkled with concern.

"Sweet pea, whatever is bothering you, we can work it out. Why don't you sit down and we can talk about it."

Rose moved forward to grasp her hand and Selena backed away.

"Maybe I should leave you two alone to—"

"No!" Selena screamed as Zoe backed toward the door. Her voice stopped Zoe dead in her tracks. "No, don't go out there, it's not safe!"

Tears filled Rose's eyes as she grasped Selena's other hand. She held both tightly and searched Selena's face.

"Selena, please. Tell me what's wrong?"

"*Everything*! Why didn't you tell me the truth about where I came from? The truth about my parents? You're not even my real grandmother, are you?"

"Okay, this seems like a family discussion," Zoe said softly as she continued backing toward the door.

"No one is going anywhere," Selena said, her voice low. "Answer me, Gram."

Rose's chin trembled as she released Selena's hands and fell back onto the couch. Her dark head streaked with gray lowered and she drew a heavy breath.

"Selena, I have wanted to tell you for so long, but I thought it would only hurt you. You see, I don't actually know who your parents are."

"What?"

"I did have a daughter; her and my son-in-law *did* die in a tragic car accident. Their two year old daughter, Abigail, died with them. They were all the family I had left and I thought I'd never be the same again. I was so alone and so miserable. But then you came along, Selena … my little blessing."

"How did you find me?"

"It's ironic how much you hate the county fair, considering it's also the anniversary of the night I found you."

Zoe, now drawn in by the unfolding drama, drifted back toward the living room and stood beside Selena, her jaw slack as she looked from her to Rose and back again.

"I was walking home from the fair that night, through that old field you like to hang out in. It's almost like your subconscious knows something special happened in that place, the way you always seem drawn to it. Anyhow, I was walking and I heard a baby crying. I waded through the grass and found you a few feet away. I estimated your age to be about fifteen months. You were sitting in a large basket on a cushion, with your thumb in your mouth and tears in your eyes. You were such a beautiful little thing and so alone. Small as this town is, I couldn't think of anyone off-hand who'd had a baby less than two years prior, and I figured someone visiting had lost track of you. So I picked you up in the basket and brought you here. I couldn't believe it, but you crawled right into my lap, stared up at me, and smiled. I never thought I could feel as happy as I did that day. It was like you knew me, chose me."

Rose paused and swiped at her watery eyes, took a deep breath, and continued.

"I called the police and told them what I had found. They asked me if I wanted to keep you while they searched for your missing parents. None could be found and after a while there was talk of placing you with a foster family. By then you and I were thick and thieves, and I knew I could never let them take you away. I kept you, promising myself every day that I wouldn't become attached, but you stole my heart, Selena. It felt like I had my little Abigail back after losing her not long before you came. When no one claimed you, I offered to adopt you and the papers were drawn up. I have presented myself to you as your grandmother all of these years because of my age, but the papers I have say that I am your mother. I have been since the day I found you and named you."

Selena squeezed her eyes shut and pressed her fist against her mouth, holding back tears and wild sobs. Zoe's hand came up to her shoulder, but her friend was thankfully quiet. When Selena opened her eyes again, Rose was reaching up into the hallway storage closet.

She pulled down the basket they'd used to transport muffins to bake sales for as long as Selena could remember.

"This is the basket I found you in," she said, extending the basket to Selena. When she took it and glanced down into it, Rose reached up into the closet again, this time coming down with a small jewelry box.

"This was the only thing you had on you other than a little green dress, which I still have boxed up with your other baby things."

She opened the black box and held it out to Selena, her wrinkled hands trembling uncontrollably. Selena reached for the box and removed a gleaming gold necklace. Amazingly, the metal had not been tarnished and seemed as if it had been polished only yesterday. The chain was long, and hanging from it was a large, red jewel—a ruby maybe—surrounded by a golden cage of leaves and flowers. Selena held the necklace up to the light, stunned by the necklace's beauty.

Zoe whistled. "One thing's for sure. Whoever your birth parents are, they're loaded."

Selena rolled her eyes at Zoe. "Yeah, cause that's what's important right now."

Zoe shrugged. "Just saying."

Selena looped the necklace around her neck. The stone settled against her chest heavily and Selena gripped it tight as she turned back to Rose.

"It's okay," she said, noticing the anxiety in Rose's eyes. "I understand why you had to hide this from me. You're right, it does hurt, but not in the way you think. You see, today I found out—"

She was cut short by the sound of pounding at the door. It wasn't exactly a knock. It was more like a booming followed by the rattle of the door in the frame, as if someone were trying to kick it down. Selena pictured the white wolf throwing its massive body up against the door, its eyes red, its teeth barred in a feral snarl.

Rose yelped as the banging started up again, this time with more force and intent. Selena stood in front of her grandmother, pushing Zoe behind her as well. She wasn't sure if she could hold her own against Titus—or that thing he had become—but she was darn sure going to try. Hearing the commotion, Freckles came hissing from the back of the house, standing beside Selena with his hair standing up on his back.

"Selena, we should call the police!" Zoe screamed as the banging continued. The door splintered under the assault, and Selena knew that in minutes it would be broken down.

"TOPD can't help us right now," Selena said, holding Rose back with one arm and Zoe with the other.

Selena trembled as the door shook and cracked. The split wood folded inward and she could see Titus, Wolf Boy, on the other side, snarling with his red eyes glowing. She could hear the scrape of his claws against the wood and the deep, throaty barks that escaped his throat. Freckles was going ballistic by now, mewling and hissing as she bared her tiny, pointed teeth at the wolf. Selena swallowed the vomit that rose up in her throat and tried to breathe. It was hard with Rose and Zoe screaming like banshees behind her.

In an instant, the door was torn from its hinges, broken in half by Titus' bulky body. He stood framed by the doorway, his fur standing on end in jagged, ferocious spikes. Selena squeezed her eyes shut as Zoe's fingernails dug into her arm.

"Oh shit, we're going to die!" she screamed as she held on to Selena for dear life.

Selena couldn't have said it better herself.

There was nowhere to run except the kitchen, and even there they'd be cornered. Selena gritted her teeth and braced herself for the inevitable. She was going to die and all before she ever learned anything about where she really came from. She braced herself for the pain, praying that Titus would make it quick and leave her grandmother and friend alone.

A splintering sound startled her and the house rumbled and shook forcibly. Selena fell to the floor, her grandmother and Zoe landing in a heap on top of her, as chunks of roof fell in on them. Selena covered her head, unable to stop the screams that tore from her lips as the house seemed to fall down around them. She curled into a tight ball, sure she was either going to be crushed by the roof or eaten alive by Titus.

Another jumble of sounds assaulted her ears and Selena snapped to attention at the sound of a thud and a canine yelp.

Then, silence.

Was this what death sounded like?

"Uh, Selena," Zoe's shaking voice called, telling Selena that she wasn't quite dead yet. "You need to see this."

Two old men stood in the middle of the living room, gazing about them curiously before their eyes landed on Selena. She looked down at the wolf's motionless body, laid out across the carpet on its side. Other than the rapid heaving of its chest, it ... he? ... was completely still. She glanced back at the two men and her eyes widened at the silver gun still smoking in one of their hands.

They were the strangest men she'd ever seen, dressed from head to toe in shades of brown and off-white: buttoned shirts, suspenders, vests, trousers, and boots. Each of them wore a pair of strange goggles, and one of them—the one not carrying a gun—wore a floppy brown hat. The one with the gun had scraggly white hair down to his shoulders. Both had bushy gray eyebrows and the hatless man had the rough stubble of a five o'clock shadow gleaming silver across his jaw.

"What the heck did you just do?" Selena screeched.

"Put a hole in our roof, for one," Rose said with a scowl in the strangers' direction as both men lifted their goggles from their eyes. Selena followed the direction of Rose's gaze and gasped, not at the hole in the roof, but at what hovered just above it. Several feet above their house was what appeared to be a floating ship. It cast a shadow over the little home and darkened the living room considerably. It appeared incredibly bulky, yet hovered over them as if it weighed no more than a cloud.

"Hope you guys have ship insurance," Zoe said, yet there was not an ounce of humor in her voice. She was eyeing the ship, Titus, the two old men, each one at a time and over and over again as if she couldn't believe her eyes.

"It's her," said the man holding the gun, pointing at Zoe with his free hand. "It must be."

He was walking toward Zoe while shoving his gun down into a brown leather holster at his right side. Zoe took a step back as he approached, inhaling swiftly.

"Selena, what's going on?" she whispered as the old man approached, eyeing her closely.

"I don't know," Selena said, her eyes still on Titus' lifeless form. Worry filled her and frustration gnawed on her insides. Why did she care if he was dead or hurt? He had just tried to kill them for God's sake! She should be thanking these two strangers, yet couldn't find the words. Especially since the one wearing a hat was staring at her intently as he removed round, wire-rimmed glasses from his vest pocket and slipped them on.

"She's not the one, Wil," he said, still watching Selena.

"Of course she is!" the one named Wil blustered in a voiced tinted by a German accent. "Look at her height and the regal features, Jake."

Jake adjusted his spectacles and sighed, rolling his eyes as if used to putting up with the other man's posturing.

"Fine then," he said with a shrug, his accent just as thick as Wil's. "Why don't we just check her for the birthmark? That will prove it beyond the shadow of a doubt."

Wil snapped his fingers as if he'd just had an epiphany and smiled. "I know! We'll check her for the birthmark. Honestly, Jake, you're supposed to be the smart one."

"God help me," Jake groaned as Wil took another step toward Zoe.

"All right then, girl, let's have it."

Zoe pursed her lips. "Have what?"

"Your birthmark, princess! Come, come, we haven't all day and that beast will only be out for so long, and then we'll all be in trouble."

"What the hell is everybody talking about? Princess? I'm not a freaking princess!"

Suddenly everyone was talking at once, a cacophony of voices that grated on Selena's nerves. Wil kept insisting that Zoe had to be the one they were looking for. Rose wanted to know who these men were and why they were here, and Zoe kept asking about the birthmark and whether being a Princess came with a castle and a pool. Jake merely shook his head and pulled his hat lower over his ears. Selena had finally had enough.

"Shut up!" she bellowed, holding her hands up, annoyance edging her tone. "Everybody just be quiet for a minute, please! There's too much going on, but I think I can help fill in some of the gaps if you give me a minute."

"Definitely sounds like a princess," Jake muttered from beneath his hat.

Selena shot him a dirty look before continuing. "This guy," she pointed at Titus, "appeared in my life the other day out of nowhere. Next thing I know, he's telling me I'm different and not from this world. He says I should be afraid of him because of what he is. Then he morphs into a wolf and chases me here. My grandmother tells me that she found me in a basket years ago and raised me as her own. So I think it's safe to say I'm the one you're looking for, although Titus didn't say anything about any princess."

"What's your name, girl?" Jake asked softly.

"Selena," she answered. "Selena McKinley."

Jake shook his head, moving forward to stand beside Wil. "If I haven't missed my guess, then your true name is Eladria. Princess Eladria of Damu. Have you a birthmark on your ribs? It would be on your right side, a brown smudge visible when you lift your arm."

Selena's heart beat in double time and the call of the familiar echoed within her chest, resounding throughout her mind. She'd always wondered about the chocolate brown patch of skin shaped like California a few inches beneath her armpit. *Eladria.* She wasn't ready to admit it out loud, but she knew deep within her heart that old Jake had called her by her true name.

"Princess," Rose whispered, staring off into space as if in deep thought. "The dress you were wearing that night was so beautiful and the material so rich. And that jewel—"

"Jewel?" Wil snapped to attention. "You have the stone in your possession? The Ruby of Damu?"

Selena reached into her shirt and pulled the golden chain and robin's egg-sized stone from its confines. "What, this?"

Wil gasped and snatched the stone from her hand, yanking Selena along with it as the chain was still around her neck. Oblivious to her discomfort, Wil studied the ruby with a smile.

"It is The Ruby of Damu! Then you must be Princess Eladria!"

"There is only one way to know for sure," Jake responded, his eyes as wide as Wil's and filled with excitement.

"Told you," Zoe muttered. "Rich parents."

Selena was so busy shooting Zoe a glare that she didn't see the dagger that appeared in Wil's hand. A sharp pain stabbed her index finger and traveled up her hand and arm.

"Ouch!" Selena yelped as Wil grasped her bleeding finger and squeezed mercilessly. "What are you doing?"

Muttering to himself about obtaining irrefutable proof, Wil held the stone beneath her bleeding finger and watched in fascination as one drop of crimson liquid fell onto it. He released Selena's finger and she quickly pressed it to her lips to lessen the sting. In an instant, the stone began to glow, casting its scarlet rays over the faces of everyone in the room.

Zoe and Rose gasped, but Selena just stared, transfixed at the glowing gem.

"What does that mean?" Selena asked breathlessly, mesmerized by the ruby's shimmer.

Wil glanced up at her with joy dancing in the depths of his blue eyes. "It means that you must come with us immediately."

"Wait just one minute," Rose interjected, snatching the ruby from Wil's thick fingers and shoving her body between him and Selena. "No one is going anywhere until we get some more answers. We do not know who you are, where you come from, or what your business is with my granddaughter."

"Our names are Wilhelm and Jacob Grimm, if you must know, and there is no time for explanations!" Wil said with a sigh. "If you come with us, we will tell you everything you need to know once you're on board our ship."

"Can I come?" Zoe quipped.

"No one is going …" Rose trailed off, her eyes rolling back into her head before she sank to the floor in a crumpled heap.

"Gram!" Selena cried as she sank to her knees beside Rose's limp form. "What's happened to her?"

Jake knelt beside her and pointed to the leg of her blue jeans. Selena hadn't noticed until now that they were stained with blood and ripped. Sometime between Titus' crashing through the door and Wil and Jake ripping the roof off, the wolf must have bitten Rose. Selena felt tears stinging her eyes as she took in her grandmother's pale complexion.

"The bite of a Werewolf is fatal," Jake said, his eyes serious behind his glasses. "You have no choice but to come with us if you want to save her."

"She's not going to turn into one is she?"

"Zoe, for the love of God shut up!" Selena pressed a hand to Rose's cool forehead and sighed. "She's so cold. Did the bite make her sick?"

Jake nodded. "A bite this deep could kill her within days. She is going to become very ill and it's not going to get better. We need to take her to Goldun."

Selena's head spun with the intake of all the new information. Werewolves, flying ships, lost princesses, her blood making a ruby glow like a firecracker, and fairytale kingdoms named Damu and Goldun … none of it made any sense, but then, it didn't have to. If she could get her grandmother the help she needed, there would be time for questions later.

"How long is the trip, and what are we supposed to do about the hole in the roof and the knocked-out Werewolf?" Selena asked calmly.

"We will use Fae magic to shield the house from human eyes," Wil said. "All who pass here will see the house as it was before. Repairs can be made later. As for the wolf, we will have to take him with us."

"Um, maybe forget what I said about coming along," Zoe said with a nervous chuckle. "I'd rather not have to share ship space with *him*."

"He will not be able to harm you," Jake said. "It'll be perfectly safe."

Selena grabbed Zoe by the arm. "My life as I know it is over," she said, stabbing her best friend with a look that said she wouldn't tolerate any opposition. "My identity, my past, everything is changing and it all feels like some kind of dream. I need something around to remind me that this is real. I need you, Zoe."

Zoe smiled and pulled Selena into a tight hug. "Well dang girl, you don't have to get all mushy on me. I'll go, okay?"

"What are you going to do about your parents?" Selena asked.

"I don't know yet." She turned to Wil. "How long will this flying ship trip take, anyway?"

Wil shrugged before bending to lift Rose into his arms. "Time does not move the same in Fallada as it does here. One day there is only a few minutes here."

Zoe nodded. "Right, so I just need a weekend alibi?"

Selena sighed. "Don't look at me, I have no idea how any of this works."

"Weekend sleepover it is," Zoe said, whipping out her cell

phone. Selena turned back to Wil, who was carrying Rose to the rope ladder dangling from the side of the hovering ship.

"I know you have many questions, Princess," he said as he paused, one foot up on the rope ladder. "All will be answered for you in time."

"That 'princess' bit is going to take a while to get used to. Be careful with her!" she added as he began his ascent.

Wil paused and grinned at her over his shoulder. "I don't think that princess bit is going to be as hard as you think."

Chapter Four

Selena stared over the side of *The Adrah*, the Grimm brothers' flying ship, her eyes wide as the landscape of Twin Oaks, Texas grew smaller and smaller. The wind whipped her titian hair around her face and neck as she leaned against the ship's railing. It all seemed like something out of a dream; a flying ship, clouds rolling by at arm's length, a Werewolf trapped in the brig below, and a mystery that was very slowly unfolding.

There hadn't been much time for talking with Jacob and Wilhelm working to get them underway. Zoe and Selena had watched them in awe, as they rapidly turned and pushed the numerous levers and buttons lining the side of the ship's engines. After coming on board, the girls were told that the ship was propelled and kept aloft by steam, which came from the engine taking up most of the deck. As they'd walked slowly in a circle around the churning machinery, steam billowed from a large chimney-like opening and up into the ship's pristine white sails. The hulking thrusters propelled them along at a steady clip through the blue sky and toward the orange, pink, and purple sunset.

"This is *so Chronicles of Narnia*," Zoe said as she approached

Selena. The two hadn't spoken much since leaving Twin Oaks behind, too wrapped up in what was going on around them.

"I guess you can just call me little Lucy" Selena muttered, "because no one back home is going to believe this."

"Who cares? You've been waiting your whole life to leave Twin Oaks." Zoe swept her hand out, indicating the stretch of blue sky and burning orange sun beyond. "Now's your chance."

Selena tried to manage a smile, but couldn't. There were still too many questions unanswered. She turned to find Jacob Grimm striding across the deck with a leather-bound book tucked under one arm. He'd removed his hat to reveal hair that was shorter than his brother's, but equally as gray.

"Jake!"

He stopped and adjusted his spectacles. "Princess Eladria," he said with a bow. "We've stowed your grandmother in a cabin below deck and given her a sleeping draught. She's resting peacefully for now, although I expect the fever to begin before the night is over. I'm afraid things will get worse before they get better until we get to Goldun."

Selena nodded. "All right. How long will it take us to get there?"

"We will enter the realm of Fallada by sunrise. We journey to Goldun for two days from there."

Selena pressed her fingers to her aching temples. "This all seems like so much to take in. Is there time for you to start from the beginning now? Can you tell me more about Damu and who I really am? And if you know why Titus was sent to hunt me, I'd be glad to hear that, too."

Jacob cleared his throat and adjusted his glasses for what had to be the millionth time. "Certainly, Princess. If you'll follow me, we'll go below deck now. Wil is there and the four of us can sit in our cabin comfortably."

Selena and Zoe followed, dodging the bustling crewmen as they moved busily across the deck. Selena was disarmed by the fact that they kept stopping their work to bow every time she walked by. She didn't think she'd ever get used to it.

Selena paused, staring through a metal grate that covered the little hold Wil and the crew had called the brig. It was barely more than a hole in which they'd stashed Titus, who lay on his side, still unconscious. Her heart wrenched at the pitiful sight. She couldn't help but notice how beautiful he was in his wolf form, stretches of lean and powerful muscle beneath a downy pelt of white and pale gray. He was also humongous, easily five times the size of a normal wolf.

"Come on, Selena," Zoe called from the stairwell leading below deck. She and Jake were already descending.

With one last look into the brig, She trailed Zoe and Jake down into a dark hallway. They found Wilhelm in a dimly lit cabin that was barely large enough to contain wall-to-wall bookshelves, two small cots, and two desks overflowing with books and stacks of loose paper. Wil sat at one of the desks, a candle flickering beside him as he hunched over a sheet of paper with a quill pen in hand. When they entered, he laid it beside the open inkwell.

"Well," he said, folding his hands on the desk in front of him. "Is Her Highness ready to hear the whole of it now?"

"Yes," Jake said as he shuffled over to the unoccupied desk. He dropped the leather volume he'd been carrying on the surface and began to unbutton his brown vest. "I thought you would delight in telling it to her."

"Wonderful! You do know how I love to spin a good yarn."

Jake mumbled incoherently and lowered his head over the book, flipping it open and taking up his own pen. He quickly lit a candle and seemed to block everyone else in the room out.

"Don't mind him," Wil said, waving his hand in dismissal toward Jake. "My brother would rather daydream and scribble in his notebooks than carry on an actual conversation. Please, have a seat … if you can find one."

Selena and Zoe shuffled through what seemed to be mountains

of paper before locating two wooden, rolling chairs. They pushed them right up to Wil's desk and sat, looking across the scratched wood at him expectantly. He studied Selena closely, a frown pulling at the corners of his mouth.

After a while Selena raised her eyebrows and cleared her throat. "Well?"

"Hmm, yes, the story. My apologies, it is just that you are a remarkable image of your mother. I cannot believe I didn't see it before. It is clear to me that you are one of them."

"Them?" Zoe questioned. "As in princesses? There's more than one?"

Wil nodded. "Yes, but we're getting ahead of ourselves, aren't we? Allow me to go back to the beginning, to a time when the world of men existed in harmony with Fallada. I know that the notion of a Werewolf or a Faerie might seem like fairytale balderdash to you, but that is because the times I speak of have been forgotten. They are recorded only by the tales written in books by men like Jake and I."

"What happened?" Selena asked. She wasn't even going to question his claims. After everything she'd seen today, there was no reason not to believe him.

"Men, in their usual fashion, ruined everything. There was a time when we were allowed to move freely from our realm to theirs, back and forth at our leisure. We were welcomed by Fallada and her people and we marveled at the world that existed just beyond our own borders. The violence and greed of mankind overruled good sense, and in time they began to covet Fallada's riches and power. Armies rose up against Fallada and invasions were planned. In his infinite wisdom, High King Endroth called his council together and proposed a solution: erect a wall between Fallada and Earth, and erase the memory of the land from their history books to ensure the safety of Fallada's people. After much deliberation, and disagreement from some parties, the decision was made and the Fae began using their magic to create the wall."

"The same sort of magic you used on my house," said Selena, remembering how Jake and Wil had walked the perimeter of her house chanting before boarding the ship for departure. They had worn odd-looking talismans around their necks and seemed to lose themselves in the task as they circled the yard, speaking a language Selena didn't recognize.

"Yes, only much more powerful. Adrah, the Queen of the Fae, led the effort, and soon the world of Fallada was closed away forever, safe from all intruders."

"Aren't you and Jake considered intruders?" Zoe interrupted. "Aren't you humans?"

Wil smiled. "Yes, but we were allowed to stay. Jacob and I could not imagine a world in which Fallada did not exist. We had already reached our twilight years and knew we wanted to spend our last moments in the kingdom we thought of as home. We staged our deaths a few years apart—it took several years for the wall to be complete—and crossed over with the help of the Fae. It was our intention to enjoy our last years in the Fae kingdom of Goldun. Things did not go according to plan."

"Is this when the war started?" At Wil's raised eyebrows Selena shrugged. "Before Titus went all Teen Wolf on me, he said something about losing his parents to a war."

"It wasn't until the wall was completed that we realized a terrible deed had been committed. You see, Fallada is governed by a High King and Queen, and below them are the rulers of the four regions. There is Goldun, the realm of the immortal Fae, Damu, the desert region, Zenun, the underwater kingdom, and Mollac, the icy expanse. The queen of Mollac, Eranna, was against King Endroth's plans from the beginning. She is a vain and selfish woman who could think of nothing other than having humans worship her. She plotted to enslave the human race and rule them with King Endroth at her side. It was her anger and jealousy that moved her to commit the great evil."

"We had no way of knowing that Eranna had taken Sorcerers

and Witches into her counsel, dabbling in dark magic arts. By the time we discovered just how powerful she had become, it was too late. She had already done away with the seven princesses."

"Seven princesses," Zoe murmured with a shake of her head. "Somehow that makes the fact that you're one feel less special, doesn't it, Selena … or Eladria?"

"Just call me Selena, Zo," she said with a roll of her eyes before turning to Wil. "What happened to them, to us?"

"Banished. Sent away, over the wall and into the world of men and scattered about. Two came from Mollac, two from Damu, two from Zenun, and the seventh is the daughter of King Endroth and heir to the throne of Fallada. Since you and the six other girls were taken, Fallada has fallen into darkness and Eranna has been gearing up for a takeover. Her dark army grows by the day and she has taken many lives and prisoners in her quest for dominance."

Wil's eyes clouded with sadness and he lowered them, leaning back in his chair and hooking his thumbs into his suspenders with a sigh.

"Even King Endroth has fallen to her evil. She holds him captive in her iron fortress."

"Why iron?" Selena asked.

"The only beings strong enough to go against Eranna are the Fae, and they are harmed by iron. Large quantities of it will suck the life from a Faerie faster than you can blink. She plans to use her iron fortress to shield herself from Adrah until she can gather enough power to rule."

"I don't get it," Selena said, running a hand through her hair. "What does all of this have to do with me? I'm guessing Eranna is the one who sent Titus after me?"

Wil nodded, his expression grim. "Yes. The Werewolves were the first to fall into slavery under Eranna's cruel hand. Those who dared to oppose her had no choice but to go into hiding. Eranna is using them against each other, pack against pack. Those loyal to her are her hunters and those who are not are slain. It is clear that this boy, Titus, is one of those loyal to her."

Selena shook her head. "No. I can't believe that."

"Do not be fooled by his pretty face girl," Wil warned, leaning forward to rest his hands on the desk. "A Werewolf's eyes are the same color whether he's in human form or animal form. What color eyes did the wolf have that attacked you, I ask?"

"Red," Selena answered, shivering as she remembered the unnerving glow.

"Exactly. He is possessed by Eranna and therefore one of her servants. He is not to be trusted."

"Then why warn me?" Selena asked, shooting to her feet. "The first day he saw me in the woods he could have killed me, but he didn't. Titus had several opportunities after that first day to take me out and he didn't! Why would he do that if he were possessed?"

"I do not know, Princess. You should consider yourself fortunate. Titus will not be the last of Eranna's minions to come for you."

"Why? What do they want with me?"

"You are different, are you not? You have abilities that are inhuman?"

Selena nodded, casting a nervous glance at Zoe, who knew nothing of her hidden talent.

Zoe lit up. "You do? Cool! Ooh, are you super strong like Wonder Woman?"

Selena sighed. "The Flash would have been a closer guess."

Zoe's mouth fell open. "Super speed? Are you kidding me?"

Wil smiled. "Yes. You possess the same power as your parents, then. The speed of the Centaurs of Damu."

"Centaurs?" Selena groaned, picturing the half-human, half-horse creature in her mind. She remembered them from Greek mythology. "One crazy thing at a time, please. Back to what you were saying about Eranna's hit men coming after me."

"Each of the lost princesses is vital to the power of Fallada. There is a prophecy that Eranna fears more than anything. She had hoped to avoid it by sending you all away, but now she knows Adrah has sent us after you. She will stop at nothing to secure her throne, and to do what she must keep you from claiming yours."

"Prophecy? What does it say?"

Wil stood and paced behind the desk. His voice took on a haunting lilt as he recited the words that had obviously been ingrained into his memory.

"When the sun turns red over desert sky, when the earth begins to shake, when the tides of the sea rise, when the clouds roll and thunder, when the phoenix rises high, when the water creatures cry, when the dreams of the white dove prophesy, then will come the sacred time. Seven souls united, seated upon thrones royal, will bring about the winds of change, and fertility to the soil. And when the great army marches, all will hear their battle cry. All will know and see the proof of their victory in the sky."

Wil stopped, his eyes fixed on Selena. "You, my dear, are the beginning of that prophecy coming to pass. 'When the sun turns red over the desert sky'… it refers to the return of the eldest princess of Damu and the coming Red Dawn. Eranna fears this, for it will signal the beginning of the war. She means to bring the fight to Damu first. You will lead the army that stops her."

"No! No way! You've got the wrong girl."

Selena jumped up from her chair and backed away from Wil and his crazy ideas. Zoe's eyes were as round as saucers.

"Sorry, man, but Selena isn't exactly a general," Zoe said. "What is she supposed to know about leading an army?"

Wil squared his shoulders and cast Zoe an exasperated glance. "*Princess Eladria* is the descendant of royalty, many of whom were great warriors. She is the daughter of King Eldalwen of Damu, one of the greatest of his time. It is already in her, young Zoe, and she will learn."

Selena felt as if a fist had closed around her lungs, it was so hard to breathe. She pressed a hand to her throat and inhaled deep gulps of air, hoping to calm her racing pulse and frazzled nerves. It was entirely too much for one set of teenage shoulders to bear.

"No," she whispered, her eyes lowered to the cluttered table between her and the eldest Grimm brother. "I can't."

"You must." Jacob Grimm spoke for the first time since bringing them into the room. He was standing, his hands resting on his desk's scratched surface. "Don't you see, Selena? This is your destiny. Your entire life, you have felt as if you didn't belong. I understand that feeling and so does Wil. It's why we left Earth for Fallada. Something in us just *knew* it was where we belonged. You will see, Selena. Once we arrive in Damu, you will understand. It is your home and those who dwell there are your people and you are responsible for them."

"I don't want to be responsible for them," Selena countered, her hands balling into fists at her sides. "Do I look like the kind of girl who's ready to throw on a cape and go around saving the universe? I'm seventeen years old! The biggest things that are supposed to be happening in my life right now are prom and graduation, not wars and evil plots!" She turned for the door, pulling Zoe along with her. "I will go with you to Goldun so the Faeries can heal my grandmother, but then you are going to take me home."

Jacob sighed and lowered his head. Wil remained silent as he crossed his arms over his chest and stared through a porthole out into the dark night.

"Very well," Jake said, his shoulders sagging. "It will be as you wish, Selena."

"ARE you ready to talk about it now?"

"No."

Zoe frowned and went back to staring out through the porthole over her cot. After leaving Jake and Wil's cluttered room, the girls had retreated to their cabin for the night. They'd been there for hours, and soon the sun would be rising, but Selena hadn't been able to sleep a wink. She had thought Zoe was asleep, but her friend's question shattered the silence in the room and reminded Selena that she wasn't the only one who'd had a bombshell dropped on her today.

Faeries, shape-shifting Werewolves, evil queens…it was a lot to take in. Selena glanced over to where her grandmother lay sleeping on her cot on the opposite side of the room and envied her. She wished someone had given *her* a sleeping potion; maybe then she could escape the frenzied thoughts taking up space in her head.

"I think you owe me at least that much," Zoe said, drawing her knees up to her chest and wrapping her arms around her legs. She stared at Selena pointedly. "I'm along for the ride here, and it sounds like this is going to get dangerous. Plus, I'm your best friend."

"You only get to play the best friend card once a year," Selena said with a smile.

"When was the last time I used the best friend card?"

"Two words: prom dress."

"It's not my fault we have similar taste in gowns. Besides, that dress looked like crap on you. Redheads can't wear red, Selena."

"Says who?"

"Says your reflection when you put that gown on. Trust me girl, I did you a favor."

"So what you're saying is, I owe you for doing me that favor."

"Exactly. I mean, you could at least tell me more about Wolf Boy."

Selena felt her cheeks going red and her face flushed with heat. She pulled her blanket farther up her chest and sighed.

"There isn't much to tell."

"So, a strange Werewolf comes into town and you don't think to tell me?"

"He wasn't a Werewolf when I met him Zoe. I mean, he was

one, but I didn't know it. Not until he went mental and chased me down. By then there wasn't much time to talk."

"Is he cute?"

A vision of onyx black hair and icy blue eyes filled Selena's mind and she smiled. "So pretty I could cry."

"Zac Efron pretty?"

Selena chuckled. "Prettier."

With a barely contained squeal, Zoe jumped up from her cot and bounced onto Selena's, taking them both back to their elementary school days of hiding beneath the sheets with a flashlight.

"This is crazy Selena. You're a freaking princess! I can't wait to see your castle. I bet you've got some fabulous clothes and—"

"Zoe!" Selena grasped the other girl's shoulders and shook her, trying not to let her friend's excitement get to her. "You're forgetting the part about the war and the crazy queen who wants my head on a pike. What about the part where I lead an army against her? Or the part where I become ruler of a kingdom? That means I'd never go home again."

"Why would you *want* to go home again? And what about the part where you get to meet your parents? Jake and Wil mentioned your father in the present tense, so that means he's alive. You finally get to know where you come from and learn where you get your freaky powers. I'm still mad at you for not telling me about that, by the way."

"What was I supposed to say? 'Hey, Zoe. Nice to meet you, my name is Selena McKinley and I can outrun a Mustang'."

"The car or the horse?"

"Why does that even matter?"

Zoe shrugged. "Just seems like the car might be faster."

"Both, okay?"

Zoe whistled. "I can't wait to see that. Soon as we land this thing I want a full demonstration."

"I don't think so."

"Selena."

She whipped the covers aside and left the bed. "Look, the only reason I haven't asked them to turn this ship around is because my Gram is going to die unless we let those Faerie people take care of her. We're staying long enough to get her better, say thank you to the nice winged people and then we're going home!"

"Where you'll go back to being a misunderstood nobody," Zoe said softly.

Selena paused, her hand on the doorknob. She lowered her head as the truth of Zoe's words sunk in. "I don't intend to stay in Twin Oaks forever. I've been saving up to move away, remember?"

"And do what? Work as a waitress somewhere while you struggle to make rent? Moonlight as a stripper named 'Chandelier' on the weekends?"

"Zoe, that's not funny."

"No, but it's worth thinking about. Everyone knows I'm not going to do much with my life. If I do go to college, I won't get much further than Baylor and that's only if my college fund covers it. I'll end up growing old in Twin Oaks married to one of the McClendon boys or something."

"Hey, that oldest one is cute. What's his name again?"

"Mark is hot, yes, but you're missing my point," Zoe said with a laugh. "I'm okay with living that kind of life, Selena. You never have been. Maybe this is the answer, this destiny Wil told you about. It might be worth it for you to check it out and see where this leads. Who knows, you might actually feel like you belong for a change."

Selena shrugged as she pulled the door open, desperate to escape Zoe and the truth. "I'm not willing to risk my life or the lives of the people I love over this, and I don't intend to change my mind."

Chapter Five

W il Grimm stood alone on the ship's deck as Selena climbed the stairwell. The wind whipped his gray hair around his weathered face and a gnarled, wooden pipe was clutched between his teeth. White smoke wafted up in a thin trail against the midnight-blue sky. The brightness of the stars astounded her, as did the size and intensity of the moon. Wil shifted and turned to face her as he heard her crossing the deck and frowned, his disapproval clear. Selena ignored him, not caring if he was angry with her. How could anyone expect her to take the fate of an entire world in her hands—a world she hadn't even known existed twenty-four hours ago? It wasn't fair, and Selena didn't think it was right for Wil and Jake to try and make her feel guilty about it.

"Don't mind him," said Jake, coming up the staircase behind her. He clutched the same brown leather volume he'd been carrying earlier. "Wil doesn't understand that you need time to digest all this information. He's always been one with a taste for adventure, diving headfirst into things without thinking. His impulsive nature is responsible for most of our escapades."

Selena was not about to get into another discussion about her so-called destiny. Instead of addressing Jake's statement, she gestured toward the metal grate covering Titus' prison.

"How long is he going to stay like that?"

"Titus is a shape-shifter and can transform at will, but the dart we shot him with is filled with a very potent Fae potion. It renders him helpless and unable to shift until the dart is removed."

Selena gasped. "You mean you left it in him? He must be in terrible pain!"

"He is the enemy," Wil said as he joined them. His pipe was gone but the scent of tobacco still lingered. "Or have you forgotten that you were almost his dinner?"

"I don't believe he wanted to hurt me. I think if you remove the dart, he would transform and he could tell us that himself."

"For the time being," Wil consented. "Do not underestimate him, he is dangerous and you are not yet strong enough to fight him off should he decide to attack you again."

"I don't think he had a choice."

Selena stepped forward, her eyes locked on the prison carved into the ship's deck. Wil's hand clamped down on her arm, surprisingly strong.

"Everyone has a choice."

Selena shrugged him off and continued forward. "Based on what you've told me about Eranna, I don't think that's the case here."

The brothers followed silently, flanking her on either side as she approached the grate and knelt. The brig was just big and tall enough to trap the massive beast lying inside. His eyes were open and glowing red in the darkness. He lay curled up on the floor, whimpering and lapping at the wound in his hip with his large, pink tongue. A silver dart stuck up out of the fur and Selena could see teeth marks around it from his efforts at prying it loose.

"Can he remove it himself?" she asked.

Wil shook his head. "There is a special instrument for removal. One of us would have to do it."

"When will you?"

He shrugged. "I had not planned on it until we reached Goldun. I must consult Queen Adrah in regards to his fate. We cannot take his attack upon you lightly. Your father will call for his blood."

Selena stiffened. "No!"

Red eyes swiveled upward and focused on her. Selena felt fear rippling up and down her spine, but calmed when she realized that Titus's whines had increased. She frowned as they increased to full-fledged yips and barks.

"Well, I'll be," Jake whispered, bending down over the grate beside Selena. "He's trying to communicate with you, Princess."

"What's he saying?"

"I do not know."

"Then take the dart from his hip so he can change back. I know he won't hurt me."

"I don't think—"

"Am I Princess of Damu or not?" she interjected, shooting her narrowed gaze at Wil.

The old man arched a silver eyebrow. "You are."

"Then open that grate and bring me the tools. Keep your stupid gun handy if you feel threatened, but I'm going to talk to him."

Jake chuckled. "Yes, Your Highness."

It didn't take long for Wil to locate the tool—a strange instrument that looked like a pair of forceps—and for the two brothers to lift the heavy metal grate and slide it aside. Selena thrust the gleaming forceps into her back pocket and threw her legs over the side of the square hole. It wasn't too deep for her to jump down. Hopefully Titus wouldn't eat her before she got the dart out of his leg. As if he'd read her mind, Wil stepped forward and thrust his silver pistol into her hand.

"Do not hesitate to use it," he said, his mouth a grim line.

Selena nodded, thrusting the gun into the waistband of her jeans and covering it with her shirt. With one last look back at Jake and Wil, Selena vaulted over the edge and landed a few feet away from the wolf. His head came up as she dropped beside him and his eyes bored into hers, glowing with silent intensity. He did not move from his spot, but watched her closely as she moved forward with slow steps. She retrieved the forceps from her pocket and held them out for Titus to see.

"They didn't want to let me come down here," she said gently, hoping to avoid setting him off. She wanted answers and Selena believed that there was more to Titus than met the eye. Something was motivating him, compelling him to do the things he'd done, and she had every intention of finding out what.

"I told them I had no reason to believe that you would harm me once you shifted back. I hope you won't make a liar out of me."

Titus lowered his head and Selena took that as a sign of acquiescence. She closed the distance between them quickly, inspecting the dart embedded in Titus' thick pelt. Her fingers ran over his soft fur and she smiled.

"You're so beautiful," she murmured, as her hand ran up over his mammoth shoulder and toward his head. He whimpered and thrust his head beneath her stroking hand. Selena giggled and trailed her fingers over his head and ears. In response, he licked her with his rough, hot tongue. Selena wrapped her arms around the wolf's neck and pressed her face against the fur.I f not for the fact that he was in pain, Selena could gladly curl up against him and sleep comfortably on his fuzzy pelt.

"Don't worry," she whispered. "I'll get you out of here. I don't know how I know this, but I believe the best of you, Titus. I know you didn't really want to hurt me."

He lowered his head again, this time resting it in her lap. Selena forced her gaze away from his face and concentrated on the dart in his hip. It took a few minutes of poking and prodding, but eventually Selena had the dart removed. Once pulled from Titus' fur and skin, it disintegrated into a silver powder right before Selena's eyes.

"Well?" she asked, staring into Titus' red eyes. "What now?"

Titus turned and began licking at the wound on his hip. Selena gasped, leaning forward on her hands and knees to watch as the injury disappeared right before her eyes, leaving no evidence behind, save for a few drops of blood. Selena leaped to her feet and moved back against the wall as the wolf rose to his feet.

He lowered his head and shuddered as his body began to contort and change shape. Fur melted away and long stretches of pale skin appeared as the wolf shrank into the boy Selena remembered. She blushed and looked away when she realized that he was naked, but not before she caught a glimpse of a broad chest, slender waist, and abs ridged with lines and bulges of sinewy muscle.

"Here, kid," Wil grumbled as he tossed something into the hole. Selena turned just in time to see Titus' naked body disappearing into the confines of a coarse wool blanket. He watched Selena intently, his ethereal eyes practically glowing in the moonlight streaming through the opening above them. Titus drew in great gulps of air, as if struggling to breathe. His chest heaved and his nostrils flared as she took a tentative step toward him.

"Selena," he said between breaths. "Where are we? I didn't hurt you, did I?"

"I'm fine. It's my grandmother you hurt."

"Damn it! I'm so sorry."

Selena could see he truly meant it as he sank to his knees on the floor. He pulled the blanket tighter around his shoulders and sighed.

"We're on board *The Adrah* and on our way to Fallada," she said. "Do you know who Jacob and Wilhelm Grimm are?"

"Of course I do. I'm certain they mean to turn me over to the Fae once we reach Goldun. It's no more than I deserve."

Selena crouched beside him. "Maybe they won't. If you tell me why you did it, maybe I can reason with them. I know you didn't want to, Titus. I saw it in your eyes right before you attacked me."

Titus shook his head. "I didn't want to, but I had a choice. I thought I didn't, but maybe I made the wrong one. Now, Eranna will kill me because I could never hurt you."

"Please, just tell me. I don't know how much pull I have in

Fallada but they say I'm a princess. I might be able to speak on your behalf or something."

Titus smiled. "Yes, you are a princess, inside and out. How could you ever forgive me for what I've done?"

Selena shrugged. "I'll find a way for you to make it up to me, Wolf Boy. For now, just tell me what kind of trouble you're in and I will do everything I can to help you."

"It's my parents, Selena. I'm sure by now the Grimm brothers have told you of the conflict between the Werewolves of Mollac."

She nodded. "They said that the wolves are divided, pack against pack, some on Eranna's side and others running away. They say that because your eyes are red, you're one of Eranna's drones."

"That is only partially true," Titus said. "I became one of her servants, but only to save my family. We had plans to leave Mollac once we realized that Eranna had grown too powerful to avoid any longer. Some families offered their services to her to save their own skins, or because they really believed in what she was doing. The others escaped to Goldun to find refuge within the realm of the Fae. My family left too late and we were captured by Eranna's other hunters. She has taken my parents and sister prisoner. She promised to free them if I traveled to the world of men and killed the princess of Damu. That's you, Selena. You know the rest."

Selena felt pity and fierce protectiveness washing over her. She couldn't explain it, but something inside her roiled savagely at the thought of Queen Eranna using Titus the way she had. Something in her wanted nothing more than to see the woman thrown down from her iron tower in disgrace, but there was only one way for her to see it done and Selena wasn't even going to consider it. Joining the war was out of the question.

Get Gram healed, go home, she reminded herself inwardly.

"You should tell Wil and Jake your story. They might not be so quick to turn you over to the Fae if they knew the truth. In fact, I think the Fae should be able to help you find your family."

Titus shook his head, his eyes wide. "Eranna keeps them prisoner in her iron fortress. No Fae can enter."

Selena lifted her head, resolution gripping her in an unstoppable hold. "Then I will help you."

❧

"PRINCESS, it is out of the question."

"Says who?"

"Say I, and Queen Adrah when she learns of your plans. You are far too valuable to Damu and all of Fallada. You cannot go traipsing about Eranna's lair looking for a family of Werewolves, when you should be preparing for the battle fulfilling the prophecy."

Selena sighed, burying her face in her hands. She had left Titus in the brig after their conversation, and was now in the ship's galley with Wil and Jake, who had offered her a warm drink. Who knew flying through space would prove to be so cold? Selena sipped the hot tea gratefully, warming her hands on the tin mug.

"Maybe you guys didn't hear me the first time. I am not going to get involved in some crazy war I don't have any stake in. After my grandmother gets well, I want to help Titus and then go home."

"Damu *is* your home," Wil insisted. "Whether you like it or not, that is where you belong."

"I'm not having this argument right now, and I'm pretty sure I don't need anybody's permission. If this Queen Adrah won't help me, then I'll find my father and *he'll* help me."

"King Eldalwen will agree with me, I think," Wil scoffed. "Your rightful place is in Damu, preparing for the Red Dawn."

"We'll see," Selena said before draining the last of her tea. "I just thought I'd give you the courtesy of telling you my plans. I was hoping you'd help, but I am going to find someone to do this with me."

"Suit yourself," Wil replied. The scrape of his chair echoed through the galley. "I am done trying to talk sense into you, you silly young creature. I will be glad to leave you to Adrah; she can talk sense into anyone."

With that, he was gone, the stomp of his boots heavy on the wooden stairs as he descended to the deck once more. Jake continued to watch her, his hands clutched around another one of his notebooks. His fingers were stained with ink.

"If you ever get the pleasure of meeting your father, you'll learn that you are much like him. Once he latches onto an idea, he does not let it go, either. I take it that you are not going to change your mind about rescuing the boy's family."

Selena shook her head. "Not a chance."

Jake smiled. "Good. We should be coming upon the portal soon. You should come up on deck, you will want to see it."

Selena watched Jake's retreating form with raised eyebrows. It was nice to know she at least had the younger brother in her corner. She followed behind him, finding both Zoe and Titus on deck. Behind them, the black night of space loomed, filled with twinkling stars. It was hard to remember that it was nearly dawn when it was so dark, yet Jake had told her it was time to enter Fallada. The portal within the wall didn't work until the sun had risen on the other side of it.

She joined Zoe and Titus at the ship's railing, trying not to notice the way the whipping wind blew his dark hair around his face. His jaw was tense and his mouth tight, but he'd never been more gorgeous, surrounded by the beauty of the universe. One of the crew had given him clothes; a white button-up shirt and brown suede pants that showcased his long legs. A tan vest hung open across his broad torso.

"The brothers let me out of the brig if I promised to behave myself," Titus said with a nervous laugh. "Your friend has been given a weapon with a poisoned dart just in case."

Zoe lifted the silver pistol and smiled. "How badass is this?"

Selena rolled her eyes at her friend and leaned against the railing between them.

"Jake says it's almost time to cross over."

Titus nodded. "You see that constellation there?"

"You mean the Big Dipper?"

Titus frowned. "In my world we call it Dynathine. That is where we're headed. Once we've passed through the brightest star of that star formation …" he smiled, "… well, let's just say you've never seen anything so beautiful."

He fell silent, propping himself on his elbows as he stared into the great beyond. Selena gave Zoe a pointed stare for a few seconds before her friend got the message.

"Yeah, um, so I'm gonna go and see the view from the other side of the deck," she said with a not-so-covert wink at Selena.

"You do that," Selena said with a sigh. She watched Zoe circle around the ship's large engine until she disappeared from sight.

Titus tensed, as if he felt her eyes on him, but didn't look her way when he spoke. "You're going to get yourself killed. This is my battle, Selena, and I won't drag you into it. You should get your grandmother well and go home."

"You don't think I should go to Damu and lead the army like everyone else seems to want me to?"

He looked at her then, his eyes shadowed and turbulent. "Do you know how long it could take them to find the others? There are seven of you, and in your world it has been almost seventeen years. Anything could have happened to those girls since then. All of you are needed and the odds of Queen Adrah tracking them all down and bringing them to Fallada are slim. It is a fool's errand."

"Thank you."

He frowned. "For what?"

"For being on my side," she replied. "Even Zoe thinks I should give this princess thing a shot. I'm sure she's thinking of all the nice clothes, castle, and handsome prince in my future."

Selena distinctly heard the sound of a low growl ripping through Titus' chest. He lowered his head and took a deep breath.

"Sorry," he said sheepishly. "The animal side of me is extremely jealous at the mention of princes. Your father will more than likely arrange a marriage for you once the prophecy is fulfilled."

Rebellion surged, hot in her veins, as Selena vowed not to let anyone control her. She had her own goals and did not intend to get suckered into a full stay in Goldun, Damu, or any other place in Fallada.

"No need for jealousy. I don't intend to stay long enough to get hitched."

Titus grew silent again, and just as Selena was about to speak her vision was overcome with a brilliant burst of light. She hadn't realized that they had approached the constellation, and now the glimmer of the formation's brightest star was enveloping the ship. Selena closed her eyes against the flash, gripping Titus' hand as swirls of color and light contorted and flickered behind her eyelids. His fingers closed around hers, and a deep, vibrating hum echoed through her body.

The ship accelerated and Selena felt pressure from all sides. The culmination of something filled her and the breath was sucked from her lungs. Just when she felt as if she would collapse from lack of oxygen, the pressure loosened its hold and air filled her starved lungs. She inhaled on a sharp gasp, opening her eyes just as the spark of white light faded. Selena's eyes widened and her grip tightened on Titus as Fallada filled her vision. She gasped and exhaled, her voice coming out in a bark of laughter tainted with disbelief.

Selena faintly heard Zoe's voice from the other side of the ship. "Holy crap!"

Selena giggled. Holy crap was right. Titus had been, too.

She had never seen anything more beautiful in her life.

Chapter Six

I t was as if someone had gone over the world with a paintbrush and replaced all of the usual colors with explosively bright hues. Beneath their soaring ship, blades of emerald green grass sparkled in the sunlight, bending beneath the gentle call of the wind. The sky was an intense shade of blue dotted with frothy clouds that sparkled like white diamonds. Trees rose up out of the ground, so tall that some of the foliage scraped the bottom of the ship. Flowers dotted gently sloping hills in shades of fuchsia, teal, and violet, leaving Selena open-mouthed and stunned. Behind the ship, the wall the Grimm brothers had told her about stretched on for miles in either direction. It glowed with a stunning mix of iridescent colors, pale blue swirling with light pink and lavender.

The Adrah slowed and the sound of a massive anchor falling to the ground below echoed across the grassy plain. Selena watched as several crewmen swung down on ropes, working to secure them.

"I thought the journey to Goldun was supposed to take two days from here," Selena said. "Why are we stopping the ship?"

"A flying vessel would draw Eranna's attention," Titus said, grabbing her hand and propelling her to where everyone was gathering around the Grimm Brothers at the ship's bow. "Now that we are in Fallada, we must travel quickly and stealthily if we're to have any chance of reaching Goldun. It will be harder for us to be found by the Eye of Mollac ... sort of a crystal ball," he elaborated at Selena's confused look. "Every region has one, and it allows the person who possesses it to locate people wherever they are. I am sure Eranna knows we have left your world by now. The longer it takes her to find us, the better. Of course, this means she will send her hunters after us."

Selena shivered as a wave of foreboding washed over her. Titus spoke of these hunters as if they were more dangerous than he was. Remembering the eerie red glow of his eyes and the gleaming white canines, Selena could only hope nothing existed in Fallada that was more frightening than that.

All around them the crew bustled, shutting down the ship's engine and preparing for the last leg of the journey. From below deck, one of the men carried Rose in his arms. Selena rushed forward to inspect her, shocked to find her face flushed and hot with fever. Rose moaned and mumbled incoherently as Selena stroked a few strands of dark, sweat-soaked hair away from her face.

"The fever has taken her," Jake said as he stepped forward to help the other man place Rose's body in a harness. Wil and two other men waited on the ground below to take her once she'd been lowered. "Don't worry, the Fae have been using their power to combat the effects of Werewolf venom for centuries. Once within their realm your grandmother will be just fine."

Selena nodded and stepped back to allow the men the space to work the harness. Once they were sure Rose had made it safely to the ground, Titus, Zoe, and Selena shimmied down rope ladders thrown over the side. Once on the ground, Selena felt dwarfed by the towering trees. Above them the branches swayed and dipped, effectively blotting out the sight of the ship and most of the sunlight. A few feet away, a chariot-like vehicle hovered inches from the ground. It was flanked by several others and some were steadily being filled with members of the crew.

Selena walked over to the nearest one and circled it, running her hands along the side. The carriage was the color of gleaming pearls and was covered in intricate carvings of branches, leaves, and flowers. A latch opened the side door and revealed three rows of cushioned benches for sitting on.

"There are no wheels. Where are the horses?" Zoe asked as she rounded the front of the hovering vehicle.

Wil leaped onto the front bench before offering Selena a hand up. "No horses here! This craft is powered by Fae magic."

Selena allowed Wil to pull her up into the chariot before reaching for Zoe's hand. Titus and Jake followed, and Rose's sleeping form was laid across the third seat. From her front row spot between Wil and Titus, Selena would have the perfect view of the passing scenery. She only wished Rose were awake to see it. The gardening fanatic would never want to leave a world filled with flowers in such vibrant colors. Selena glanced to where her grandmother lay in the back. Rose's breathing was steady, if not a little rapid, and Selena prayed silently that they would make it to Goldun without incident.

Wil reached into one of his many vest pockets and retrieved a gleaming silver key. He placed it into a slot on the … dashboard? … and turned it. A low humming met their ears and the vehicle vibrated gently as it rose up a few more feet from the ground. The chariot lurched and sped forward, pushing Selena back against the cushioned seat as it careened and dipped through the trees.

"MY QUEEN, I have news for you that is most disturbing."

Eranna sighed as she slid into her silk robe, turning to face Ushma, who had interrupted her nightly beauty ritual. Hours of soaking in a concoction of milk, honey, and enchanted herbs stolen from the forests of Goldun kept her skin young, healthy, firm, and kissed its paleness with a luminescent glow. Next would come another hour of treating her hair with the same mixture and brushing it until it gleamed. It wasn't a bother to her; tending to her beauty brought her nothing but peace and happiness. She looked forward to the day when the pesky business of war had ended and she could spend her days reveling in others' admiration of her exquisiteness.

"What is it, you hag?" Eranna snarled as she slid her feet into matching silk slippers. "Can't you see that I am busy?"

"I would not have disturbed you if it were not important, My Queen," Ushma said, inching farther into the room but keeping her head bowed in reverence. "It is about the boy you sent into the human realm."

Eranna smiled at her reflection, smoothing one hand over a high cheekbone. A tiny shiver of satisfaction shot though her as she remembered the raw terror she'd incited in young Titus.

"He is quite delicious, isn't he, Ushma? He is young, but moldable. Once his assignment is done, I might keep him around a while longer just for fun."

"That is what I'm trying to tell you! The lookouts you posted on the wall have reported seeing him enter Fallada in the company of the Brothers Grimm."

Fury swirled low in her gut and exploded from her lips in a ferocious roar. Her fingernails ate into her palms as she whirled on the hunchbacked Witch, her eyes glowing with the pale, white light of her rage.

"Princess Eladria was with them, was she not?"

The calm tones of her voice wavered with the force of her anger, causing Ushma to cower and fall to her knees.

"Yes, My Queen. They are traveling together toward Goldun. What would you have me do?"

Eranna brushed past Ushma and moved through the open door of her bedroom, to the chamber containing the Eye of Mollac. She welcomed the frigid winter blast that met her through the room's open windows. It stirred the stark white curtains with bursts of swirling snow and filled the room with white flakes. In the center stood a full-length mirror in a gilded silver frame, covered by a sheer, white cloth. Eranna pulled away the cloth and felt serenity calming her turbulent thoughts at the sight of the swirling arcs of light within the mirror, her all-seeing Eye. She faced it determinedly.

"Mirror, mirror, show me the traitorous Werewolf and his companions."

She focused all her mental energy on Titus and called up his image using the Eye. It shuddered and glowed with a blinding white light as her vision was filled with that of a shady glen only one days' journey from Goldun. By the afternoon of the next day, Princess Eladria would have made it to the realm of the Fae—out of her reach until she'd be transported to Damu. Once surrounded by Adrah and her warrior Fae, Eladria and her party would be more than adequately protected.

The traveling party was sleeping peacefully in the little corner of the woods. Eranna shifted her energy from the sleeping form of Titus, to that of Eladria. Revulsion and envy twisted in her chest as her eyes traveled over wide, doe eyes, a pert nose, and a full, pink mouth. Locks of vibrant red hair fanned out beneath her head and thick, brown lashes rested against her cheekbones. Deeper than her outer beauty was a quiet strength. It boiled just below the surface, waiting to be unleashed.

She couldn't have that. If King Eldalwen got hold of his daughter, the seasoned warrior would no doubt turn her into a fierce fighter, unlocking the full potential of her power. It would be the beginning of the end for Eranna, but she was not going down without a fight.

Turning away from the mirror, Eranna reached for the cloth and quickly covered it. Ushma waited outside of the chamber, cowering as Eranna stormed back through the doorway.

"Your hunters await your orders, My Queen," Ushma said as

she followed her mistress through the winding corridors of her iron fortress. "Ruen has assembled them in the hall."

Eranna turned left down the corridor leading to the hall Ushma had mentioned.

"Perfect," she purred as she swung the doors open.

The faces of fifty of the most frightening creatures in all of Fallada greeted her. The Minotaurs were hideous apparitions created by her Witches, with the bodies of strong males and the heads of horned oxen. They were unintelligent, great lumbering brutes, but they served their purposes well as trackers and ruthless killers.

They parted for her as she moved into their midst, watching her with shining black eyes as she held her hands up for silence. The light of a dozen torches cast an eerie orange glow over their deranged faces and the sounds of their snorts and heavy breathing echoed from the high, arched ceilings.

Ruen, the head hunter who could be identified by the three golden rings puncturing his wide nostrils, stepped forward.

"We are ready to serve you, my beautiful queen," he said, the deep timbre of his voice echoing through his massive chest. "What do you require?"

"Princess Eladria has been brought into Fallada by the Grimm Brothers and Titus, that treacherous Werewolf."

The snorting and growling grew louder as the hunters expressed their mutual rage. Eranna smiled her pleasure as she grasped the beefy shoulder of Ruen.

"My hunters, I want the traitor brought to me alive. As for Eladria …"

Their breaths stilled in anticipation as every heart within the large hall skipped a beat. Eranna's grin widened.

"Kill her!"

The roar that met her ears was thunderous as the eyes of every beast flashed red. Their stomping and grunting preceded them from the hall like a mighty earthquake, causing the walls around her to shake. Eranna crossed her arms over her chest and watched them go.

"Worry not Ushma," she said to the Witch, who had stood in the doorway, watching the entire exchange. "In me, Queen Adrah of Goldun has found her match."

❧

TITUS HALTED MID-STRIDE, his every muscle stiff and his eyes narrowed. Selena came up short, confusion knitting her brows as she studied him. It was sunset, and their group had made camp for the night. The Grimm Brothers refused to travel after dark, stating that this time of day was when Eranna's minions were at their most powerful. They promised arrival in Goldun by the following afternoon, and as far as Selena was concerned, they couldn't get there fast enough. Rose was not awake often, but when she was fits of delirium consumed her. The hallucinations, sweating, and mumbling were so bad that after they'd managed to get some water down her throat, Selena begged the brothers to give her more of their sleeping potion. It was the only thing that seemed to bring her peace.

She and Titus had just left a nearby stream, where they'd washed their hands for a picnic dinner, when he suddenly became stiff, silent, and alert.

"What's wrong?" Selena asked, only to be shushed by Titus.

She fell silent, and he dropped his finger from his mouth while keeping the rest of his body perfectly still. His nostrils widened and he inhaled as he slowly scanned the line of trees surrounding them. Titus shifted his eyes toward Selena, and she felt anxiety creeping up her spine at the fear she found in his.

"Minotaurs," he said, his whisper snatched away by the wind. "At least six of them."

Selena tried to recall her Greek mythology. Jake had told her that many of the creatures written about in myths and fairytales were a reality in Fallada, immortalized by those who had lived during the time when the two worlds were one. Acid rose up in her throat as she recalled her junior high school English class study on the Greek legends. Minotaurs were the stuff of nightmares, and she definitely did not want to be around if one of them was about, let alone six.

"What do we do?" she whispered back, deciding to follow Titus' lead and not speak loudly or make any sudden moves.

"You're going to have to really trust me," he said as their eyes locked once more. "I'm going to shift."

Selena felt herself stiffen involuntarily as memories of Titus' attack came rushing back to her mind. He reached out to grasp her hand and gave it a reassuring squeeze.

"I'm not going to hurt you," he said gently. "Never again, Selena, I promise. It's the only way I can take them on and give you a chance to escape to camp. Warn the others and get away."

Selena shook her head. "No!" she said a little louder than she'd meant to. "You can't, you'll be killed!"

He smiled and shrugged. "I'll be fine. Just do it. As soon as I shift, they'll be on me and you need to make a break for it. Run like you never have in your life."

It was then that she heard the sound of low growls from different points around them. The demonic glow of red eyes peered at them through the brush and foliage, making Selena's blood run cold.

"Okay," she agreed as she released his hand. "I'm ready."

Titus closed his eyes and inhaled deeply, expanding his chest with the motion. In a flash, the sound of realigning bones and cartilage met her ears and Titus was bending and transforming, sprouting fur and dropping to all fours until he was a fearsome beast once again. Selena stood, mesmerized, unable to take her eyes off the white-furred animal. He turned to her, his eyes burning red, and growled before nudging her leg with his muzzle. The roar of the Minotaurs echoed across the forest and threw

Selena into action. She hurled all of her strength into a single burst of speed, propelling herself away from Titus and the menacing creatures.

Through the blur of trees ahead of her, she witnessed a sight that stole her speed and punched the air straight from her lungs. Behind her the sounds of struggles and growls assaulted her ears, while in front of her, six more Minotaurs held her entourage hostage. The Grimm brothers stood with Zoe between them and were surrounded by the members of the ship crew. Rose was limp in Jake's arms. The Minotaurs encircled them, rendering them helpless with massive, sharpened axes.

Their enormous bodies rippled with hard muscle, their biceps like tree trunks. The hands gripping the axes were as meaty as Christmas hams. Their grotesque faces were further mauled by various piercings: gold rings that punctured their nostrils, eyebrows, eyelids, and ears. A stripe of dark hair ran from the top of each one's head and down between their shoulder blades. Long, curved, pointed horns gleamed menacingly in the moonlight. Selena skidded to a stop, her every nerve on edge as the sixth beast, one sporting three dangling rings in his nostrils, came toward her.

Selena met Zoe's eyes and felt her heart lurch at the fear she found there. Wil's hand was on the butt of his silver pistol, but his expression told Selena that he was not stupid enough to try to fire. By the time he took one down, the other five would be on him in a second. She could tell he was angry over feeling helpless. So was she. What was she supposed to do against six Minotaurs? She wasn't sure, but for the sake of Zoe and the sleeping Rose, Selena knew she would have to try.

The sixth Minotaur rested the staff of his axe on the ground and leaned forward, his glowing red eyes narrowed as he studied her. His nostrils widened as he chuckled, sending Selena's head reeling as the stench of his acrid breath curled around her.

"Princess Eladria, I presume," he said, the deep bass of his voice sending chills through her core. She refused to show her fear.

Instead, she placed her hands on her hips and narrowed her eyes at the creature.

"My name is Selena," she hissed.

"It does not matter what you choose to call yourself. By entering this realm you have sentenced yourself, and your companions, to death."

"They haven't done anything," Selena argued, her voice wavering with fear. "Let them go."

The beast laughed again. "You have yet to take the throne, and already you issue orders like a royal. I have a queen, little girl, and she is far more magnificent, powerful, and beautiful than you. You are no match for her."

"Obviously I am," Selena scoffed with false confidence, "if she felt the need to send you to kill me!"

A low rumbling growl rippled from the Minotaur's chest. "You are foolish to mock my queen!" he roared. "And now you will suffer before you die. Bring the old woman forward."

"No!"

Selena lurched forward as one of the Minotaurs wrestled Rose from Jake's arms. She was abruptly brought up short by two of the creatures, who had crossed their axes in front of her in a blocking maneuver. A strong pair of hands grasped her arms and forced her to her knees as he held the staff of his axe to her throat. She ceased her struggles as the unforgiving wooden pole pressed against her windpipe.

The leader stood over Rose, axe raised and his eyes gleaming with glee.

"You will watch each one of your cohorts perish before meeting your end, Eladria."

He raised the axe higher and Selena felt panic ripping through her as she realized they were all going to die. She wanted to close her eyes, but could not look away from the gleaming axe blade raised high over the Minotaur's head. With one last defeated cry, Selena tossed her head back and screamed her anguish.

A rush of what could only be described as intense energy exploded in her chest and rippled out from Selena's body in waves. A gale of forceful wind whipped around them, propelling all six of the colossal creatures into the nearby trees. Selena met Zoe's stunned gaze as her friend ran toward her.

"What did you just do?"

Before Selena could answer, the whooshing sound of gigantic wings rang out overhead, drawing the eye of every member of their party. Large birds of every breed swooped down upon them, several times the size of any bird Selena had ever seen on earth. Their loud screeching seemed to enrage the Minotaurs, who were slowly picking themselves up off the ground.

As the oversized birds drew closer the Grimm brothers, along with the bedraggled sailors, began waving their arms in celebration and whooping with joy. Selena looked back and forth between the celebrating men and the hovering birds in slack-jawed question.

Jake chuckled at her confusion and pointed toward the bird leading the flock. His smile was wide and his eyes twinkling as he uttered the one word that flooded Selena with hope.

"Faeries!"

Chapter Seven

The Faeries were nothing like Selena had imagined they would be. Disney had it all wrong and Tinkerbell was nothing compared to these magnificent creatures. Silver armor etched with tree branches and flowers adorned the torsos of both male and female Fae. They were tall, willowy creatures with luminescent skin and eyes that glowed in every shade of green imaginable. Gleaming silver headpieces in a variety of shapes boasted gems, jewels, and dangling strings of pearls, and covered hair that ran in various lengths and boasted a spectrum of color between pristine white and shimmering gold. Pointed ears showed beneath the helmets, but Selena was surprised to see that the Fae were wingless. Their garments and hair flowed about them as if possessed of a life of their own, creating a beautiful streak of glowing color and light as they swooped from overhead.

As they plunged down with various weapons raised and leaped from the backs of their birds, they engaged the Minotaurs in a battle that lasted only minutes. The ugly creatures were outnumbered and forced to retreat. The Fae did not give chase, but instead, surrounded Selena and the others in a protective circle. Selena turned slowly, hypnotized by twenty pairs of green eyes set in angularly shaped, angelic faces. The largest male stepped forward and removed his helmet, revealing shoulder-length silver-blond hair. He placed a fist to his chest and dropped to one knee in front of her. The other nineteen Faeries followed suit, falling to one knee and laying their weapons in the grass, heads lowered and hands fisted over their chests.

"Dude," Zoe whispered as she took in the bowing Faerie circle. "This is too weird."

The emerald green eyes of the male Fae met Selena's and he stood.

"Princess Eladria, I am Rothatin, general of the Fae Warrior class. We were sent by our queen to rescue you from the hand of the Minotaur. It is an honor to be in your presence."

Selena stuck one hand out to the Fae, who towered nearly an entire foot over her. "Uh, yeah, nice to meet you Rothatin. This is—"

"I know the members of your party," he interrupted with a gleaming, magnetic smile. "Our queen is wise and all-knowing. She has been watching your journey with great interest and is anxious to meet you. We will provide an armed escort for the remainder of your expedition to Goldun."

"Wait!" Selena cried as Rothatin turned toward the trees, where the flock of birds awaited their masters. "What about—"

"General, we've found the traitor!"

Selena whipped around to find two more male Fae holding Titus by the arms and dragging him toward their little circle. He had shifted back to his human form and besides his tousled hair and a little blood running from a cut on his forehead, be seemed to be unharmed.

"He is not a traitor!" Selena defended, glaring at the Faerie who had made the accusation.

Rothatin's jaw hardened as he brushed past Selena and walked to where the two warrior Fae had forced Titus to his knees. He looked up at the approaching general silently, his blue eyes as calm as a still river.

"You know little, Princess," Rothatin said, his eyes never leaving Titus. "This boy will be made to pay for his crime against you and Queen Adrah."

"He saved my life," Selena countered, refusing to be intimidated by someone who went flying around on …. good Lord, was that an owl? Selena shivered and avoided the sharp, yellow gaze of the predator bird and focused on Rothatin. "Doesn't that count for something?"

Rothatin's lips pursed as he glared at Titus, his emerald eyes cold and hard. "We will leave that up to Queen Adrah. For now, your grandmother is in need of her help, is she not?"

"How did you know that?"

"As you've been told, Adrah sees and knows all," interjected Wil as he stepped forward to scoop Rose's still form from the ground. "Stop questioning the man … er, Fae … and let us be on our way, Eladria."

Selena blew her bangs out of her eyes, deciding that it was a waste of breath to continue to ask people to call her Selena. With another glare at Rothatin, she moved back toward Wil and Jake, who had started rounding everyone up and directing them toward the waiting chariots.

"Very well," said Rothatin. He whistled for his owl, and the bird swooped from its perch in a tree to his master's side.

Rothatin climbed onto the creature's back as the other warriors whistled for their own rides. Selena found Titus seated on the back of an eagle the size of a Mack truck, with his arms shackled behind his back. A powerfully built Fae female was seated on the bird behind him. Selena gave him a tiny smile.

"Don't worry," she said with a reassuring nod. "I'll have you out of those handcuffs in no time."

Titus's sad smirk told Selena he didn't believe it. She squared her shoulders and raised her chin to show him she meant business.

Queen Adrah sounded like a reasonable woman. Selena would tell her about Titus' bravery against the Minotaurs. If that didn't work … well, there was always begging.

Selena joined Zoe, Rose, and the Grimm brothers in their horseless chariot. Once they were surrounded by their escort, Rothatin lifted a white horn to his lips. The instrument hung from a leather strap that went across the Faerie's wide chest and was edged in gold.

"First a fight and now music?" Zoe said with a snort. "These people are very entertaining."

Selena giggled as Rothatin lifted the horn to his lips. The sharp sound of the instrument bellowed overhead and suddenly Selena felt the odd sensation of floating. Zoe gasped.

"Holy crap, we're flying!"

Selena tore her eyes away from Zoe's shocked expression and looked over the side of the carriage. Sure enough, a substance that Selena mentally dubbed 'stardust' was shimmering around the vehicle in a pinkish haze and seemed to have lifted them clear off of the ground. They were steadily moving upward, and within seconds the trees that had once towered over them were now beneath them. Selena gripped the side of the carriage and held on for dear life.

"You'd think they would install seatbelts in this thing," she muttered as Zoe grabbed her waist and held on tight.

"You think that Faerie cloud will protect us if we fall out?"

"I don't know, Zo. Why don't I push you and we'll find out?"

"Unless one of these Fae boys decides to grow wings and catch me … Hmmm, on second thought …"

"Don't even think about it."

"What? That Rothatin dude is hot!"

"He's a jackass."

"He's a jackass, but he saved *your* ass."

Zoe giggled over her little quip, but Selena tuned her out. Rothatin *was* handsome; very Chris Hemsworth. However, he could prove to be a thorn in her side when it came to the matter of gaining some sort of immunity for Titus. She needed the Fae warrior to be with her, not against her.

Selena soon forgot all of that as the landscape of Fallada whizzed beneath them. From their present height, she felt as if she could see all four corners of the land she had been born in. It was breathtaking with its incredible scenery and vibrant colors. Ahead of them sat the northern city of Goldun. It floated miles above the ground in one, gigantic solid mass of earth, almost as if it had broken away from the rest of the world. On top of the floating island was a city that gleamed gold in the moonlight and was surrounded by trees and plants, the likes of which Selena had never seen before in her life.

To the east sprawled an endless ocean. It rolled with waves, but boasted no towering buildings or signs of life. Selena supposed that Zenun was literally underneath that massive body of water. To the west was Mollac, with its jagged mountains and cliffs, and endless stretches of pristine, white snow. Sadness stabbed at her heart as she glanced over at Titus. Even from where Selena sat, she could see the anguish that homesickness brought to his eyes. Selena glanced back toward the icy kingdom and located the towering fortress of ice encased in what appeared to be an iron cage. She supposed this was what kept the Fae from invading Mollac. She trembled as she remembered that Jake and Wil wanted her to be the one to lead the first siege.

Definitely not happening.

Finally, to the south was Damu. Its sienna sand rolled and dipped toward buildings that reminded her of the castle from Aladdin. With their domed ceilings all boasting different shades of purple, red, and gold, the city appeared to be one of great wealth.

"Just think," said Wil from his perch on the front seat, "that is where your parents are."

Selena blushed at having been caught staring. She whipped around in her seat, focusing on the floating city of Goldun.

"Why would I care about that?"

Selena didn't want to acknowledge the twinge of something low in her gut, the thing within her that desperately wanted to see the faces of her real parents. The child inside her wanted answers, but she had already decided. If Adrah would lend her aid, then Selena would help Titus find his parents and leave Fallada. End of story.

Wil smiled knowingly at her and shook his head. "You are a stubborn one, Princess, much like King Eldalwen."

Selena pressed her lips together, refusing to take the bait. Zoe continued staring at the landscape, trying to pretend she wasn't listening in. Wil sighed and turned to face forward again.

ᚦ

AS THEY ASCENDED TOWARD GOLDUN, a gate made of twisted, gnarled branches intertwined about each other barred them from entering. Flowers in every color conceivable dotted the green foliage growing from the curling branches. The gate wrapped around the entire floating island was so tall that even if she and Zoe both climbed onto the shoulders of one of the tall Fae, they still wouldn't be able to see inside. A phrase spoken in the language of the Fae caused a shift along the gate branches. They uncurled and slipped out of their intricate pattern, parting to create a gap large enough for their party to enter. Bright, blinding light met their eyes, gleaming from the surfaces of buildings that stretched up toward the sky and sparkled with iridescent light. As Rothatin led their flying party through the gates, Selena knew Zoe was experiencing the same awe that she was.

The vibrant colors of Fallada seemed more ethereal here, kissed with a shimmering glow that appeared to be as alive as the flora and fauna that surrounded them. Trees seemed to sway to a soundless rhythm as one, and flowers danced and curled in the waving grass, seeming to turn toward them as they passed, lifting their petals and twirling in a hypnotic waltz. Nature surrounded them, interspersed with massive pillared buildings with domed roofs. Every building was etched with carvings that depicted the surrounding nature, and some buildings even had the tops of trees growing straight up out of their roofs. It seemed that, unlike people who bulldozed every tree in sight to build their citics, the Fae had respected Mother Nature enough to build around it. The effect was stunning.

"We go first to the royal Fae court," Rothatin said as he guided his owl alongside their floating chariot. "My queen will be expecting you."

Rothatin pulled the reins of his bird and banked left, guiding the rest of their entourage toward the largest building nestled at the center of Goldun. It was made of smooth white marble and its domed roof was solid gold. Stretching up from the rooftop was the shimmering statue of a Fae woman draped in a Grecian-goddess style gown. Her face was calm and serene, her jaw set and determined. Her hands clutched a bow and held a notched arrow to it. The weapon was pointed toward Goldun's entrance, as was the statue's gaze.

They came in for a graceful landing in a courtyard filled with plants and trees, surrounded by an ivory gate. Everyone dismounted from their carriage or bird, and Jake took Rose into his arms once again. Zoc gripped Selena's hand and gave it a reassuring squeeze as they followed their escorts through one of several open, pillared archways leading into the building. Titus was guided along by two of the warrior Fae, hands still bound behind his back.

Through the archway was a long corridor with pink-veined marble floors and walls depicting life-like scenes of nature. Music, voices and laughter could be heard coming from behind the gilded double doors at the end of the hall where Rothatin paused and turned to them

"Be advised, Queen Adrah is a very powerful being. She sees all and knows much, and you must remember to always be honest with her. Chances are, she already knows the truth before she asks a question."

"Then why even ask?" Zoe mumbled under her breath.

The sharp-eared Faerie turned his narrowed gaze on Zoe. "To measure the character of the person being asked for answers."

"Well excuse me," Zoe whispered.

Rothatin tensed as if he'd heard her, but didn't respond. He merely turned to the heavy-looking doors and pushed them inward. The room they entered was more stunning than Selena could have ever imagined.

The sound of babbling water reached her ears, and as they moved farther into the room, she spotted a circular pool with a fountain at its center. A statue of four female Faeries standing back to back rose up out of the water. Each Fae wore a gown in a style similar to the statue on the roof and each one held a large urn, tipped over to pour water into the rippling pool. Inside the pool, members of the royal Fae court frolicked and swam, their gossamer garments hanging from their bodies, moving and shifting around them of their own accord. Some even lounged on the pool's edge with their legs dangling in the water, jeweled goblets clutched between slender fingers.

On couches and chaise lounges placed haphazardly around the room, more royal Fae lounged; some with books in hand, others with plates of food. Near the corner of the room, a group of Fae sat gathered in a circle, making music with wooden instruments. Drums, rattles, flutes, and guitars created a haunting and peaceful melody that all the other Fae seemed to enjoy. The music held an energy all its own and wafted about the room in the same hypnotic motion as the garments of the Fae. Selena felt all of her cares melting away at the very sound of the music. It seemed to have the same effect on everyone in the room, including the Grimm brothers and the Fae. Even Rose's complexion brightened and her moaning and writhing ceased. The lines across her forehead smoothed as her facial muscles relaxed.

On the other side of the pool sat the most beautiful woman Selena had ever seen. *This must be Queen Adrah*, she decided, as she was a match for the statue on the roof. Her statuesque body stretched up tall and proud, and her figure was that of warrior blended with a curvy woman. A white garment draped and dipped across her body, flowing around her ankles in a wave-like motion, giving her the appearance of floating as she moved about the room. Her skin shimmered beneath the stark white dress and her feet were bare. Her body was adorned with silver jewelry, from the series of chains draped over her sparkling blonde hair, to shining silver cuffs on her wrists and sparkling anklets and toe rings. A series of silver chains hung from her neck, each sporting a pendant representative of nature: flowers, trees, butterflies, birds. Her features were strong yet delicate, fierce yet calm, haunting yet beautiful. Beneath her light blonde eyebrows were eyes that could only be described by comparing them to spring. The green of her irises swirled with iridescent light so that the shade of green varied depending on the lighting or her position. Selena was mesmerized by them as she locked gazes with the queen from across the room.

Selena felt frozen in place as Adrah seemed to float across the room toward them. Even without Rothatin's warning, she would have known better than to lie to this woman about anything. The wisdom and knowledge in her gaze were too obvious to miss.

"Selena, Zoe, welcome!" she said warmly, looking both girls in the eye as she greeted them. "It is an honor to meet you both."

Her voice echoed from the tall walls and high ceilings, putting the music to shame with its lyrical sound. All noise in the hall ceased and every Fae stopped what they were doing to turn and gaze upon the newcomers. Adrah took Selena's hand, her piercing green stare seeming to strip her down to her soul.

"You are your mother's daughter in appearance," Adrah continued with a slight upturning of her lips. "Yet I feel your father's warrior spirit within you, child. He will be so pleased."

Selena cleared her throat. "About that …"

"There will be time enough for that later, Selena," Adrah said with a pat on her hand. "We must see to other matters first, such as your grandmother's health. I am sure you are all hungry and tired as well after your long journey. You have my hospitality for as long as you need it."

"Thank you," Selena mumbled as she lowered her head. The fact that Queen Adrah was being so nice to her was only making this harder. The Fae queen was counting on her to play her part in the fulfilling the prophecy and Selena was only going to let her down.

We shall see. All has not yet been decided, Princess.

Selena's eyes widened as she looked back up at Adrah, who had turned and began talking with the Grimm brothers. She was certain she'd heard the queen's voice in her head. As Selena stood gawking, Adrah glanced at her out of the corner of her eye. They twinkled knowingly, filled with mischief. Selena shivered and turned away, watching as the Fae royals who had been swimming left the pool and began converging around them.

"How long since Rose was bitten by the Werewolf?" Adrah asked as she reached a hand out toward the limp figure in Jake Grimm's arms.

"Three days," Wil answered. "The fever has been raging for two and she's delirious. The venom is spreading."

Adrah ushered one of the burly swimmers forward. Selena watched as the male Fae plucked Rose from Jake's arms as if she weighed no more than a baby, and turned toward the pool with her.

"What is he doing?" Selena asked as he waded into the pool with Rose.

Adrah gave her another little half-smile. "Do not fear, Selena. Fae royalty are blessed with healing powers through nature. Daxos's gift is healing by water and he is one of the most powerful among his kind."

They looked on as three other Fae—two females and one male —joined the one named Daxos in the pool. They helped him spread Rose's body out in the water, each of them keeping one hand beneath her to keep her afloat. Each Fae closed their eyes and tilted their heads back while moving their free hands in the air above

Rose's body. They chanted in unison, Fae words that sounded more like a song. Its melody caused ripples in the still pool, which swirled around them gently, gurgling in answer to the Fae's power.

The other Fae watched silently, reverently, as the four chanted and sang. Slowly, Rose began to come back to life as a black, smoke-like substance exited her nostrils and dispersed on the air. Within minutes, her eyes were open and she was staring in wonder at her surroundings. Selena felt tears of joy stinging her eyes. They didn't even try to stop her as she rushed forward. Rose was placed on her feet and waded through the water toward Selena with her arms spread wide. Selena didn't hesitate as she dropped into the pool and launched herself against Rose. They hugged, jumping up and down in their excitement. Selena pulled back and looked down into Rose's smiling face with wonder. Her grandmother was a healthy woman, but she'd never looked so beautiful. The healing hands of the Fae had obviously done wonders for her.

"Sweet pea," Rose whispered, stroking Selena's bangs back from her face affectionately. "Did we make it? Is this the land of the Faeries?"

Selena nodded. "Yes, Gram, we're here. Come meet the queen, she's beautiful!"

They left the water hand in hand, flanked by Daxos and his three helpers. Selena pulled Rose toward Adrah, who stood waiting by the edge of the pool with her arms clasped in front of her.

"Welcome, Rose, to Goldun."

"Thank you," Rose said as she wiped her wet face with a towel provided by a nearby Fae. "It is such an honor to meet you."

"No, dear Rose, the honor is all mine, for you are the one who has safeguarded our dear princess all this time. I am eternally grateful to you for what you have done."

Rose beamed with pride and grasped Selena's shoulder tightly. "She's my girl, Your Majesty. No matter what."

Adrah gave another little smile. "Yes, she is. Now come, I wish to see you all settled and well rested. There will be time enough for politics in the morning."

"With all due respect, Queen," Selena objected, "we would like to return to our world as soon as possible."

Adrah nodded, her eyes narrowed and thoughtful. "Yes, I am aware of this. We will talk later, I promise. But first, rest and a warm bed for you and your family, as well as the Brothers Grimm."

"My Queen, what of the traitor?" Rothatin spoke for the first time since entering the hall.

Adrah swiveled her cool gaze to Titus. "He will be brought to my chambers for questioning," she commanded. "First, I want him released from his bonds."

Rothatin's eyes widened and darkened to almost black, and his jaw hardened. "Your Majesty, he is very dangerous!"

Suddenly, the air around them grew icy cold and Adrah's eyes swirled with iridescent color before going silver. If at all possible, she drew herself up to an even greater height as she stabbed Rothatin with a piercing glare.

"You dare to question me, General?"

Rothatin lowered his head, properly chastised. "No, My Queen. Please, forgive me."

As quickly as it had come, Adrah's anger melted away and her serenity had returned.

"You are forgiven. Now, please do as I have asked. Titus of Mollac and I have much to discuss."

Chapter Eight

Queen Adrah's chambers were reflective of everything she represented. Light and air were ever present in the room with open archways leading out to circular balconies overlooking Goldun at the height of Osbel tower, the castle inhabited by the Fae ruler. Furniture in shades of white and pale yellow adorned the chambers and billowing, sheer curtains shielded the bed and other sections of the quarters from view. The Fae Queen sat in a high-backed chair across from Titus, who perched stiffly on a matching couch. Everything about the room screamed serenity and calm, yet he overflowed with turbulent fear.

Adrah was even more powerful than Eranna, and her wrath was great when she chose to exercise it. Titus hung his head, refusing the meet the Fae queen's knowing gaze. He had a feeling that if he did, the dam incasing his emotions would break and he would fall at her feet in a sobbing mess. He studied the intricate pattern of the tiles printed with sunflowers beneath his feet instead.

"You must be thirsty," she said.. Her lyrical voice wrapped around him and echoed with resounding authority. She gestured toward the gleaming silver tea set laid out on the table between them.

Titus shook his head in refusal. "No, Your Majesty. I'm fine, thank you"

"Not one for pleasantries?" Adrah smirked and shrugged, pouring her own tea with refined movements. "Very well, young man, we shall come straight to the point. I am told that you are possessed by the Queen of Mollac."

Titus reached for the back of his neck, running his fingers along the black, cursive letter E tattooed across his skin. The brand had seared itself there the day he pledged his service to Eranna in exchange for his family's freedom.

"Yes," he admitted, knowing the Fae queen was already aware of the truth.

She lifted a small teacup to her lips, her face fixed into an expression of thoughtfulness.

"The wolf packs of Mollac are now set against each other, with many taking refuge here in Goldun. While the rest, like you, have chosen to serve on the side of evil."

Titus did not miss the coolness that seeped into Adrah's eyes, turning them a wintry shade of green that bordered on shimmering white.

"I did what I thought was necessary for my family to survive," he said, fighting down the growl that emerged in his throat. His canines throbbed and he felt the anger that welled up in him, as if he were suddenly filled with molten fire.

In an instant, Adrah had crossed to sit on the couch beside him. She rested a hand on his knee, her eyes wide and piercing as she captured his gaze. Coldness rushed through him like an arctic blast and his anger abated as quickly as it had welled up. Adrah brought her warm palms up to his face. She held him, gazing deep into his eyes as a rush of power flowed through him from her fingertips.

"Show me, Titus of Mollac, those things which I have not seen."

A flash of light blinded him as the tentacles of Adrah's power seeped into his mind and latched on, giving her full access to his memories and he knew she could see what he was seeing. Tears filled his eyes as images of himself running with his pack in wolf form flitted through his mind's eye. His father, the pack Alpha male, ran alongside him. He was muscular, proud, and covered in a pelt of mingled white, black, and gray. His sister and mother brought up the rear. The other wolves of the Awcan pack surrounded them, flurries of snow swirling around like fairy dust.

Another flash of light brought the image of Eranna's Minotaurs, as they invaded the cavernous cliff where the Awcan pack lived, taking them all captive after a bloody fight that left many of his pack mates dead. He relived it all so Adrah could see the Witches and Sorcerers taking him from the cell where his family was held and bringing him to Eranna, who'd offered him a deal. His skin tingled as he recalled kneeling before Eranna and accepting the wicked queen's mark. The rest followed in a speeding blur up until his arrival at Goldun with the Grimm brothers and Selena.

Adrah snatched her hands away from his face and fell back onto the arm of the couch, her chest heaving with effort as she adjusted her draping gown's neckline. She watched him pensively as he quickly swiped at the tears running down his cheeks. Titus sniffled and turned away, embarrassed.

"It is as I suspected," Adrah said after a few minutes of silent reflection. "You have a strong heart, Titus. Circumstance has dealt you an unfair turn, but I shall do all I can to see things put right."

Titus couldn't help the hope that blossomed in him as he met her gaze. "You do not wish to punish me?"

"These are desperate times, and I cannot fault a man for doing what he thought was best for his family. I do wish you had come to me first, but I am willing to forgive you the oversight. I will help you as much as I can, but first you much pledge your loyalty to me, King Endroth, and Fallada."

"You have it!" Titus proclaimed emphatically, dropping to his knees and lowering his head.

Adrah's laughter was sweet, and not condescending in the least as she reached out to ruffle Titus's hair.

"The mark of a good wolf is his loyalty, and I can see you have plenty of that. It is no wonder she is so enamored of you."

Titus shivered as Selena's warm, brown eyes flashed through his thoughts. Adrah lifted his chin until their eyes met.

"She means to leave Fallada," he said, his voice hitching and his breath racing at the thought of losing Selena forever. He wanted her to stay; not just for Fallada, but for him. Just as Fallada would be cast into darkness without the princess of Damu, so would Titus be flung into a lifetime of loneliness.

Adrah squeezed his chin gently, that half-smile curling at the corner of her lips once more. "Princess Eladria's journey is not yet complete and all is not lost. Now, to deal with that pesky mark on your neck."

Her hands were on his shoulders then, holding tightly as her eyes burned into his. The mark on his neck warmed until Titus felt as it his skin were on fire. He groaned and writhed against the agony. She merely tightened her grip, eyes flashing white and searing Titus to his bones as she worked her magic within him to remove Eranna's poison. It seeped out of his ears and nostrils like black smoke, curling around them before dissipating onto the air.

Titus collapsed to the floor with relief when she was done, caressing the back of his neck to find it smooth and unblemished once more. Adrah stood and moved to leave the room in ethereally graceful motions.

"You will find clothing on the bed that should fit you perfectly. There is a bath prepared in the washroom adjacent to this one, and I hope after you are clean and suitably attired, you will join us for a celebration in the ballroom."

"I'd be honored, Your Majesty."

She paused in the doorway and flashed him her knowing smile. "Good. Never fear, young Titus. I have seen much through the Eye of Goldun. It may not seem like it now, but I promise you that in time, all will be well."

🍂

"YOU LOOK LIKE A FREAKIN' Greek goddess!"

Selena tugged self-consciously on the skirt of the soft pink gown that had been provided to her by Adrah's Fae servants. After leaving the house of the royal court, Rothatin and his flying warriors had escorted their party to Osbel tower, where they were promptly provided rooms. They'd indulged in tea—which had a very mysterious calming effect when Selena drank it—and hot baths filled with fragrant bubbles. The tub, which was more like a small swimming pool, was lined with hand-painted tiles bearing the images of exotic birds and plants. Selena had been reluctant to leave the hot water and invigorating bubbles, but Adrah's beautiful servants had coaxed her out by showing her the gown she would be wearing and the promise of food.

Pink wasn't exactly her favorite color and she hardly ever wore dresses, but even she had to admit that she'd never looked better. The gown's plunging neckline made her a bit self-conscious, but the silver clasps at her shoulders and matching belt at her waist were stunning against her sun-kissed skin. The dusky shade of pink complimented her coloring nicely and the sweeping, draped skirt of the gown made her feel as if she were floating instead of walking.

Her hair had been curled and pinned up on top of her head, and decorated with silver combs sporting jeweled dragonflies. A pair of silver earrings shaped like flat disks dangled from her ears. Zoe was outfitted in a similar dress in sky blue with gold accents rather than silver. Her blond bob was accentuated by a golden headband featuring a cluster of jeweled flowers. Selena wrapped her arm around her taller friend's slim waist as they studied their reflection in the mirror.

"We both look pretty awesome," she admitted. "I wonder if they'll let us take this stuff home."

Zoe pulled away from Selena's embrace to lift an ornate silver hand mirror from the vanity table where they'd both had their hair done.

"*Let* us? Girl, I plan on slipping this dress, this headband, and this mirror into my purse!"

"You didn't bring a purse."

"I'm going to slip it somewhere," she said as she replaced the mirror on the table. "Besides, *you* don't have to leave. I have a feeling Queen Adrah would give you anything you asked for as long as you promise to be their savior."

"I am not anybody's savior," Selena argued, an edge to her voice. Why couldn't everyone just leave her be? "Anyway, what would you and Gram do without me?"

"I guess you're right, but what about that hunk-a burnin' Werewolf down the hall? You can't exactly take him back with you."

Selena turned her back and pretended to inspect a mural of a forest taking up an entire wall in their shared room.

"Why would I care about that?"

"Hmmm."

Zoe didn't elaborate but Selena could hear the doubt in her tone. It wasn't exactly unwarranted; along with a desire to help Titus rescue his family was an even deeper want. She was grateful when an opening door and the sound of Rose's enthralled gasp interrupted them. She turned to find her grandmother wrapped in a more modest, long-sleeved and high-necked gown in yellow satin. Her dark, silver-streaked hair was left to tumble down her back.

"Oh, you girls look so beautiful. Selena, you look like …"

"A princess?" Zoe offered shamelessly, a mischievous smile curling her lips.

Rose chuckled and grasped Selena's hands. "That's exactly what you look like." Her blue eyes were soulful and filled with tears as she gazed up at her granddaughter. "I always knew you were special, sweet pea. Now I hope you know it, too."

Selena's answer was a smile and a hug. She grasped the hands of her grandmother and best friend before turning to lead them out of the opulently decorated room.

"Come on. Let's go party, Faerie style!"

Glad to have distracted everyone from all the princess talk—at least for now—Selena followed Adrah's servants, who led the way to the ballroom where the celebration was taking place. More of the same music the Faeries had been playing in the royal hall came flitting through the doorways and greeted them, only this tune was livelier. Selena felt excitement pulsing through her as the bright lights of the ballroom enveloped them. It would be hard to forget that these people were celebrating because they believed she had returned to Fallada to take her rightful place as Damu's eldest princess. For now, though, she would try to enjoy herself as much as she could. Adrah had promised that they would talk later.

The scent of fresh flowers was the first thing Selena noticed. The colorful buds were everywhere, blooming from long chains of ivy that looked as if they had naturally overtaken the entire ballroom. The greenery and flowers climbed the room's massive white pillars and some sections of wall, creating a colorful and awe-inspiring display. Lanterns made from the thin branches of trees hung from the ceiling, and as they moved farther into the room, Selena could see that they were lit by swirling fireflies.

More lights danced about the room on their own accord and Selena gasped to find that those particular creatures were not fireflies, but small winged people. Two of them twirled right in front of her, glowing from within and surrounded by a shimmering, golden haze. They were male and female, clutched together in a hypnotic waltz, the skirt of the tiny woman's gown floating around them like a silken banner. Selena watched as they twirled back up toward where the other little lights had gathered close to the ceiling. They converged as one glowing mass before dispersing, bursting out across the room in a display of light and color that left everyone in the room breathless.

"They are Pixies," said Queen Adrah as she appeared beside them from out of nowhere. She was dressed in another pristine white gown, but this one was embroidered with blossoms matching those adorning the ballroom. Real blooming petals decorated her upswept hair and she carried the same entrancing glow as when Selena had met her earlier. "They are distant relatives of the Fae; mischievous, but beautiful and important to our way of life as the keepers of nature. Our other cousins have joined us as well. The Elves have come all the way from Inador Forest to attend."

Adrah gestured toward a group of beings very similar in appearance to the Fae. Their coloring varied from pale to ebony, but each and every one possessed eyes as blue as the ocean. Their ears were a bit larger, but just as pointed as their Fae counterparts. Their garments were as flowing and beautiful as the Fae's, but trimmed in brown leather and feathers. Many wore bows across their bodies and sheaths of arrows on their backs. Their figures were thicker and more robust than those of the Fae, as if they were born from Amazon warriors.

"And, of course, there are also many Werewolves present," Adrah continued as she led them toward the corner of the room boasting tables full of food. Her smirk widened into a smile as she placed a full goblet in Selena's hands. "Perhaps you will find a familiar face among them."

Selena lifted the goblet to her lips as she turned to locate the group Adrah had spoken of. They gathered in clusters among the Fae, easily recognized by their muscular builds and un-pointed ears. Like the Elves, their looks ranged from blond haired to dark with eyes from shades of crystalline blue to black onyx. A pair of electric blue ones pierced her as her stare came to rest on a lone figure dressed in shades of white and chocolate brown.

Zoe was at her side in an instant. "I never thought I'd be saying this, but that is one yummy Werewolf."

Selena had to agree as she eyed Titus' lean and muscular build from across the room. His attire was much like that of the Fae males; long-sleeved tunic with leather vest and matching pants. His shirt was unbuttoned at the top and Selena felt her face growing hot at the sight of exposed chest muscle and the shining silver necklace resting against smooth, pale skin. His dark hair fell across his eyes in a haphazard way that lent him an air of mystery. Selena took a long gulp from her goblet, trying to concentrate on the sweet and fragrant drink instead of Titus, but failed miserably.

"Those were your exact words when *Breaking Dawn* came out, remember?"

"I meant I never thought I'd be saying that about a *real* Were-wolf. Jacob doesn't count, he's not real. That, on the other hand ..." Zoe trailed off and lifted her eyebrows, jerking her head in Titus' direction. "That is real. I suggest you take advantage of it while you can, since we'll be leaving soon and all."

The last sentence was said with a shrug and knowing smirk before Zoe was disappearing into the crowd with Rose on her arm. The last thing Selena heard was something about going to the buffet table before she lost sight of them both.

"Damn you, Zo," Selena muttered as she drained what was left in her goblet before setting it down. Conveniently, Queen Adrah seemed to have disappeared from sight as well, leaving Selena completely alone. Titus was watching her from across the room, his hands in his pockets and his gaze intense. As if drawn magnetically, Selena felt her feet moving her in his direction until they were standing face to face, just inches away from where Fae, Elves, and Werewolves frolicked on the dance floor.

"Hey," Titus said in that gravelly tone of his, reminding her of the day they met in the grassy field.

"Hi," she responded, for lack of anything better to say. Titus' eyes swept over her, from her pinned-up hair and down over the gown draping across her body. Her heart leaped up and lodged in her throat.

"You look …" he trailed off and inhaled deeply, his Adam's apple bobbing forcefully as he swallowed. "Stunning."

Selena lowered her eyes from his probing stare. Guys never looked at her the way he did and the effect was unnerving; she just didn't know how to handle it.

"Thank you," she mumbled.

And then his hand was in hers, the warmth of his palm brushing up against hers. His gentle squeeze on her fingers forced her to look back up at him. He smiled.

"You want to dance?"

Selena eyed the twisting and turning bodies crowding the dance floor and felt fear gripping her chest. No one was doing the shuffle or the running man, so she was sure to stand out. Add that to the fact that she had absolutely no rhythm and two left feet, and Selena was terrified at the prospect.

"I don't know how," she admitted.

Titus smiled, flashing his pearly whites and pointed canines. "There aren't really any rules. Fae music is very unpredictable, like nature. It's what rules this realm. So, the dance moves are just as unpredictable. I can show you."

Selena didn't have time to protest before he was pulling her toward the crowd and right to the center of the dance floor. Nerves prevented her from really enjoying it at first, but Titus' genuine smile put her at ease and relaxed her. He showed her the steps, which reminded her of something out of a movie set in medieval times. Arms linked, they spun in circles before joining in with a series of claps and turns, before coming together again with hands touching. Titus's eyes never left hers, crinkling at the corners and twinkling with humor as he watched her catch on to the steps. By the time the song ended, Selena's forehead had broken out in sweat and her heart was pounding in her chest.

"Had enough?" Titus asked as he wrapped an arm around her waist to protect her from the jostling crowd.

"Yes!" Selena shouted to be heard above the boisterous Faeries, Elves, and Werewolves.

Titus grinned and grasped her hand, pulling her swiftly through the crowd. "Come on," he said once they'd reached one of the open archways leading out from the castle. "I have something I want to show you."

Selena's eyebrows furrowed as she glanced over her shoulder to find Adrah watching them. "Are you sure it's safe?"

Adrah's nearly imperceptible nod was timed with Titus' exclamation. "Of course. Unless you're worried that I might hurt you."

Selena looked into his eyes and saw guilt there, along with worry. Impulsively, she stood on tiptoe and wrapped her arms around his shoulders, hugging him tightly. The feel of him against her felt natural, like something falling into place, and Selena closed her eyes against the feeling of oneness. Feeling right with Titus meant accepting her place in Damu, in Fallada, and she just wasn't ready to do that. Still, she held on tight as she reassured him.

"I know you would never do that."

Chapter Nine

"You should know that I am free from Eranna's possession."

Selena turned to look at Titus as she walked alongside him, away from the towering castle of the Fae queen.

She smiled. "That's great! So that means …"

"When I shift into my animal form, I am in complete control."

"So, no more freaky red eyes?"

Titus laughed. "Absolutely not."

Soft grass swayed beneath their feet, shimmering green in the light of the crescent moon. It invited her to take her sandals off and dig her feet into the soft blades, an impulse she gave into without hesitation. She sighed and wiggled her toes in the grass, the blades like silk between them.

"You know," he said as he grasped her hand again to pull her along, "I thought you were beautiful when I met you, but seeing you here … it's as if you coming home has enhanced your beauty. You're glowing, Selena."

She knew it was true. In the moonlight, her skin had taken on a luminescent glow and she was filled with an energy she'd never possessed. With her bare feet in the grass, all she wanted to do was run. But she didn't want to admit it, so she decided not to respond.

"Where are you taking me?" she asked, desperate to change the subject. Titus lifted his arm and pointed to a ring of trees in the distance. The branches seemed to be reaching for each other, closing the area between them in a cocoon of lush green leaves.

"See that copse of trees over there?"

Selena nodded, a slow smile spreading across her face. "Wanna race?"

Titus snorted. "You don't stand a chance."

Selena folded her arms over her chest. "Oh really? Why don't you put your money where your mouth is? Or, your snout. If you think it'll give you the edge, you can morph into your wolf form. I bet you still couldn't beat me."

Titus' eyes flashed and glowed as he smiled back at her. "You're on!"

In the blink of an eye, the boy Titus was gone and his wolf form stood before her. Instead of that frightful red, his eyes now glowed the same hypnotic blue as they did in his human form. They were familiar and comforting, leaving Selena with no doubt that he'd been set free from the evil queen's hold.

Titus bent to gather his fallen clothes in his mouth and turned toward the circle of trees, waiting for Selena to start the race. She dropped her borrowed sandals onto the grass and gathered the hem of her skirt in her hands.

"Ready—" she said with a sideways glance at Titus, "—set, go!"

They were off like a shot of lightning, neck and neck as they sprinted across the open green field. Selena felt the rushing of wind on her bare arms and face. She closed her eyes, breathing deeply as her feet sank into plush grass. Every few steps, her speed allowed her to leave the ground and Selena savored the sensation as if she were flying. After a while it became less about beating Titus and more about the thrill of running in the open, unashamed and unafraid that someone might see her. Here, everyone was as strange as she was. So much so that being strange was actually normal. It was a feeling Selena had never experienced.

With a final burst of speed, Selena reached the shaded glen just a few seconds before Titus, who was panting heavily when he came to a stop beside her. Selena smiled smugly at him and received a yipping bark and playful snap at the hem of her dress in return. She ran her fingers over the wolf's beautiful fur and dropped to her knees, pressing her face against the soft pelt.

"You get an A for effort," she said jokingly, before tugging his ear teasingly. His hot, rough tongue lapped at her cheek and Selena pushed him away with a chuckle. He took his pants into his mouth and disappeared into the trees at a run. A minute later, his human figure appeared on the edge of the trees, wearing the pants and running a hand through his dark hair.

"I am not ashamed to admit when I've been beaten," he said with a grin as he bent to retrieve his shirt and vest. Selena was salivating like a dog looking at a juicy steak as she studied Titus' lean and lithe form. The broad chest and shoulders tapered in to a narrow waist, showcasing the ripples along his abs perfectly. Selena bit her lower lip and tried to find something else to look at. She was grateful when he had his clothes back on and was leading her toward the trees.

"What is this place?" she asked as she allowed Titus to take her hand once more and led her between the thick circle of trees. She'd never seen trees growing so close together, as if they were protecting something within their little circle.

"It is one of the many homes of the Pixies," Titus said softly as they cleared the trees. What Selena found on the other side stole the air from her lungs. Though the foliage of the trees blocked out the light of the moon, a soft, golden glow illuminated the space. The tiny lights were coming from inside the petals of hundreds of tulips, which dotted the ground around them in shades of pink, purple, and white. As Titus led her closer, Selena realized the glowing lights inside the flowers were the same Pixies that had been dancing at the

Fae ball. More of them dotted the trees above them, creating the same effect as roped Christmas lights. They twinkled above, creating a glowing cocoon separate from the rest of the world.

In the midst of the glowing field of flowers stood a still pond on which even more of the glowing creatures played, skidding across the water and creating glowing rings that rippled out around them.

"Oh," Selena gasped, unable to say anything else while surrounded by so much beauty.

Titus smiled and directed her toward one of the trees. "This is the main reason I brought you here," he said as he reached up toward the branches. He came back down with two pieces of strange-looking fruit. They were a deep, rich red, and large enough that Selena had to hold hers with both hands. It looked like a very large, firm tomato.

"There is a lot of good food in that banquet hall," Titus said. "But you'll never taste anything like the fruit from a clutzia tree."

Selena watched as Titus sank his teeth into the fruit's skin, groaning with pleasure as the ruby red juice spilled over his fingers.

He chewed and nodded fervently, his eyes wide. "It's heavenly, taste it."

Selena shrugged and brought the fruit to her lips. She had already been attacked by a Werewolf, rescued by two old German fairytale writers, been on board a flying ship, rode in a flying chariot, met Faeries and Elves, and been attacked by Minotaurs. This was easy.

The sweet juice of the clutzia filled her mouth, like the perfect blend of pomegranate, blueberry, and pineapple juice. There was something else there that Selena couldn't describe, but it was almost like a touch of honey. The sweetness danced on her tongue and the meat of the fruit provided a feeling of fullness that Selena did not expect.

"I'm full from just that one piece of fruit!" she exclaimed once she was finished.

Titus nodded. "That is one of the best things about clutzia," he said. "Even one bite could bring a starving man back from death. It is found only in Goldun."

Selena licked the addictive juice from her fingertips. "Now my hands are sticky."

"Well, that's what the pond is for."

He led her over to the water, where the Pixies seemed to ripple out over the water in an effort to make room for them. Many of them watched curiously as Selena and Titus knelt at the water's edge. Selena dipped her hands into the water, surprised at its coolness. She watched as Titus cupped his hands together and came up filled to the brim with water.

"It's the best water you'll ever drink," he promised as he held his hands out to her. Selena glanced down at his glistening fingertips, squeezed tightly together to keep even a drop from escaping. Her pulse thumped against her throat as she leaned forward to accept his offering, grateful for the coldness of the sweet water as it rushed down her hot throat. It *was* the best water she'd ever tasted, pure and clear with just a hint of sweetness.

Selena wiped her mouth with the back of her hand as Titus finished off the water and wiped his own hands on his pant legs. He stretched his long limbs out and leaned back onto his elbows, gazing up at the dancing Pixies above their heads. Selena joined him, gazing up at the tiny dots blanketing them like golden stars.

"Tell me about Mollac," Selena asked, laying back to rest her head against the grass. "Do you miss it?"

Titus sighed, his chest heaving as he closed his eyes. "There is a harsh sort of beauty about a place covered in ice and snow," he said softly. "It's like living inside of a diamond; everything is so pure and wrapped in shades of white and pale blue. There are soft hills and jagged mountain peaks, forests full of trees that appear dead, but are brimming with life inside."

"What about your family?"

"There are my parents and my sister, and then there is my pack. We live together and hunt together. We were happy before ..."

Selena reached across the space between them and touched his hand. "We will help them, Titus. I promised you that I wouldn't leave until I helped you rescue your family, and I meant it."

Titus turned onto his side to face her. "You should go. If you're not going to remain in Fallada, then tomorrow you should have Jake and Wil take you back to your world."

Selena turned on her side as well, panic ripping through her at the thought that Titus would want her to leave.

"What do you mean? I thought you wanted me to be here."

"I want you to stay!" Titus said with a low growl rumbling at the base of his chest. He reached out and grasped Selena's shoulder tightly. "I want you to stay and take your place in Damu. I want you to meet your parents and your people. I want you to be here when this war ends so I can take you home to Mollac, and introduce you to my family and the wolves in my pack. More than anything I want …"

He trailed off, dropping his eyes from hers with a heavy sigh. Selena searched his face for any sign of what was coming next, her heart already soaring from what he'd said.

"What, Titus? What do you want?"

Titus shook his head and pulled his lips into a tight frown. "I know you don't know much about Werewolves, but there is one thing you should be aware of, especially if you intend to stay here even for a short time. Werewolves are pack-oriented. We find a sense of belonging by being surrounded by those who we consider our extended family. But when it comes to love, it's not so simple. Werewolves can have only one mate, and it can't just be anybody. I can't simply choose a woman and ask her to marry me. The pull of a Werewolf male to his mate is a powerful one, and when he finds her he just … knows. He feels it in his gut and it's like being kicked in the stomach."

Selena shivered under Titus' intense gaze. "What are you trying to tell me, Titus? I mean, I'm not even a Werewolf."

"You don't have to be. I'm telling you I feel that pull toward you.

I have since the first time I saw you running across that field in your world. I didn't want to believe that it could be you … a girl who's not a Were and a princess to boot, but I can't fight it anymore. And it won't get any better. The longer you are here, the worse it will be until I'm miserable with knowing you're leaving and never coming back. So you see, you have to leave. I'm grateful that you want to help me find my family, but if you're not going to stay permanently then you shouldn't stay at all. I don't think my heart could take it."

Selena forced herself to swallow past the lump in her throat. She gently stroked the fine strands of dark hair that had fallen over his brow, her fingertips grazing his forehead gently.

"I don't know what to do," she whispered. "Everyone is watching me, wanting me to be their savior. I just don't know if I can. I've wanted to know about my family and my past my whole life, and now that I know where I come from, I don't think I can live up to what everyone expects from me. I'm just a girl, a seventeen year-old girl."

Titus' hand came up to grip her wrist. He held it tight before bringing it to his mouth. His lips grazed the back of her hand gently, leaving tiny shivers that ran up her arm.

"You, Selena, are more than just a girl."

Before she knew it, he was hovering over her, his arms trapping her between them as he leaned down. Selena felt a flush of embarrassment as she realized that this was to be her first kiss. She felt like such a loser for almost reaching her eighteenth birthday before a boy had been interested enough to kiss her. Then, as Titus' full lips closed over hers, and the scent of tulips wafted up around her, Selena realized that no stolen peck behind a school locker could have ever compared to this. No clumsy, wet smooch with an overeager teenage boy with busy hands could come close to Titus' lips, firm yet supple and the solid weight of his chest against hers and his arms on either side. Not even the bright stars over Texas could compete with the soft glow of Pixie dust as it rained down over them.

Selena opened her eyes as the warm dust fell into her face and hair, holding on to Titus' shoulders and laughing happily as the little winged creatures swirled around them. Their laughter sounded like tinkling bells as they danced and frolicked overhead. Titus smiled down at her and ran his fingers through her hair, which was now loose from its updo and trailing down her shoulders covered in gold Pixie dust.

"See?" he said with a laugh. "Even the Pixies know we're destined to be together."

As Titus lowered his head toward hers again, Selena wrapped her arms around his neck and surrendered to the warmth of his mouth and the sweetness of the clutzia fruit on his tongue. Even if she didn't want to admit it, she felt deep within her heart that he was right. After a night like this, how would she ever be able to go home again?

❧

"ARE you ready for that conversation now?"

Selena paused, her fingers tightening around Titus' as they crested the sloping hill leading up to Osbel tower. Adrah was waiting for them, her own aura outshining that of the moon. With her hands folded in front of her and her facial expression serene, she appeared unruffled, but Selena could see the fire dancing in her eyes, darkening them to jade. That dark green gaze was fixed firmly on Selena, her eyebrows raised as her gaze swept over the Pixie dust covering them both.

Silently, Titus released her hand. "I am sure you two want your privacy." He stopped and nodded respectfully toward Adrah. "Your Majesty."

Adrah touched Titus' shoulder gently as he walked by. She was silent, but Selena was sure the Faerie queen winked at him. Selena brushed it aside and tried not to gawk at Titus' broad back as he left them behind for Osbel tower. The humor in Adrah's expression was gone the moment Titus had disappeared inside.

"Come with me."

Selena obeyed without question. The queen's tone indicated that she would not take no for an answer, and Selena couldn't avoid this forever. Now was the time to tell Adrah that she had no intention of becoming the savior of Fallada.

"Perhaps," Adrah said, causing Selena to halt mid-stride. Adrah shrugged as she waved her hand toward a tall, narrow stone door at the side of the tower. "But then, perhaps not."

Selena heard a strangled sound emitting from her throat and realized it was her own shock, rising up to choke her. Had Adrah heard her thoughts? Selena cleared her throat and shook her head. No, of course she hadn't. That sort of thing was impossible, wasn't it?

"And yet, I know you are going to request my aid in the rescue of Titus' family, while at the same time telling me you have no intention of returning home to Damu."

That was it, she was officially losing her mind. Adrah waved her arm again and the door slammed behind them. The sound of a bolt scraping into a lock resounded through the pitch-black chamber they were standing in. Adrah's glow cast just enough light around that Selena could see a few feet in front of her face. She stood in front of a stone pedestal, Adrah on the opposite side with her hands resting on the edge of the round surface. A shimmering white cloth concealed what appeared to be a globe resting on the table.

"I have been watching your world for a long time, Selena," Adrah began, her voice filling the chamber. "And while you were not born of the human race, I believe that you possess many of their qualities. Humans are, at first glance, a weak species—easy to manipulate, control, and trick. Yet there is an inherent instinct for survival and the tendency to band together as one when necessary. It is in the darkest of times that men truly come into their strength and as a people, becoming far greater than they once were. I see these things in you, Princess. Honor, bravery, mettle … these are all qualities fitting a royal daughter of Damu."

"You have my Gram to thank for that," Selena said with a shrug. "What can I say, Texas chicks are tough."

Adrah chuckled. "Yes, our dear Rose was instrumental in your upbringing, was she not? I could not have asked for better. Eranna thought sending our princesses into the world of men would weaken them, render them helpless and defenseless. Her goal was to cheat you all from achieving your full potential. Her mistake was in underestimating the resilience of the human race. You see, throughout the course of man's life on Earth, we have watched them kill, hurt, and disrespect one another, and Eranna has seen this as an advantage in her quest to enslave mankind. What she has not seen, is that spark of unpredictability, that essential humanity that pushes men to achieve their greatness under adversity."

"What does any of that have to do with me?"

Adrah's eyes twinkled and danced to a shimmering, silver-tinted sea-green. "Oh my dear Selena, it has everything to do with you."

Selena shook her head. "Sorry to disappoint you, but I'm not exactly hero material. As a matter of fact, if it weren't for Titus biting Gram I wouldn't even have come to your world. I was doing just fine in Twin Oaks."

One of Adrah's silvery-blonde eyebrows rose. "Were you now?"

Selena's cheeks stung with embarrassment as she thought about her growing savings account and plans to leave Twin Oaks on the first thing smoking after graduation. *To do what*, her inner voice taunted. Besides running, she wasn't good at anything, and she never did have any idea what she wanted to do with her life. On career day, she had always been that girl standing in the middle of the room with confusion on her face.

"That is because, in your heart, you always knew you didn't belong."

"What makes you so sure I belong here?"

"Think about it, Selena. Do you believe Titus bit your grandmother by chance, or that the Brothers Grimm reached your home in enough time to save you from being killed by a possessed Were-wolf by sheer coincidence? Do you think I just happened to decide to send my warriors for your protection on a whim? My dear, our lives are guided by destiny, a course that has already been set for us. Our actions can sometimes divert us from that path, yet somehow our feet tend to bring us right back to where we are supposed to be. You, Princess, are exactly where you are meant to be at this moment in time. Titus was exactly where he was supposed to be when he found you running in that field."

Adrah reached for the silky, white cloth and pulled it away, revealing a clear orb settled against the stone pedestal. Within the orb, swirls of color mingled and danced with barely-contained energy. It was as if by uncovering it, Adrah had awakened it. Selena took a step forward, entranced by the swirling lights.

"This is the Eye of Goldun," Adrah said as she stepped forward as well, placing her hands on either side of the Eye. "For millennia I have watched the past, present, and future through it, and because I wish it, you shall see what I see. What you will witness is the future of our land should you depart, or if our mission should fail."

Before Selena could respond, a flash of white light filled her vision, and the colors at the center of the orb parted to reveal the images inside. Fire swirled and raged as the sounds of clashing metal filled her ears. Creatures fought to the death before her eyes, Centaurs battled Minotaurs, Elves and Fae fought Witches and Sorcerers. Blood splattered across once-green fields, now gone dry and brown. Fire rained from the sky and enveloped the battlefield in a raging inferno, and a crumbling castle fell to pieces in large chunks behind the fighters, raining slabs of stone down along with balls of fire.

The most heartbreaking image brought tears to Selena's eyes. Wolves tore at each other, and even though Selena didn't know them, she instinctively knew these animals were of the same packs and families, torn asunder by Eranna's schemes. Brother fought brother in flashes of sharp teeth and claws, ripping out throats and entrails with a single swipe or bite. On one side the eyes glowed red, on the other, various shades hinting at the humanity of the shifters still inside. Selena's heart squeezed as she beheld the white wolf with the glowing blue eyes.

He charged to the front of the pack, a nearly identical, larger wolf at his side—the Alpha male, Titus' father. The two were magnificent in battle, taking down Eranna's possessed wolves along with Centaurs and other unsightly creatures. A sudden puff of black smoke brought the battle to a halt as a woman that could only be Queen Eranna rose up out of the mist.

All around her grew still as she stepped down from her chariot of ice, a double-edged spear gripped in one pale hand. On her side of the battlefield, her red-eyed followers roared and leaped gleefully, spittle rolling from their mouths and their expressions dazed as if they were all drunk from power. Silence swept over the field as a pounding roar filled Selena's ears, her eyes zeroing in on the wolf that rose up from the ranks of the side of good to challenge her. Titus was beautiful, proud and formidable as he leaped into the air, soaring with all four paws off the ground toward the beautiful yet horrendous Eranna. Pain lanced through Selena, as with a flick of Eranna's spear, Titus was impaled. Selena fell to her knees, covering her ears and closing her eyes against the sound of howling wolves, and the sight of gore and blood that stayed with her even as she lost sight of the Eye.

Swiftly, Adrah covered the orb with the cloth once more, casting them back into darkness except for her ethereal glow. She slowly rounded the pedestal and stood over Selena, who was cowering against the wall, shivering against the cold stones and crying for Titus of the future. Watching someone die, even in a vision, was not something she'd been prepared for.

Selena glared up at Adrah accusingly, tears spilling over her eyelids and splashing her cheeks. "Why did you show me that?"

Adrah offered Selena her hand, but she refused, choosing to stand on her own.

The queen sighed. "That is the fate of Fallada as it is now set by destiny. However, I have seen an alternate destiny, one that hinges completely on the fulfillment of the prophecy. The very same prophecy that begins with you, Eladria."

Selena felt rebellion welling up in her at the mention of her birth name. Her hands curled into fists at her sides. "I don't like being manipulated into doing things I don't want to do."

Adrah's tone was gentle when she replied. "My dear, I have the power to bend others to my will on a whim, yet I am offering you a choice. Should you wish it, I would put you back on board *The Adrah* tonight and send you home."

"Why? Your world is in trouble and you need me." Selena lowered her gaze and felt her fingernails digging painfully into her palms. "Titus needs me."

"Without you, he will take it upon himself to lead the rebellion against Eranna. Soon, she will be too powerful to be stopped without the lost daughters of Fallada. We need your combined powers to destroy her. Nothing else will do."

"I do not have any great power!" Selena exclaimed. "Everyone keeps talking about how powerful I am, but all I can do is run really fast. What am I supposed to do if Eranna comes after me?"

Adrah's grinned, eyes twinkling with a thousand secrets. "I think it is past time you met your father."

Chapter Ten

Selena tore her eyes away from the looming, dense, rock formation that was Goldun, as it grew smaller in the distance. From her perch on the back of a soaring owl, she felt as if she could see just about every corner of Fallada. The thick arms of the warrior Fae, Rothatin, were holding the reins of the owl on either side of her. And while they offered security, they offered none of the warmth she felt when being held by Titus. Her place in front of Rothatin was necessary, though, as neither she nor Titus knew the first thing about guiding an owl.

The eagle bearing Titus and another warrior Fae swooped close to her and Rothatin's owl, close enough for her to see Titus' warm smile and expression of sympathy. Selena lowered her gaze. She'd been hoping he wouldn't be able to tell that she'd cried her eyes out all night, but Titus was entirely too perceptive for that. He reached out for her hand and she placed her palm in his. The two warrior Fae exchanged glances and nodded, keeping their birds close enough so they could talk.

"You did the right thing," Titus said gently. "It wasn't safe for them to continue on with us."

Selena knew he was right, but that didn't make her feel any better about having sent Zoe and Rose back home that morning. Yet, looking at Titus now only reminded her of what Adrah had shown her within the Eye of Goldun. It reminded her of his fate if she were to leave like she wanted to. That, coupled with the long talk she'd had with Rose the night before, had sealed the deal. Her grandmother's words stuck with her now, hours later.

"I DIDN'T SEE much of you at the party, sweet pea."

Selena looked up from where she sat on a silver, cushioned stool in front of a low vanity and mirror, brushing her tangled hair. She felt a smile curling at her lips as Pixie dust rained down onto the table and into her lap. Even after the terrible things she'd seen within the Eye of Goldun, Titus' kiss remained on her lips, tingling with remembrance.

Rose chuckled. "Oh, so that's where you've been. I should have known."

"It wasn't like that, Gram."

Rose shook her head and sat on the edge of Selena's bed. "Of course it is. Just because I'm old doesn't mean I can't remember the good ol' days when Jeb McClendon and I used to park his Chevy at Lookout Point and neck."

Selena swiveled on her stool and turned to face Rose. "Okay, first, no one calls it necking anymore. Second … Jeb McCendon? Ew! And third, is there even a place in Twin Oaks called Lookout Point?"

"I will have you know that Jeb was the quarterback of the football team and best looking guy in school in his day. And if there was a place in Twin Oaks called Lookout Point, I sure as shootin' wouldn't tell you where it is."

Selena shrugged. "Well in Goldun they call it Pixie Point and it's magical."

Rose's face was suddenly serious. "Making out with that cute Werewolf boy isn't the only thing that happened, is it? I saw you coming back to the party with Queen Adrah. Something is wrong."

Selena frowned. "Gram, how do you do that?"

Rose shrugged. "Years of practice. Besides, I raised you! I know you inside and out and I definitely know when something is bothering you."

"It's this whole princess of a nation thing. And the long lost parents thing. And the prophecy thing. So really, it's everything."

"Feeling a little uncertain, huh?"

"Uncertain is an understatement. I'm downright scared, Gram. I mean, these people expect me to fight and I don't know the first thing about fighting. All I know is running, and as far as I know running away never helped anyone."

"Honey, you've just solved your own problem."

"What do you mean?"

"Think about what you just said. 'As far as I know, running away never helped anyone.' If you get back on that ship and let those Grimm fellas take you home, that's exactly what you'll be doing."

Selena stood, too restless to remain sitting. Her feet itched to move and she paced to keep the urge to run at bay.

"I don't understand. You want me to stay here with these people; lead them into battle? Gram, that means I can't go home with you. I may never come back."

Rose nodded. "I know. I'm prepared for that."

Her voice was sure, but Selena detected the sadness in her eyes. It glistened in the form of tears.

"I can't leave you, Gram. You're all I have in the world."

Rose shook her head. "No. You have a mother and a father who lost you tragically. They didn't abandon you, Selena, you were stolen from them. Seventeen years later they now have a chance to see you, to know that you're all right. As a mother who has lost a child, I know exactly how they must feel. I could never take that hope away from them and be so selfish as to ask you to come back with me. You belong here, Selena."

"How can you be so sure?"

"Because for years I've watched you struggle to fit in with the other kids. I've watched you try to deal with being different, and I could see that you felt like less than the rest of them. Granted, I didn't know why you were so different until a few days ago, but still. You can be yourself here, Selena. You can reach your full potential. You say that you don't know how to fight, but I wonder if maybe you're wrong about that. How could you know when you've never had the chance to learn?"

"Adrah thinks I should travel to Damu and meet my father. She believes the journey will change me somehow."

Rose nodded. "I agree with Adrah."

"You can't go with me, Gram … you or Zoe. It's too dangerous."

Rose stood and wrapped Selena in her arms, transporting Selena back to the days when she was a kid with pigtails and her head only came up to her grandmother's waist. Now, her chin rested on Rose's shoulder.

"I love you, Gram."

"I love you, too——" Rose pulled away and stared up at Selena with tear filled eyes "—Eladria."

THE MEMORY of the conversation and the resulting farewell almost brought tears to Selena's eyes again. She choked them back and tried to focus on the positives. Her grandmother and best friend were now safely on their way back to Earth; Jake and Wil had seen to that. Their ship departed from Goldun first thing that morning, after Selena had taken the time to explain to them, Zoe, and Adrah that she had decided to stay.

"If there's going to be some kind of Werewolf wedding, I want an invitation," Zoe had said jokingly before boarding the Grimm brothers' flying steamship.

Selena shook her head and laughed. "You are seriously twisted."

Zoe shrugged. "Someone's gotta keep things interesting in Twin Oaks." Her friend was suddenly serious as she leaned in to grasp Selena in a tight hug. "It won't be the same without you."

Selena hugged Zoe back and tried not to cry. She'd already spent hours the night before mourning the loss of the familiar.

"No, but if Adrah is right, neither will this place and neither will Titus."

Zoe pulled back and swiped tears away with the back of her hand. She attempted a smile. "Oh, the things we do for boys."

Selena had glanced over her shoulder to where Titus stood, leaning against a tree and watching the exchange. She shivered and looked quickly away from the all-too perceptive gleam in his eyes.

No, Titus was definitely *not* a boy. His talk of mates and destiny scared the crap out of her, while thrilling her at the same time. She wasn't sure what it all meant just yet, but if staying in Fallada meant more kisses with Titus under the Pixie tree, then maybe it wouldn't all be as terrifying as she thought.

"There's a lot more at stake here," she answered, even knowing that Titus had been the main reason she chose to stay.

Zoe nodded. "I know. Give 'em hell, Selena."

And just like that, they were gone; on board the steamship and streaking across the morning sky. For Zoe and Rose it was the journey home. For the gray and wrinkled Brothers Grimm it was a double assignment. The Eye of Goldun had possibly located another one of Fallada's missing princesses. They were hoping to return with her. Selena had tried her best to ignore the smug expression on Wil's face as he wished her good luck. Darn him, he had known all along that she would choose to stay!

"Princess." Rothatin's deep voice intruded upon her thoughts. "We are nearing Damu."

All thoughts of flying ships and smug German writers disappeared as Selena turned toward the horizon in front of them. The gasp that escaped her throat gave voice to her awe at the beauty that was the desert of Damu.

The light of the sun seemed to take on several colors at once, adding to Selena's amazement over Fallada's vibrant hues. The sky was a stunning mix of pink, wispy clouds against a blue backdrop. Sand glittered like gold as far as the eye could see, and sloping dunes dotted the horizon beyond. The gleaming city sat miles away, its curved rooftops reminding her of pictures she'd seen of India. The largest building had to be a royal palace, she decided, as her eyes fixed on the towering, red-domed rooftops. They matched the ruby dangling from the chain around her neck. Setting eyes on the building caused something to resonate within her. It expanded outward from her chest until she was vibrating with it. Her gaze remained fixed there as the Fae landed their birds right on the line where the green grass ended and the golden sand began. Selena frowned as Rothatin dismounted and offered her his hand.

"Why are we landing here?" Selena asked as she reluctantly reached for Rothatin's hand.

"The heat of Damu is too much for them without the protection of adequate cloud cover," Rothatin answered, stroking the feathers of his owl affectionately. "They will return to Goldun and we will continue on foot."

Selena eyed the city in the distance and sighed. It would take a full day, maybe more, to reach it. Titus hopped down from his eagle and the rest of their party—twelve warrior Fae in all—followed suit.

"You know, if you guys hadn't created that wall, Fallada would probably have cars," Selena grumbled.

Rothatin shot her a glance that told Selena he was not amused.

Selena shrugged. "Zoe would have laughed."

Titus came up beside her and threaded his fingers through hers. *I thought it was funny.*

Selena leaped nearly a mile in the air at the sound of Titus' voice. He was smirking at her, his blue eyes twinkling mischievously. His lips hadn't moved and Selena was pretty sure that voice had been in her head.

"Did you just do what I think you did?"

Titus nodded and his voice intruded again. *Yes.*

"Do all Werewolves have the power to talk to people inside their minds?"

No. It is a psychic bond shared by Were-males with their mates.

Selena's heart hammered in double time as the weight of what Titus had just said settled in. Her hand trembled in his.

"I don't understand."

When a male Werewolf comes in contact with his true mate, the bond is almost instant. Over time, it grows stronger, until the two are able to communicate telepathically. As it grows stronger, emotions can even be shared.

Selena swallowed past the lump in her throat and resisted the impulse to run screaming for the hills.

"So, you're saying that I have this ability, too?"

Titus smiled and squeezed her hand. He pulled her closer and wrapped his free arm around her waist.

"You have to concentrate," he said out loud. "After a while it will become like second nature to you, but at first you will have to think about it. Reach out toward me with your mind and form your thoughts. Project them at me ... sort of like throwing a ball to someone. You throw it, my mind catches it."

Selena stared up into Titus' sapphire gaze, locked in by the intensity of his stare. He looked back at her, his arm tight around her as he waited.

Like this?

Selena's voice echoed between them, resounding from the walls of her mind as if she'd spoken aloud. She could tell by Titus' smile that he'd heard it, too.

You did it. You're a fast learner, Selena.

This is unreal. I don't know how I feel about all of this.

I know. It's hard for you right now with so much going on. Soon, you'll be meeting your parents and that is what's important right now.

This feeling I have when I'm with you ... that seems pretty important, too.

Titus smiled as he drew her closer, resting his forehead against hers. *It is.*

Selena closed her eyes, inhaling Titus' masculine, woodsy scent. It filled her with security, reminded her that someone was with her on this wild adventure, someone who truly cared about her.

Titus?

Yes.

I'm afraid.

Don't be. I'm here.

Titus shifted against her and Selena braced herself for another one of his mind-bending kisses. Her lips were parted, her breath caught between them and her lungs bursting to contract as she waited. The second his lips brushed hers,

Rothatin's booming voice intruded their haze of telepathic conversation and touching lips.

"We have a long day's travel ahead of us," he said with a dark glare in Titus' direction. It was obvious the Fae male still did not trust him. "We should keep moving."

Titus returned Rothatin's glare. "By all means, let us go."

With another dangerous glance at Titus, Rothatin moved to the front of their procession, a doubled-edged, curved spear clutched in his slender fingers. The others followed without question as Rothatin crossed over into Damu. Selena and Titus fell in behind them, their hands still clasped between them. Disappointment stabbed Selena in the gut and she grimaced at the back of Rothatin's blond head. Titus's laughter rang out inside of her head.

There will be time for that later, my princess, I promise.

Selena blushed and stared down at her feet as they trekked over the sand. *I have no idea what you're talking about.*

Another laugh from Titus. *Sure you don't.*

THE NEWS COULDN'T BE good. Eranna could tell, just by the slump of Ushma's shoulders and the dragging of the horribly ugly Witch's feet. She supposed an hour in the bathing pool was long enough. She waded through the pool and accepted the towel that Ushma clutched between her gnarled fingers. After drying off, Eranna draped a white silk dressing gown over her shoulders and belted it at the waist.

She stabbed her most loyal Witch with a narrowed glare and frowned. "You've brought news."

"Yes, My Queen."

"The expression on your loathsome face says it all. I am not going to like this, am I?"

Ushma shook her head, keeping her gaze averted. Eranna knew her eyes were beginning to glow red, a side-effect of anger that had begun happening only recently. Eranna reveled in the feeling of rage as it raced through her veins with cold fury. Her hand curled into a fist at her side.

"Let's have it."

"Ruen has returned with only a handful of Minotaurs. They have failed you, My Queen."

Eranna's fingernails bit into her palms, drawing blood, but she was heedless to the crimson stain running down her bathrobe.

"I will deal with him later," she said, her voice laced with deadly promise before stalking over to her cherished mirror. She paused and took a deep breath, unclenching her fists and allowing her body to rapidly heal the tiny half-moon gashes she'd created with her fingernails. She inhaled deeply and focused on her reflection in the gilded mirror.

"Mirror, mirror, show me Princess Eladria of Damu," she commanded.

Eranna's reflection faded in a swirl and flash of light, and in the center of a swirling haze appeared the image she'd been waiting for. The princess was escorted by the Warrior Fae and accompanied by that traitor Werewolf. Eranna shook with barely controlled rage.

They had already set foot on the sands of Damu, which meant King Eldalwen was more than likely aware of her presence. His Centaurs would protect her with their lives and add strength to her escort of Warrior Fae. Eranna could not risk losing valuable soldiers when she had been gathering them for her army. The Battle of the Red Dawn was coming. Now that Eladria had crossed over into her home realm, Eranna could no longer prevent this part of the prophecy. Ushma shuffled up beside her, giving voice to what Eranna already understood.

"It is useless trying to stop the battle, My Queen," Ushma said.

"Then we will focus all of our energies on winning, my faithful Witch. You will begin work on your protection spells and talismans.

Adrah's warrior Fae will be the greatest asset to our enemy's forces. Instruct Ruen to see to the construction of iron weapons and gather the wolves. It is time to prepare for battle."

THE JOURNEY WAS EXHAUSTING, so Selena was grateful when they finally made camp for the night. She was also grateful for the tents provided by Queen Adrah, which did a more than adequate job of protecting them from the swirling sand whipped about by the wind.

"The winds blow strongest at night," Rothatin had told her when she commented on the increase in the air's current. "You will learn more of this once we bring you to King Eldalwen, but the people of Damu draw their power from the wind."

She thought over this now as she sat, alone in her tent. If what Rothatin said was true, then maybe her power was not that of speed, but control of the wind. That was hard enough to wrap her brain around without the added pressure of knowing she was about to meet her parents for the first time. Even though she missed Rose with a deep and resounding ache, she couldn't help excitement and a sense of rightness about going to Damu to meet her parents. While she still hadn't quite come to terms with a lot of things— Titus claiming that they were true mates, the fact that everyone wanted her to be the catalyst for an impending war—she knew meeting her parents was the right thing to do. Selena only hoped she wouldn't be a disappointment to them.

She'd been told that her mother was a great beauty. Would the queen of Damu be disappointed in Selena's average looks?

And what about her father? Would King Eldalwen feel let down because she wasn't tougher? Surely a great warrior like him would expect his daughter to be able to kick some ass. The idea that he could expect something from her that she did not possess terrified Selena.

"You look as if you are a thousand miles away."

Selena glanced up to find Titus standing in the open flat of her tent. He was smiling, but he also looked concerned. She tried to return his smile and motioned for him to join her on the thick, cushioned floor of the tent.

"I'm right here," she answered as he lowered himself beside her. She instinctively reached for his hand, trying as hard as she could not to even think about the fact that it came so easy to her. Almost as if what he said about their mated destiny was true.

"Yes, but I can see your thoughts have taken you somewhere else."

His eyes searched hers probingly, and Selena felt invaded to every corner of her soul. She shivered.

"Stop that," she said, lowering her eyes. "I feel naked when you do that."

"I'm sorry," he said. "I can't help it. It is just that your emotions are so bare to me. The connection is getting stronger, Selena. If you try, you can read my feelings, too."

Her gaze jumped back up to his. "Really?"

Titus nodded. "Sure. If you want I'll go first." He pierced her with his intense gaze again for several seconds before speaking again. "You are thinking about your parents. You're worried you will fall short of their expectations. You're wondering if you'll fit in at the palace and with the people of Damu. You are worried that if you take your place as princess and lead the charge against Eranna that you will fail. You fear failure most of all because you know that you are powerful. You feel your power, even if you don't know the full extent of what it is, and you fear falling short when the time comes to use that power."

Selena's jaw went slack and she was afraid she'd have to pick her chin up off the floor. "Okay, that's freaky. That's exactly what I was feeling and thinking!"

Titus smiled. "Of course it is. Now you try."

"I don't think I can."

Titus sighed and shook his head, sending a lock of dark hair falling into his eyes. "You haven't even tried yet, Selena. One thing you will have to learn is that you can't give up before you even try. You're setting yourself up for failure. If you tell yourself you can do it, then you can. The bond is already created between us. You must trust it and yourself. Look at me and tell me what you see. Don't be afraid to give voice to exactly what you feel coming from me."

Selena took a deep breath and shifted until she was fully facing him. She folded her legs under her and rested her hands on her knees. She leaned forward and found Titus' gaze, locking her eyes with his. Selena blocked out the sounds of the Fae moving around outside, cooking and making camp outside her tent, the sounds of wind and swirling sand, and even her own beating heart. She lost herself in the blue depths of Titus' eyes, zeroing in on the dark pupils and the rim of lighter blue that edged them. Suddenly, her heart squeezed tightly as everything he felt poured into her. She was seized by it, as if gripped by an unbreakable force, a tight band that squeezed the very air from her lungs. Tears came to her eyes uncontrolled.

"You are afraid Eranna has learned of your switching sides, and that she has killed your family in retaliation. You worry you will never see them again, and that you have failed them. You want me to meet my parents and take my place in Damu, but you don't believe that a war with Eranna's forces will bring about change. You don't think I should be the catalyst for this war and you worry that I'll be hurt or killed. You do not think Adrah and the Grimm brothers will be able to find all seven of the lost girls. You worry that this world will forever be lost to darkness and evil."

She paused and took a deep breath as the tight band of emotion squeezing the life from her loosened, but she could not break her gaze from Titus'.

"Do you really think there is no hope?"

Titus's jaw tightened and his lips were a disappearing, white line. "It is a small hope, like a single star in a black sky. I am skeptical, Selena, I can't lie to you about that. I hope you don't think it's any indication of what I think of you and your abilities. I think that if there is a war, and if it does begin with the Red Dawn of the prophecy, maybe you are the best chance we have of at least getting my family back and liberating the other wolves in captivity. Beyond that ..." Titus trailed off and shook his head. "I just don't know what will happen and it scares me, especially if you are choosing to stay. The selfish part of me is ecstatic at the thought of having you as my mate for life. Another part of me wonders just how long those lives will be. With Eranna's reign of terror growing by the day, we would find ourselves hunted like animals. I would never ask you to live such a life when I know you would be safe in the human world."

Selena leaned forward and placed her hands on either side of Titus' face. "I won't leave you, Titus, not like this. Not without knowing that you've gotten your family back."

Titus's hands covered hers. "And I won't leave you, no matter where you go. I may not believe in the start of a war, Selena, but I believe in you, and I'll protect you from anything."

With all her heart, she believed him. She stroked his smooth cheek with the pad of her thumb. "What am I thinking now?" she asked with a mischievous smile.

Titus' eyes widened. "Really?"

She nodded and lowered her hands to his firm chest. "Rothatin has rotten timing, and I got cheated out of a kiss earlier. I don't see any overbearing warrior Faeries around, do you?"

Titus's grin matched hers as he grabbed her by the waist and pulled her practically into his lap. "No, I don't."

His lips were insistent but gentle as he gave her more of what she'd been wanting since their time under the Pixie tree. He held her, one hand at the nape of her neck, the other at her back, his fingers biting into her skin. Selena clung to him, her comfort in an otherwise troubling time, and drank from his mouth, hoping to forget everything else, even if only for a little while. When he pulled away, she was dizzy and knew that if he let her go, she'd fall into a heap on the tent floor.

He stroked her hair affectionately and kissed her forehead. "Enough," he said with a chuckle. "Any more and I won't be able to stop."

Selena's face went hot and she shivered, a contradiction of hot and cold that ra

ced through her body with both craving and apprehension. She swallowed and cleared her throat. "Not that it wouldn't be awesome but—"

You're not ready, his voice said in her mind. His smile was genuine and full of understanding. *Not to worry, my princess, the time is not yet right for us. Such a physical bond would seal our connection as mates forever. I don't think you're prepared for that.*

I wish I was … I want to be.

He kissed her again, slowly and achingly sweet. *You will be.*

I'm just glad you're not one of those jerky guys that tries to put the pressure on. It's definitely making me feel better about this whole 'mate' business.

I take the fact that you haven't told me to go to hell yet as a good sign.

Selena laughed out loud. "Never."

"It's getting late," Titus replied. "Tomorrow will be a long day and I want you to get plenty of rest."

Selena frowned. "They didn't exactly give me a pillow. I know we're traveling light, but you'd think a Fae tent would have a Sealy Posturepedic in it or something."

Titus moved away from her with a shake of his head. "I believe I can remedy that."

Within seconds, the beautiful white wolf was seated before her, his blue eyes glistening invitingly. He lowered himself onto his stomach and crossed his front legs, laying his head on them before nodding toward his furry back in invitation. Selena crawled across the space between them. She leaned down to nuzzle Titus' soft pelt and scratch his ears before curling up against his strong, soft body.

Oh God, not the ears! his voice resounded in her head. *If you do that again, I'll be forced to shift back to my human form and finish what I started earlier.*

Selena pinched him playfully. *Sorry. Didn't know the ears were so sensitive.*

Haven't you ever pet a dog before? Same thing here. In human terms it's the same as your grabbing me by the—

"Good night, Titus!"

His chuckles resounded through her head.

Chapter Eleven

Selena was grateful that the royal palace was only another day's walk away. The heat in Damu was oppressive; much like Texas, only dryer. As she walked beside Titus, surrounded by her Faerie guards, Selena reached for the hood of the red cloak Adrah had given her before she departed from Goldun. The gift had seemed ridiculous at first. Who wears a heavy cloak in the desert? But now, Selena was grateful for the long material, which she wrapped around her shoulders and used as a veil over her nose and mouth. She'd swallowed enough sand to last her a lifetime. With only her eyes peeking out from behind the red material, Selena was baking inside the cloak, but decided it was better than eating a gritty sand sandwich.

The clay walls surrounding the city were fortified by gates that gleamed gold in the morning sun. Beyond walls that seemed to stretch on forever, the city of Damu almost blended in with its surroundings with its red clay buildings, the only exception the jewel tones of the gleaming, domed roofs. As they drew closer throughout the day, the exotic smell of spices met her nostrils. Selena felt butterflies swirling and dipping in her stomach. Even when they stopped for lunch, she couldn't eat, couldn't think beyond what would happen when she entered the gates and finally stood on the steps of the home she'd been born in.

Titus was silent as well, seeming to respect her need to be left alone today. Selena could have kissed him for it, if she hadn't been so focused on the meeting that would occur by the end of the day. So deep were her thoughts that she barely registered the sound of hooves pounding against the sand until the Centaurs were almost upon them.

The Fae warriors drew their weapons and moved into a protective circle around Selena and Titus, who grabbed her arm and shoved her behind his back. She caught just a glimpse of the creatures from human myth before the wall of broad-shouldered Fae blocked them out and her jaw dropped uncontrollably. The Centaurs were possibly the most complex and beautiful creatures she'd ever seen.

The gleaming, bare torsos of the men rippled with muscles that bulged and swelled against skin in shades of olive, tan, and deep, dark brown. The women wore iron breastplates studded with rubies over shoulders and chests that were equally as muscular and impressive as their male counterparts. Hair in shades between blond and midnight black fell down to each one's waist, and many had adorned their tresses with feathers and charms fastened to silver chains. Piercings dotted their ears, noses, and eyebrows; sienna brown markings lined their arms, chests, and some of their faces. The tattoos were in an intricate pattern that Selena instantly recognized as some system of lettering. Something within her latched on to the symbols, recognizing them as familiar. Just before Titus blocked the undoubted leader of the Centaurs from view, she could have sworn she recognized the letters running down the side of his arm. They spelled the word 'Warrior'.

From the waist down, of course, the Centaurs possessed the hindquarters of horses. The four powerful legs of each one were strong, their coats gleaming just as beautifully as the skin across their chests and arms. Long, flowing tails swished behind them and massive hooves pawed the ground. Their ears flicked and moved toward sounds and voices, and they were very horse-like as well.

Selena peeked from behind Titus to watch Rothatin separating from the group. He moved forward to meet the leader of the Centaurs, a male with skin like dark ebony wood. His dark hair was streaked with feathers and his chest was lined with the reddish-brown markings.

"I am Tinutai, general of Damu's army, and servant of King Eldalwen. You will identify yourselves and state your business if you wish entrance into the city."

Rothatin removed his silver helmet and stepped forward, his chest swollen with pride and indignation. "You dare to question a servant of Queen Adrah? She is second only to King Endroth himself. Certainly neither she, nor I, need answer to you."

Selena stifled a gasp as the menacing Centaur took a step toward Rothatin. His nostrils flared as he leaned toward the unmoving Fae.

"Your arrogance is likely to get you and your party slaughtered right here and now, Faerie. If you are who you say you are, then you will state your business and offer proof of your intentions. You will not be given entrance to the city otherwise."

Rothatin leveled his double-edge spear at Tinutai. "You will step aside, pony, and allow my men and I to pass."

Tinutai's fists curled at his side and his front legs left the ground as he advanced on Rothatin with a deep, guttural roar.

"Stop!" Selena cried without thinking, shoving Titus aside and running to Rothatin's side. Tinutai landed with a thud, sending sand flying up into Selena's face. She shielded her eyes, but didn't back down from the intimidating creature. Once the sand and dust had cleared, Selena fixed Rothatin with an angry stare.

"If you just tell them why we're here, you might not get trampled to death by the Arnold Schwarzenegger of all horses."

Rothatin rolled his eyes. "I am more than able to hold my own against a Centaur, Princess."

"That's not the point! A fight is unnecessary."

"Princess?" Tinutai eyed her incredulously, his eyes locking on hers through the material shielding her face. "What trickery is this?"

"This is no trick," Titus said, coming to Selena's side. She did not miss the protective stance or determined set of his jaw. "We are the escort of Princess Eladria, daughter of King Eldalwen and Queen Axonia, and you will allow us entrance into Damu."

A second Centaur, a reddish brown-kinned female, stepped forward beside Tinutai. "Impossible. Princess Eladria is lost to the world of men. They are lying."

"Would you look Queen Adrah in the eye and call her a liar?" Rothatin argued. "How about her beloved scribes, the Brothers Grimm? Are they liars as well?"

"How do we know she has sent you?" the female Centaur asked. "The fact that you are of the Fae does little to convince me. Eranna's power is great enough that even you are susceptible to it."

"I can prove it," Selena said, stepping forward and unwinding the cloak from around her face. "I am who they say I am."

She felt surprisingly lighter after making that statement. It was the first time she'd ever owned her identity as Eladria.

"We're waiting," the female Centaur replied, her arms crossed over her gleaming breastplate. She eyed Selena with undisguised disbelief.

Selena reached down into the shirt of the getup she'd borrowed from Adrah, and retrieved the large ruby from its place against her chest. Gasps rang out among the Centaurs, and the female's eyes widened. Tinutai stepped forward, inspecting the ruby as Selena dangled it from its chain. She held her free hand out to him, offering it with raised eyebrows.

"Go on," she challenged. "I have nothing to hide."

With a grunt and a nod, Tinutai stepped forward and removed a dagger from the leather cross-braces creating an X across his chest.

Titus stiffened beside her but Selena stepped forward, allowing Tinutai to draw her blood with the blade. She squeezed a drop onto the stone, smirking at Tinutai and his girlfriend smugly as it started to glow.

"By God, it's true! That means that you ..." Tinutai folded his front legs in front of him, bowing as low as he could get on four legs. He placed on fist over his chest and lowered his head. "Forgive me, Your Majesty, we had to be certain."

The other Centaurs promptly followed his lead, bowing in the same graceful way as their leader. All except for the skeptical female.

"But it cannot be!" she exclaimed. "The princesses of Fallada were lost! Everyone knows that the Brothers Grimm were sent on a fool's errand."

"This is real," Titus said, his mouth tight. "The scribes have succeeded in finding the first of the lost daughters of Fallada."

Selena glanced over at him and smiled, realizing that just a few days ago, the female Centaur's words had been the same as his. He had no more believed that the retrieval of seven lost girls would be a success than she had. Perhaps time would change both their minds.

Tinutai glared at his companion. "Dargha! You dare to question the daughter of King Eldalwen? We have seen the proof. Where is your respect?"

Dargha promptly fell into a bowing position, her cheeks red with embarrassment. "Forgive me, Your Majesty."

Selena felt all eyes on her and grew uncomfortable as she realized everyone was actually waiting for her to forgive Dargha or condemn her to ... death? Torture? Banishment? She cleared her throat and shifted uncomfortably.

"It's all right," she said. "No harm done."

"We will, of course, escort you to Damu immediately. King Eldalwen will be more than joyous at your return."

The massive Centaur bent all four legs beneath himself and motioned Selena toward him. "Come, it will be much faster if your party rides rather than try to keep up with us."

Selena wanted nothing more than to challenge the creature to a race. Tinutai could be the second four-legged beast to be beaten by her, but Selena knew now was not the time. Besides, she could hardly expect Titus and the Fae warriors to keep up. If the Centaurs were as fast as Jake and Wil had led her to believe, they would be within the walls of Damu in no time.

A low rumbling growl sounded the moment her hand was in Tinutai's and Selena shot an annoyed glance at Titus, who had stepped forward to bare his teeth menacingly.

"Seriously?"

Titus at least had the decency to look embarrassed. "Sorry. Animal instinct."

Selena smiled. "He's not *that* good looking."

Titus raised an eyebrow and returned her smile, crossing to the beautiful Dargha, who had offered her back to Titus.

That is so not cool! Selena whined inwardly as they both mounted their Centaur escorts. *She's freaking gorgeous!*

That may be, but I am not interested in half-wolf, half-horse babies, Titus responded with a visible shudder. *Besides, as far as I'm concerned, you are the most beautiful woman in all of Fallada.*

Selena raised her eyebrows at him as the rest of their party mounted up—even Rothatin, though he did so a bit reluctantly.

What about in the human world?

I wasn't there long, but I did see plenty of photos of the one named Megan Fox. Not bad ... not bad at all.

Careful. We're in my territory now, Wolf Boy. I could have you deserted right here.

You wouldn't do such a thing.

What makes you so sure?

Simple. Because you love me.

Selena was jolted physically as Tinutai started off at a run with the other Centaurs falling in behind him. She was jolted emotionally as well by Titus's bold accusation. She closed her mind off to him, refusing to respond to what she'd already realized the night before while curled up against him in sleep.

❧

THE CITY of Damu surrounded Selena and her party in a stimulating haze of sights, smells, and sounds. Once within the high, clay walls, the wind and sand were mostly blocked out, enabling her to lower her veil and hood and take it all in. The red clay buildings were high and close together, creating a maze of roads leading toward the very center, where the palace loomed highest of all with its towers and domed tops.

Centaurs mixed with people on the street, moving in and out, as much a part of Damu as everyone else. No one spared them a glance, as if it were an everyday occurrence for the half-horses creatures to be walking around in broad daylight. Among them also were a few Elves, Satyrs, and Faeries. Every eye turned toward their party in curiosity, yet Tinutai and his guards remained stone-faced, clearing a path for her and her traveling companions as they wound their way through the village. Selena wondered what they thought of her, if they had any inkling who she was and what her arrival could mean for them. She tried not to focus on that, and went back to taking in her surroundings.

The smell of spices grew stronger, further enhanced by the heat, as they reached what Selena assumed was a marketplace. Beneath beautifully woven tents, open to the view of everyone walking past, women baked and stirred spicy-smelling concoctions in large kettles. Fires roared as the scent of roasting nuts and meats mingled with the fragrance of coconuts, saffron, nutmeg, cinnamon, and something spicy that reminded Selena of chili powder. Her mouth practically watered at all the different smells and the sight of a whole boar being roasted over an open flame. She'd never tasted boar, of course, but if it was anything like barbecued pulled pork, she was down for trying it.

Just like any other place in Fallada, the colors were beyond Selena's imagination or anything she'd ever seen in her world. The deep, rich hues of Damu swirled around her in shades of crimson, plum, golden yellow, and royal blue.

And then there was the music.

It seemed to call to her in a mixture of floating flute notes, pounding drums, and tinkling chimes. The rhythm was intoxicating, as was the choreography of the dancers gathered near the palace. Their skin was bathed in sunlight, much of it showing through their nearly sheer harem-style pants and wispy tops. Banners and flags were clutched in their hands and painted the air around them in beautiful streaks of color as they dipped, swayed, and turned in time to the music. Selena had to be nudged by Titus, not realizing she had stopped dead in her tracks and stood, motionless and open mouthed, watching the dancers.

Their dancing makes me want to join, she confided in Titus.

I'm sure they'll be here later. I'm even more certain that there will be some sort of celebration in your honor and those dancers are likely to be a part of it.

I don't dance in public, Selena scoffed. *That Faerie ball was a onetime occurrence. I was just saying that their dancing makes me feel like dancing … alone … when no one's watching.*

Titus laughed out loud. *I think you will find over the days to come that you are going to do a lot of things you've never done. You might surprise yourself, Selena.*

You're right, she countered with an inward laugh of her own. *After all, last week I'd never have been able to say that I'd kissed a Werewolf.*

Titus raised his eyebrows. *Nice to know I won't have to go hunting down any of my own kind.*

Jealous much?

No more jealous than you were watching me climb on the back of that Dargha.

Hmph. I was not jealous.

Right, Selena. Don't worry, if you had a horse's ass, I'd happily jump on for a ride.

That sounded so dirty.

I meant it to.

Selena punched him in the arm and they both fell into a fit of laughter, earning them a confused glance from Rothatin and a smirk from Dargha.

"You are the Werewolf's mate," she said, leaning toward Selena as they neared the palace.

Selena's eyes widened. "No. What made you think that?"

Dargha shrugged. "You communicate silently, do you not?"

Selena sighed. "Yes, but we're not actually … I mean we … it's complicated."

Dargha's smirk turned into a smile that transformed a face that had been hard and stony before. Selena found her to be absolutely beautiful when she did.

"It always is," she said with a nod.

Selena did not have time to reply before they were on the front steps of the royal palace. Her heart leaped into her throat and her pulse raced. Everything within her tensed and strained, knowing she was now setting foot within the place where she'd been born. Titus' fingers threaded through hers and she felt instantly at ease.

The front doors were flanked by golden pillars carved with figures of men and Centaurs marching off to battle. The double doors matched the pillars and stretched high over their heads by several feet. They were pushed open by two men wearing open vests with nothing underneath and loose-fitting pants. Selena's cheeks turned red at the sight of rippling chests and abs on display. She supposed she ought to get used to it; when the air was as hot and dry as it was in Damu, a guy couldn't exactly walk around wearing layers—or a girl, she soon realized as they passed servant girls in attire just as skimpy, but in fabrics even richer than those she'd seen on the streets. Selena's eyes widened and her jaw fell open as they entered the main hall.

Tinutai brought their party to a halt there. "You must wait here," he said. "The king and queen will have to be informed of your presence. As you can see, nearly everyone here recognizes you as their daughter."

Selena returned some of the awed gazes, with confusion. "Yeah, what's up with that?"

Dargha pointed at the wall across from them. "You are the very image of your mother, Princess."

Confusion melted into something else as Selena laid eyes on the floor to ceiling portraits hanging on the wall Dargha had pointed to. The gilded frames held paintings depicting two faces Selena had been longing to lay eyes on her entire life. Emotion welled in her chest and lodged in her throat, thick and smothering. Sadness, anxiety, elation; all three of them washed over her suddenly and without warning until tears were filling her eyes.

The woman in the photograph *did* look a lot like her, only more stunning. Her tanned skin and vibrant red hair were a match for Selena's and so were her deep, brown eyes and mahogany eyelashes. Her mouth was tilted into the barest hint of a smile, but her eyes, even in portrait, were tinged with sadness. Selena knew that years of mourning two lost daughters had done that to her.

Her father was everything she had imagined. His face was broad and chiseled, with a jagged scar running across it from forehead to jaw. His lips were firm and hard, as was the gleam in his green eyes. Blond hair hung down to beefy shoulders. Everything about this man screamed 'fighter', causing Selena to shiver just by looking at him. Her heart sank as she realized that this was the man whose spirit everyone assumed she possessed. This was the man whose disposition she was supposed to have. Everyone would be watching to see if she measured up. Selena feared she never would.

Just then, the sound of a gasp filled the hall and Selena turned to find a young man standing at the bottom of a winding staircase. He was tall and just as beefy as the man in the photo, with the same bright red hair as Selena and the same piercing green eyes as her father. Her heart told her the truth before anyone else had a chance to. This man was her brother.

He wore a loose-fitting, long-sleeved tunic embroidered in gold that dipped down over a tanned chest. The same loose fitting trousers as the servants covered his legs and fell down over sandaled feet. Tattoos much like those of the Centaurs showed through the vee in his shirt. There were more on his hands. Selena recognized the lettering on his left hand as the word 'Prince'. Her conclusion was further confirmed.

No one in the room moved or spoke as the prince walked forward, his eyes locked on hers, his chest heaving with the quickness of his breathing.

"Eladria?" His voice was deep, but unsettled and wavering, thick with the same emotion that choked Selena. "It can't be!"

"It is," said Rothatin, making his way toward the front of their group. He stood on Selena's other side—Titus still held her hand on the other—and addressed the prince of Damu. "I am General Rothatin Longspear of Queen Adrah's court. I have been sent to inform your parents that their eldest daughter has been found."

He fell silent as the prince stepped forward, his head cocked slightly to the side as if he were measuring her up. Selena squared her shoulders and returned his gaze, silently daring him to find offense with what he was seeing. Finally, a lopsided grin broke out over his face as he rushed forward and swept Selena into a back-breaking hug. He twirled her around with a laugh and a loud 'whoop' before setting her on her feet again.

"It *is* you! I cannot believe it! After all these years, you've finally been returned to us. Mother and Father will be ... oh my God, they'll be so happy, Eladria!"

"Selena," she corrected, with a smile of her own. It was hard not to when her brother was beaming so proudly. His joy was infectious. "I prefer Selena."

His face grew serious. "Of course. I hadn't thought to ask the name you were given on Earth. Selena. I like it! I am Thaddeus, your elder brother by four years. It is a pleasure to meet you."

An older brother. Selena had been expecting parents, and knew that there was still another sister lost out there somewhere, but the big brother she'd always secretly wanted was an added bonus.

"Prince Thaddeus, I was just on my way to inform your parents of this joyous news," Tinutai said with a smile. "I am sure you know what this means."

Thaddeus' smile changed and became one of someone who was itching for a fight. "The Red Dawn approaches. We must prepare."

"Perhaps we should see to the reunion of parents and child first," Titus said with a protective hand on Selena's shoulder.

Thaddeus frowned at the movement and glanced back and forth between the two of them. After a while he nodded in acquiescence. "Of course. Right this way."

He led them to a room that was separated from the corridor by sheer red and purple curtains. Beautifully patterned rugs covered the floors and heavy curtains draped from floor to ceiling over windows that held no glass. The warm, spice-scented air wafted in from outside, mingling with the fragrance of incense that smoked from every corner of the room. Selena dropped into a plush, gold brocaded armchair. Titus and their entourage followed suit.

"The servants will see to your comfort while I fetch Mother and Father," Thaddeus said to Selena. "Anything that you wish, you have only to ask. You are home now, sister."

With that, he was gone with Tinutai and the other Centaurs hot on his heels. A servant girl in billowing, sheer silk was instantly in front of her, thrusting a gleaming silver tray under her nose with a friendly smile.

"Tea? Water?" she offered. "Perhaps you would like something to eat."

Selena was way too nervous to eat anything, but accepted a cup of water gratefully. She sighed happily as she realized the water was just as sweet here as it was in Goldun. She gulped it down greedily while the servant girl made a trip around the room to the other occupants. As if she sensed Selena's insatiable thirst, she reappeared at her side with a pitcher once she'd drained the cup.

"Thank you," Selena said before downing the second cup just as quickly. The servant girl bowed with another smile before leaving the room. The silence that followed only made Selena more nervous. The seconds seemed to drag by as they waited. Selena's eyes remained locked on the door until the second it opened and she lost her nerve completely and lowered them to the floor.

The first glimpse she got of her parents was of their shoes.

Chapter Twelve

Queen Axonia was stunning, and not in the runway model sort of way. Hers was the kind of beauty that was warm and inviting; that made a person feel at ease the moment her lips split into a smile. Selena's rapid heartbeat slowed as she looked into a face that was a lot like her own, only more intensely stunning. Brown eyes widened and a heart-shaped mouth parted as the woman who'd given birth to her rushed forward with an audible cry, her arms outstretched. Selena was immediately enveloped in emerald green silk as Axonia hugged her tightly. She smelled like exotic spices and her embrace was warm and possessive all at once. Selena felt tears choking her as she glanced over her mother's shoulder and met her father's eyes.

King Eldalwen could only be described as a big bear of a man. Blond hair fell down to broad shoulders and framed a weathered, stubble-roughened face. Deep, emerald green eyes stared at her from beneath bushy blond brows and the scar that had been so perfectly depicted in his portrait, slashed across his hardened, chiseled face. His chest was as wide as two barrels stacked side by side, and his arms were so humongous that a bear hug from him would likely kill her. Selena was not expecting the large, calloused hand to be so gentle when he rested it on her shoulder and joined her and Axonia in a group hug. Thaddeus stood to the side, watching with a wide smile on his face.

Finally, her parents released her from their joined grasps. Axonia gazed at Selena with tears in her eyes and Eldalwen eyed her appraisingly.

"Welcome," Axonia said, her voice hoarse from her tears. "Welcome home, my daughter."

"Thank you," Selena said, fiddling with the hem of the leather vest she wore over a dusty white shirt. Standing beside her richly dressed mother, Selena felt drab and dirty. "Your palace is beautiful."

"It is also *your* palace," Eldalwen said, patting Axonia's shoulder lovingly as she wiped her tears. "Your home. You cannot know what you coming here means to us."

Selena cleared her throat nervously. "Um, actually I do. I was hoping we would get to talk about that."

Eldalwen nodded, his expression grim. "We will, in due time. Thaddeus says that Selena is the name given to you in the world of men? This is what you prefer to be called?"

"You can call me whatever you want," Selena said with a wobbly smile. She felt at any moment as if she would burst into tears. Seventeen years of wondering and waiting had ended and she now stood face to face with her birth parents. How could she deny them anything? If they wanted to call her Dixie, she'd let them.

"Selena is a beautiful name," Axonia said. "I love it. I know my husband is anxious to speak to you about some very important matters, but first I will see to your comfort and that of your guests. I hope you will all stay for a while and rest before returning to your homes. Rothatin, it is wonderful to see you again. I am sure you would be more comfortable allowing my husband to see you to your usual quarters in the warrior's compound? Your lady soldiers may come with me."

Selena had no choice but to follow Axonia, her mouth agape in slack-jawed wonder. Was this what being queen was like? This woman knew how to command. Not one person questioned her authority or her requests. Everyone just fell in to do as she asked. Selena caught Titus' gaze before turning the corner. He smiled and nodded.

Go and get to know your mother, he said into her mind. *I will find you later.*

Selena and the four female Fae Warriors followed Axonia up a white-and-pink veined marble staircase and down wood-paneled halls. Selena was hoping for a bath and change of clothes so she could stop feeling so out of place in such a decadent setting. Her prayers were answered after Axonia had shown the Fae women to their rooms and left them in the care of her handmaidens.

"Come, I will take you now to the family wing of the palace. I hope you like your room. I haven't changed the décor since you were born, only changed the furnishings in hopes that you would be found someday."

Selena remained silent, but smiled encouragingly and nodded. She didn't know what to say. While she had been living a comfortable, albeit somewhat boring, life in Twin Oaks, her family had been waiting for her return for almost two decades. That had to be exhausting. Selena tried to concentrate on memorizing the turns they were taking as Axonia led her through winding hallway after winding hallway, but it was futile. By the time they stopped in front of a carved oak door, Selena was completely lost.

The room was just as decadent and fine as the rest of the palace, and when Selena stepped into the chamber she almost wished Zoe was with her. Her friend's estimation over her parents' wealth had been seriously understated. The room was done in rich shades of red, yellow, and gold. Gleaming solid gold was everywhere, edging the furnishings and frames of paintings lining the walls. A raised platform sat in the center of the room with three steps leading up to a massive canopy bed. The oak posters held red and gold embroidered curtains that were tied back with red tasseled ropes. Just like everywhere else in the palace, the windows held no glass and allowed the mugginess and spicy smell of Damu to filter in. Yet, somehow the room was still a comfortable temperature.

Black tiles lined the floor beneath her feet, each one hand-painted with red or gold depictions of birds. A sitting area near the large, open windows held a couch, two armchairs, and a chaise. In another corner of the room, a floor-to-ceiling window held a cozy window seat that was lined with cushions and pillows. A large, oak armoire rounded out the room with another oak door leading to the room beside it.

"What do you think?" Axonia asked, after Selena had turned and inspected her surroundings.

"It's so beautiful," Selena said, suddenly feeling even dirtier. "I've never owned such expensive-looking things before. It's funny, I feel so at home here, but out of place at the same time. I hope that makes sense."

"Absolutely. It will take time for you to adjust to your new life … that is, if you plan on staying?"

Selena didn't miss Axonia's questioning tone and hopeful gaze. She sighed. "I honestly don't know what I want to do yet. I came here to ask Eldalwen for help. You see, my friend—"

Axonia stopped her with a wave of her hand. "There is no need for us to speak of this now," she said gently. "I know you must have many doubts and fears, but I also know what you are capable of, what you can become. I hope to be able to show you what I know before you make your decision. But for now our priorities are a bath, clean clothing, and a meal for you and your companions."

Selena nodded. "Okay."

Axonia gestured to the second doorway. "Through this door you will find your private bathing room. My handmaidens have already prepared it for you. Take all the time you need. You will find clothing in your size in any color and style you could imagine in this armoire. When you are finished, simply pull the bell rope near your bed to call on a servant. Someone will come to escort you to the dining hall for the evening meal."

Axonia quickly exited the room, leaving Selena standing alone in the middle of it. Glad to finally be within reach of a bath, she nearly ran for the door leading to the bathing room. The floor and bathing pool were lined with more of the painted black tiles and the walls were splashed with beautiful murals depicting Damu's desert. Near the pool stood a servant girl swathed in pink. She gestured toward the small, round table beside her.

"There are towels here as well as scented oils for your use. Just a few drops of whatever fragrance appeals to you in the water will do."

"Thank you," Selena said, waiting for the girl to leave before rifling through the vials. Five minutes later she was undressed and neck deep in water that was scented with a combination of oils that made the water, and her skin, smell very much like the scent of spices that seemed to cling to the air here.

Selena didn't want to leave the hot, relaxing water, but knew she couldn't avoid the dining room and her new family forever. There was still that talk with her father to get out of the way. And of course there was Titus. They still had to come up with a plan for saving his family. Selena left the pool reluctantly and reached for a towel.

❧

SELENA HAD NEVER BEEN FULLER in her life. The people of Damu sure knew how to put out a spread. Roasted meats, cheese and crusty bread, toasted nuts, rich custards and sauces, and fragrant rice and beans filled the massive dining hall with tantalizing smells. Then there were the desserts; more of the nuts dusted with cinnamon, tiny tartlets dotted with fresh cream, and a variety of fruit that Selena had never seen or heard of. When her fingers closed around a plump clutzia fruit, her eyes met Titus' and the two shared a private laugh over memories of their first kiss. There was also wine, which her brother kept pouring into her goblet. Selena had never tasted wine, being under the age of twenty-one, but she supposed there were no such laws in Fallada because no one seemed inclined to stop her.

It was sweet, but she could taste the vinegary alcohol behind it. Intriguing. She took another long swallow and felt dizziness rushing straight to her head. She set it aside after the first initial buzzing raced through her veins, deciding to take only small sips until she was used to the potent brew. She didn't want Titus to have to carry her back to her room.

It would be my pleasure to do so, Titus' voice was teasing, but his eyes were full of heat as he watched her from across the table.

How did he do that, manage to turn her knees to jelly with just one look? He made her feel beautiful; which, for the first time since the Fae party in Goldun, Selena actually embraced. The garments she'd chosen from her armoire were a lot like Axonia's and the other servants. A navy blue silk top with long, sheer sleeves stopped just above her belly button, while fluttering harem-style pants flowed around her legs. The matching slippers were dotted with clear gems, and a silver headpiece covered her head and ended in a point between her eyebrows, draping down over her hair in delicate silver chains. Zoe would be green with envy.

You certainly look the part, Princess, although I do like you in leather and a vest, Titus said with a chuckle that echoed in her head.

Selena smirked. *I still have that vest and those leather pants somewhere … unless the maids carried them off and burned them.*

Titus frowned. *Now that would be a pity. Although, I could get used to watching you walk around in that getup. I especially like your … ahem … shirt … if you want to call it that.*

Selena's cheeks grew hot as she tried to turn her thoughts back to food. It was hard, but she managed to get through the meal with dignity. Once the food had been taken away, Eldalwen turned to her from his place at the head of the table.

"It pleases me to see you seated at the family table, daughter."

"Thanks," Selena said, still a little uncomfortable around the guy she was supposed to call 'dad'. He was just too intimidating for words. "I'm happy to be here."

"Thaddeus and I would like to take you on a tour of the palace this evening. You might find the war room to be of particular interest."

Selena's breath caught in her throat at the same time a flicker of annoyance sounded off in her head. Eldalwen certain hadn't wasted any time.

"War room?" she asked, trying not to get off on the wrong foot with her dad and brother.

Thaddeus smiled and took a sip of his wine. "A history in portraits, weapons, and armor that depicts the warrior past of our family. I'm sure you'll be interested in some of the wind-harnessing tools."

Selena sat up straighter at his mention of wind. Her earlier questions surfaced and her need to avoid all talk of war was pushed away.

"Wind-harnessing?"

Eldalwen wrinkled his brow. "You do not know about wind-harnessing?"

She shook her head. "No. All I know is that I can run really fast. I discovered it when I was about ten."

Eldalwen's laughter was hearty and full. "My dear, the strength of Damunians is not in their speed, but in their power to feel and manipulate the very air around them. Wind, is your gift, Selena."

Selena gasped. She remembered clearly the night that the Minotaurs had attacked. A rush of power surging all around her as she screamed had surrounded her like a gushing wind. It had knocked the ugly beasts right off their feet.

"Oh my God," she whispered. "So there is more to my abilities than just running away."

Thaddeus leaned toward her from his place beside her at the

table. "Whenever you run, you are pulling on the strength of the wind to propel. It pushes you along, makes you faster. It can do the same for your fighting skills. It can be used to strengthen and quicken your blows, and it can also been used as a force against your opponent."

Selena's eyes widened as she realized now why everyone had been waiting for her return, why she was so important to them.

"They think I can fight," she whispered as she stood. Her chair scraped the marble floor noisily and her fingers gripped the chair's edge tightly. "You think I can fight!" she exclaimed, louder this time.

Axonia stood as well and began circling the table toward her. "Darling, no one expects anything from you."

"Of course you do!" Selena bellowed, backing away from Axonia's comforting hands. "It's all I've heard since I got here. The Red Dawn, the battle against Eranna, and the return of the first-born daughter of Damu … it's all pointing right at me!"

"Selena, it is your destiny," Thaddeus said, standing at her side. "It is what you were born to do."

"Look at me!" Selena cried, gesturing toward herself wildly. "Do I look like a warrior to you? Well, I'm not! I can't fight. I've never even been in a schoolyard girl fight. I can't throw a punch let alone use a weapon. You're going to have to find somebody else to fight your battle. I only came here because I wanted to solve the mystery that's been plaguing me since I was a kid. I wanted to know who my parents are and where I came from. And I wanted to help Titus rescue his family."

Eldalwen's jaw was tight and his lips pressed tightly together as he stood also. "A lot has changed in your life over the past few days, and I understand that you have some reservations—"

"Reservations? No, try this one on for size. I. Can't. Do. This. Can't do it. Won't do it. Got it?"

No one answered, and no one tried to stop her as she turned and fled. She half expected Titus to try, but even he hung back as she stormed from the room. The hallways began to blur into one long maze as she tried to find her way back to her room. She stopped and turned, trying without success to find her way. After a while, she found herself wandering aimlessly and feeling pretty guilty. She was sure her parents and brother only had the best intentions. Besides, it was their home that would be destroyed if this Eranna person succeeded. Their way of life would be destroyed.

So would Titus's, she reminded herself.

Then why was this so hard? Why couldn't she just put on her big girl undies and be the woman Damu needed her to be? She didn't know why, and hated herself for it. Not just for not knowing, but for being so damned scared.

After roaming for quite some time, Selena came to a dead end. The hallway she was in lead to a stone door. Selena frowned. It was strange, since none of the other doors in the palace were made of anything other than oak or gold. Curiosity gripped her and propelled her toward the door. There was no handle, yet when Selena got close to it, it swung open on its own. Selena stared up a dark staircase, knowing that if she were in a movie theater she'd be yelling at the idiot standing at the bottom of a dark stairwell to run. She'd never believed in ghosts, but then she'd never believed in Faeries either. Yet here she was, in a palace in the desert in a magical fairytale land. Weirder things just had to be on the horizon.

With a shrug, Selena made her way up the stairs, deciding that once she found her way out of here she would have to find her parents and apologize for her outburst. Maybe even take them up on that tour of the war room. As she neared the top of the curved stairwell, a soft glow lit her path, making her feel a little less creeped out. When her feet hit the landing at the top of the stairs Selena realized that she had climbed one of the palace's many towers. The circular, one-room tower held a stone pedestal covered in a red, silk cloth and no other furnishings. Axonia stood behind the table, a wide, nearly flat bowl and silver pitcher of water resting in front of her. The glow of the moon filtered in through the skylight above and kissed the queen of Damu with an ethereal glow.

Selena paused in the doorway. "I'm sorry, I didn't know anyone was up here. I got a little lost on the way back to my room."

Axonia smiled. "I understand. When I first married your father and he brought me here, it took me weeks to learn my way around. Come in. I am glad you're here."

Selena entered the room and stood on the other side of the table. Everything about this situation reminded her of the meeting she'd had with Adrah in a very similar room. Axonia answered her unspoken question immediately.

"This is the Eye of Damu," she said gesturing toward the bowl.

Selena frowned. "It's a bowl."

Axonia laughed. "It is. It was forged from the silver of the first Eye, which was destroyed. It was reshaped and now this bowl serves as the Eye. I was just preparing to look in on Mollac and Queen Eranna. Would you like to join me?"

"I don't know. The last time I looked into an Eye, I saw something terrible."

"Yes," Axonia said with a nod. "It can be that way often. It is a heavy responsibility for the royals of Fallada to bear, being the keepers of the Eyes. However, you must know that nothing you see within the Eye is set in stone. The future is controlled by our present actions, which means we can change the course of our history with a single step in any direction."

Wow. Not only was Axonia beautiful, but she was wise as well. What she'd just said sounded like one of Rose's life lessons. It made her heart swell with that feeling of being at home again.

"Okay," she said. "Let's have a look."

Axonia reached for the silver pitcher and tipped it over the bowl. Crystal clear water filled the bowl and Axonia set the pitcher aside, and waved her hand over the water once. The liquid responded by lifting up to form a dome over the open top of the bowl. It was within the center of this water dome that the vision was shown.

"The iron weapons are being prepared as we speak, My Queen," said an atrociously ugly and misshapen creature as she hobbled into what

looked like Eranna's bedchamber. The haughty queen was reclined on a black settee, draped in a bright yellow nightgown and matching robe, her long, dark hair spilling over the back of the chair and sweeping the floor. Eranna paused, a silver wine goblet inches from her blood red lips.

She smiled. *"Excellent. I assume my army of Minotaurs is ready to march? What of the others?"*

"They have come from every corner of Mollac, ready to serve and protect their queen. They will be ready."

"And the wolves?"

"Awaiting you in the courtyard."

Eranna rose to a sitting position, stretching her long legs before draining her goblet. *"Wonderful. I will address them now."*

Her billowing nightgown and robe fluttered around her ankles as she moved on swift feet down the corridor that led out to the courtyard. The stones glowed nearly blue in the moonlight from their coating of ice and snow. Barren trees surrounded an iced-over fountain and cast their shadows over the sculptures of swans frozen over unmoving water. The wolves came in as if drawn to the center of the courtyard by Eranna's very presence. From the darkness of the night they came; a mass of white, black, and grey fur, sharp claws, gleaming canines dripping saliva and glowing, red eyes, narrowed and fixed upon their leader. At the front of the pack, a large white wolf that Selena recognized as Titus' father lowered his head in reverence. The other wolves followed suit.

Eranna looked out over them, proud, her chin high as a sinister smile curled at the corners of her lips. She walked forward until she was face to face with the massive Alpha wolf. With a throaty purr of laughter, she reached out and stroked his fur.

"At last, the mighty Alpha Orem, leader of the Awcan wolf pack, is mine. You and the other loyal packs have made a very wise decision in serving me. The Day of the Red Dawn approaches in one week's time, my lovelies. You will join my armies and crush the ranks of those who would rise up under Princess Eladria's reign."

Eranna walked through the gathered wolves. They sat on their haunches, eyes locked on her attentively as she waded through them, petting a head here or there, locking eyes with individual wolves and nodding her approval as she inspected them.

"I can see that I have recruited the strongest of the strong, those among your kind who are smart enough to understand survival. As for those who have chosen the other side … " Eranna shrugged and sighed heavily as if troubled by a heavy burden *"… yes, I know that they are your children, your brothers and sisters, your pack mates. But you will no longer think of them as your family. They are no longer your friends. They are your enemies, and they seek to destroy the kingdom I have built from nothing with my own hands! They seek to steal our victory and protect those insipid creatures from the other side of the wall! They are weak, clouded by their loyalties and attachments. You are above them, stronger, greater. With me as your ruler, you will annihilate them. We will rise above them, a testimony of true strength and superiority!"*

At the end of her speech, Eranna threw her arms up into the air as if embracing the universe, her head thrown back dramatically, her hair blowing wildly in the snow-dotted wind. Then the howling began.

It started with Orem, who threw his head back in imitation of Eranna's theatrical pose and let loose with a spine-tingling howl. The lone note stretched on forever, carried and magnified by the howling of the wind. The other wolves joined in, one by one, and then in groups of two or three. Soon, the entire hoard was singing Eranna's praises. The dark queen kept her hands lifted, her eyes glowing as red as her wolves and wild with power.

"We march on the eve of the Red Dawn."

The vision suddenly faded, and the water dome dissolved, leaving nothing but white vapor at the bottom of the silver bowl. Selena's eyes met Axonia's over the stone table. Selena was surprised at the serenity still present on her mother's face. Hadn't she heard Eranna's plan of attack? Hadn't she seen those massive wolves, all with the glowing red eyes that hinted at their state of possession?

"You are frightened by what you just saw."

"Uh, yeah," Selena snorted. "Why aren't you?"

"Because I have lived for hundreds of years, and have seen the passing of three Red Dawns. They only occur once every one hundred years, you know. They mark a time of strength for our people, a time of rejuvenation. Our power comes to its height the moment the red sun rises and sets the sky on fire. Is it any wonder Eranna wishes to attack on the eve of this day? She knows as well as I do what the Red Dawn means, what this particular one will cause if she does not defeat us."

"What are you saying? Are you telling me that Queen Eranna is afraid of me?"

Axonia smiled. "Exactly."

Selena pressed her fingertips to her forehead, knowing a headache was in the making. It had been an epically long couple of days.

"What about Orem, Titus' father? Titus told me his family was being held hostage. Now Orem is leading Eranna's wolf death squad? It doesn't make sense."

Selena fell back against a stone wall and sank to the floor, running her hands through her hair. Axonia joined her, arranging her skirts primly around her legs as she spoke.

"It is possible that Orem has sacrificed himself for his wife and child. He might have been told that Titus is dead. I know Orem of the Awcan pack well. If he thinks Titus has died, then he will see no other option. He will do what he must to save his family, which means his wife and daughter are likely safe in Goldun."

"Safe? For how long? It sounds as if this battle on the Day of the Red Dawn will only be the beginning. No one will be safe."

"Now do you see why we need you so badly?"

"I still don't fully understand."

Axonia stood and offered Selena her hand. "I know you don't, but I have something to show you that will clear it all up. Come with me."

Chapter Thirteen

"What is this place?"

Selena studied her surroundings in awe, taking in the stone statues and wall-mounted armor and weapons as Axonia led her down the center of a long corridor that served as a gallery.

"This is the war room," Axonia said. "Thaddeus and Eldalwen will be very irritated with me when they learn I've brought you here, when they were so intent on showing it to you themselves, but you need to know the story."

As they approached the end of the room, Selena gasped at the spectacular statue looming over her. It was made of solid gold, an image of a woman seated on a throne, wearing a crown of stars and holding a scepter in one hand and an odd-looking staff in the other. Behind her, a mural of the desert covered the entire wall. Unlike the other murals of Damu that seemed so prevalent in the palace, this mural depicted a blood red sun, casting its rays over an equally red sky which melted into orange and then yellow at the horizon. Selena approached the statue and reached out to touch the figure's golden scepter. As its coolness seeped into her fingers, Selena looked up into the lifeless eyes of the statue. Now, this woman looked like a warrior.

She looked like she was more than capable of leading an army to victory.

"This is Princess Nyioa. She brought the very first Red Dawn, hundreds of years ago."

"What happened?" Selena asked, unable to tear her gaze away from the image of Nyioa.

"It all occurred by chance, really. It was before the creation of the wall, when our world mingled freely with the world of man. This particular year marked the beginning of our troubles with humans and their constant war-making. Damu was a particularly attractive target for those out for profit or power. Our caves produce Fallada's jewels and precious metals."

"Is that why everything here is covered in gold?"

Axonia nodded. "Our caves are brimming with it. Our ancestors were constantly at battle to protect it from the humans. It was on one such occasion that the first Red Dawn occurred. According to the legend, our ruler at the time, King Sirus, was worried that the human forces would overwhelm ours. Many of our people had been killed or captured by those in the human world, and he despaired that they would finally succeed in taking over our lands once and for all. It is said that in his desperation, he underwent a ten day trek in the desert, to the Lucan Rocks."

"Lucan Rocks? Are those the tall rock formations that I saw in the distance?"

"Yes. The red rock structures are ancient and have been here since the dawn of our world. A band of seers live there, women with the power to cast spells and enchantments."

"Like Witches?"

Axonia shuddered. "No. Those unsightly creatures that lend their power to Eranna are Witches. These women are a race all their own. Prophets. They are the ones that spoke of the coming of the first Red Dawn. They told King Sirus that every one hundred years, as long as Damu's eldest royal daughter was seated on her throne and wielding the scepter of power, the Damunians would be blessed with power over the winds. Every one hundred years, our powers would strengthen on the Day of the Red Dawn, marked by a morning sky kissed with a blood red sun. If you hadn't noticed by now, red is the color of Damu, our royal heritage. It adorns our flag, our temples; it is the color of our people, and every first born daughter of Damu has been blessed with hair as vibrant as the Red Dawn."

"So what happened after Sirus went to the prophets?"

"He returned to Damu full of hope and told the people of the prophecy. On the day that our enemies attacked, Princes Nyioa was seated on her throne, wearing that starry crown and holding that very scepter—the scepter that will soon be yours. The moment the sun touched the horizon, the sky was filled with red light. It is said that the Damunians' power was so great, they created a massive sandstorm that wiped out the enemy and struck fear into all who would dare to trespass in search of riches or power. And it has been that way every one hundred years since, and from that day we have been blessed with the power of wind."

Selena paused, taking this all in. It was fascinating, the history of the people she'd come from. She glanced back up at the statue of Princess Nyioa and felt pride swelling in her chest. In one week's time, thousands of people were depending on her to fill this girl's shoes. Her parents, her brother, her sister, who was yet to be found—and of course there was Titus. Her hand curled into a fist at her side.

"What about the other prophecy, the one about the Red Dawn, the storms and earthquakes, the dreams of a dove? Where does that factor in?"

"That prophecy came at our darkest hour," Axonia answered, tears welling in her eyes. "Not long after you and the other six princesses were lost, the rulers of Fallada—minus Eranna—met at the Lucan Rocks. We went to the Prophets for answers, for we could see no hope with the loss of our daughters. King Endroth was distraught, a hollow shell of himself, which allowed Eranna to cast her spell over him not long after. But I am getting ahead of myself. We visited the Prophets at the Lucan Rocks. They prophesied the return of you and the other lost girls. They told of a time of strength and vitality in Fallada, a long road, but one that was necessary for Eranna's defeat. All seven of you must be returned to your thrones, and each of your restorations will be another blow to her power, the High Princess' return the final defeat. Eranna will not win, Selena. Thousands of lives are at stake here, including those you love."

Selena pressed a hand to her quaking stomach as she thought of Rose and Zoe. "If we don't stop Eranna, she will find a way into the human world."

Axonia nodded. "Yes, now you understand. She wants to enslave the human race, and that includes your friends, your family."

"My grandmother," she said. "She found me in a field seventeen years ago. She found me and raised me. She's the only person who's ever loved me up until now. I have to protect her. I have to protect everyone."

"You are stronger than you think, my daughter. With your father and brother at your side, you will learn the true extent of your strength. You will be the savior of us all, the savior of the one you love."

Selena gasped, her eyes widening as Axonia grinned knowingly.

"You do love him, don't you? Titus?"

Tears filled Selena's eyes and she swiped at them with the back of her hand. "I think I do. I can't explain this thing that's happening between us, this connection."

"The bond of a Werewolf and his mate is a powerful thing. A bond that cannot be broken. Your father and I would be proud to see you take such a husband. The alphas of the Awcan wolf pack are strong, noble, and loyal."

"Yes, all of those things are true about Titus. But I know we can't think about marriage right now. There is so much at stake; not just for me, but for him, too. His father is in trouble and that's what's important right now."

Axonia nodded. "Yes, you're right. There will be plenty of time for Titus to speak with Eldalwen about an engagement after the Red Dawn has passed, if this is what you truly wish. For now, let us find your father and brother. They will be anxious to begin your training first thing in the morning."

ELDALWEN AND THADDEUS were ecstatic at the news of Selena's willingness to train for battle. Selena's father had expressed his excitement with a crushing hug and loud roar of laughter. The three promised to meet immediately after breakfast the following morning in the war room. Selena only hoped she wouldn't lose her nerve before then.

Now, the palace had gone quiet for the night with everyone heading to bed. Selena was still too restless to sleep, even though she knew tomorrow would be a long day, so she decided to try and use their mental connection to find Titus. She found him in one of the palace towers, standing on the stone balcony. He stood, shirtless and barefoot, in a pair of the loose silk pants characteristic of Damu, the moonlight glinting off his dark hair and giving it an ethereal bluish tint. He rested his hands on the railing of the balcony, his head bowed and his shoulders bulging with sinewy muscle. Selena felt guilty for not being able to take her eyes off his naked back when it was obvious that he had a lot on his mind. She tried to still her racing heart before stepping out onto the balcony.

You should be resting, Selena.

She smiled and crossed to stand beside him and covered his hand with hers. "I know, but I wanted to talk to you before I turn in. It's important."

Titus turned and reached for her, pulling her into a tight hug and resting his chin on top of her head. "What could be more important than what is about to take place here, one week from today? You might just become the savior of us all, Selena."

She shook her head, half in disbelief and half because his bare skin felt so nice against her cheek. "I thought you believed the fulfillment of the prophecy was a long shot."

"It is," Titus said, "but everything has changed for me now. I may not believe much in prophecy, but I have come to believe in you. I mean, if the Grimm Brothers can find you, then maybe they can find those other lost girls. Maybe all hope isn't lost after all."

His arms tightened around her and he trembled. "Maybe there is still hope for my family."

Selena stiffened, bringing her hands up to his chest and pushing gently. She hated to ruin the moment, but Titus had to know about Orem.

"About your family …"

Titus' brow furrowed with worry. "What is it? What do you know?"

"My mother came to me after I left dinner. She showed me the Eye of Damu and we looked in on Eranna in Mollac. Titus, it's not good."

He clenched his jaw and sighed. "Just tell me."

"Your father … he's … he's one of them now, possessed by Eranna. She has an army of shifter wolves, some of them may even be from your pack. She has them brainwashed, and their eyes are glowing red just like yours were. She has them breaking all their loyalties to their own kind. When she marches on Damu next week, they're going to be with her and your father will be at the forefront."

Titus covered his mouth with his hand, squeezing his eyes shut as shivers caused goose bumps to break out over his skin. "My mother? My sister?"

His voice was a raw whisper and his pain ripped through her in a jagged slash of pain. She clutched her heart and felt tears coming to her eyes uncontrollably. Was this what it meant to be bound to someone? Selena didn't think she'd ever get used to sharing someone else's emotions.

"They weren't there. Axonia thinks your father might have sacrificed himself for their release. They could be safe in Goldun, but we don't know for sure."

Titus's hands rested on the stone railing again and he bowed his head, eyes closed, hair falling haphazardly over his brow. Selena came up behind him and placed her hand on his back.

"We will save them, Titus. You just have to give me a chance to save them. I won't let you down."

Titus's laughter was bitter. "My little princess, taking the weight of the world on your shoulders."

He stood erect and turned, backing away from her and bending to shift into his animal form. The silk trousers ripped in two and lay in tatters on the floor as the white wolf emerged. The blue eyes were mournful, boring into her soul in a single glance that left her feeling invaded and crestfallen all at once.

We all have our parts to play in the time to come, he said, turning to prance down the tower stairs on all fours. *I have just realized what mine will be.*

Where are you going?

Do not worry for me, Selena. I will return well before the Red Dawn. If you need me, you know how to reach me.

You mean this telepathic communication thing has a long-distance plan?

Wherever I am, you can always reach me. Always remember that, my love.

Titus?

Yes.

I think … I love you, too.

A chuckle. Selena could already see his white form disappearing away from the palace at a run.

Selena?

Yeah?

I know you do.

❧

TITUS HATED TO LEAVE SELENA, but he his mission was crucial. With only seven days left until the Red Dawn, time was of the essence and the journey back to Goldun would be a dangerous one. Hopefully, he wouldn't run into any of Eranna's hunters. He didn't fear a fight, but he didn't exactly have time to stop and play around with the Minotaurs.

As he ran, surety gripped him. It urged him on, reminding him what was at stake here; his home, his family, his pack mates, and now, his love. Her parting words stayed with him, warming him from the inside out. That she would voice her feelings out loud, even being unsure of them, gave Titus hope. Hope that she would not abandon him; that even if the battle was lost and Damu were to fall into ashes, she would find a reason to stay. It took everything he had to focus on the task at hand and not lose himself in daydreams of Selena as his mate and a shared life. That a future with her in it was possible would sustain him for now. Everything else would have to wait.

Titus traveled through the night, stopping to take water and rest whenever he could. When hunger overcame him, he hunted and ate, remaining in his wolf form. His respites were brief, then he was back on the trail again, making his way stealthily down the lesser known paths to Goldun.

Adrah had mentioned other wolves, shifters who had retreated to the Fae realm seeking refuge. It was for this reason that Titus traveled there now. Not just to search for his mother and sister— although knowing they were safe was important to him—but to gather those lost wolves, those separated from their families and packs, those looking to come out of hiding and join the fight.

Like him, many of the wolves had thought of the prophecy as a long shot. Titus only hoped he could convince them otherwise. It was clear to him now that winning this battle on the day of the Red Dawn could mean the difference between life and death for many of his kind. It might just be the start of something big; the Falladians taking back their world and saving the unsuspecting human world from enslavement. He knew many men who would want to join him, and hoped they would be instrumental in convincing others. Titus knew each and every man would count against Eranna and her hoard. He had been to Mollac and knew firsthand the kind of army her Witches and Sorcerers had crossbred in their dark lairs. Despite the thick fur running down his back, he shivered.

❧

WHEN MORNING CAME and Titus still hadn't returned, Selena couldn't help being worried. She tried not to think about it too much, especially since he'd specifically told her not to worry. She'd dropped a pretty big bombshell on him the night before, and he'd been through a lot in the short time they'd known each other. Maybe it was best this way, being apart while preparing for what next week would bring. Selena had to do what she had to do, and so did Titus. It would be awful hard to concentrate on training for battle if she was constantly around him, staring into those fathomless, sky blue eyes, or longing to run her fingers through that silky dark hair. And if he was going to keep walking around without a shirt on, then she and Damu were both going to be in really big trouble, because she couldn't seem to focus on anything else when Titus' naked chest decided to make an appearance.

Selena shook her head as she once again donned her leather pants, tunic, vest and boots from Goldun. She hated to give up her silky, gem-studded Princess wardrobe, but these clothes were better for what she'd be doing this week. Thankfully, someone had washed them and hung them up in her wardrobe. After getting dressed and pulling her hair up into a ponytail, Selena met her mother in the dining room for a quick breakfast. Then the two started off for the war room, where Thaddeus and Eldalwen waited eagerly for their arrival. Axonia happily left her in their care.

Nerves created a tight knot in her stomach as Eldalwen and Thaddeus showed her the various wind-harnessing weapons lining the walls of the war room. After the time she'd spent with Axonia last night, Selena felt closer and more comfortable with her mother. Thaddeus and Eldalwen intimidated her, which she figured she'd have to get over sooner or later since they'd be fighting side by side. Still, it was hard to get over that fear of not measuring up to two men who obviously knew their way around a war room.

Selena's eye caught on a long, golden-handled instrument and she paused, ignoring the surrounding blades, swords, and other oddly shaped apparatuses in favor of it. The staff was long, nearly as tall as she was and carved with the same markings that lined her brother's and father's arms and chests. At the top a golden cage of branches held a red ruby, much like the one that dangled around her neck.

"What about this one?" she asked, reaching out to touch the engraved gold's smooth surface. "It's beautiful."

Thaddeus and Eldalwen smiled at each other and chuckled, stepping up to lower the weapon from the wall.

"What's so funny?"

"It is not funny so much as it is ironic," Eldalwen said as he held the staff out to Selena. "You have chosen the very same weapon used by the previous daughters of the Red Dawn. Every last one of them has wielded that staff."

Selena grabbed the staff and felt a jolt of awareness rushing up her arm and straight into her heart. A vibration began within her and slowly rippled outward, pulsating with an undeniable energy that Selena couldn't have ignored if she wanted to. A whisper of something moved over her skin, creating a chilling effect that left her shivering.

Thaddeus smiled proudly and nodded. "The power of the staff calls to you. Even if we had any doubts about your status as our eldest princess—which we do not—this would prove it beyond the shadow of a doubt. That weapon carries the spirits of the previous owners. They live now in you. You are the daughter of the Red Dawn."

Tears filled her eyes and Selena allowed them to spill uncontrolled. This moment felt like something out of a movie—like Rocky making it to the top of the stairs, or Neo learning how to dodge bullets while in the Matrix—one of those moments that would be immortalized in her memories until the day she died. She didn't understand how or why, but Selena just knew this occasion would mark the defining moment of her life. For as long as she could remember, she'd felt as if she didn't belong, like something was wrong with her because she didn't fit the same mold as the other kids. Selena knew better now. She turned her tearful eyes to Eldalwen and found identical ones staining his weathered cheeks.

He smiled. "I have waited for almost two decades to see you holding that staff. What do you say your brother and I show you how to use it?"

Selena wiped at her tears with the back of her hand and nodded. "I'd like that."

Chapter Fourteen

Titus waited impatiently in the sitting area of Adrah's chambers, nursing a cup of tea he didn't want. He had arrived in Goldun that morning after a long night of nonstop running, and he was exhausted. He wanted a meal, a hot bath, and a cool rock to curl up on and sleep, but he wanted something else more. His need to know what had happened to his mother and sister kept him going. He wouldn't be able to close his eyes until he knew that they were safe in Goldun.

He was just reaching the edge of his patience when the door swung open and the Faerie queen came gliding in. She was clothed in white and silver as always, her nearly white hair unbound and flowing almost to her ankles. That secretive grin curled her lips as she swept into the room and came toward him with open arms.

"Titus!" she exclaimed, her voice a lyrical and soothing balm. It eased the tension from his shoulders the second he heard and it, and Titus released the breath he'd been holding as she kissed both of his cheeks warmly. "How wonderful it is to see you, my dear. I have been waiting for you."

"You have?"

She nodded. "Of course. I knew that once Axonia told Selena the news of your father's unfortunate circumstance, you would return here to inquire about the rest of your family."

Titus' eyebrows shot up. "Is there anything you cannot see, Your Majesty?"

The coy smile was back, crinkling her iridescent eyes at the corners. "Your mother and sister are here," she said, instead of answering his question. "I will, of course, take you to them straight-away. First, there is something else that you and I must speak of, something of the utmost importance."

This time, Titus was one step ahead of Adrah. "You want me to lead an army of the shifter refugees against Eranna in the Battle of the Red Dawn."

Adrah lifted on eyebrow and dipped her chin. "My, now who's seeing things clearly?"

"We have to take a stand against her, to give the wolves under her possession a fighting chance. There has to be a way to break her hold over them and give those who want it a choice. You have already offered so many of us refuge. Could I trouble you to take in a few more?"

"Anyone seeking refuge during these dark days is welcome here and I am more than happy to gather those who have already come for you this evening. It would be best if they were to hear it from you; you are their leader now, Titus."

"I will do my best to guide them."

"And what of Orem? If the Alpha of the Awcan pack should choose the other side?"

Titus's jaw tightened and he shook his head. "He won't."

"But if he should? I have to know that you will do what you must when the time comes, Titus. You must put your loyalty to the other shifters, your faithfulness to Fallada above all else; even familial ties. Can you do this?"

Titus felt his heart breaking at the thought of having to face his father on opposite sides of the battlefield, but Adrah was right. There was always the chance he would have to kill his own father. He squared his shoulders and forced a show of confidence that he did not feel.

"Of course," he said. "I will do what I have to."

Adrah nodded, seemingly satisfied. "Very well. I will take you to them now. Then you will rest. Tonight, you shall have your time to speak and select those who will follow at your side. There are six days until the Day of the Red Dawn. You will leave here with all shifters willing, as well as a contingent of my own Warrior Fae. They will travel with direct orders from me to defer to you, and in your absence, King Eldalwen."

Adrah turned and guided him from her chambers and through the maze of corridors lining Osbel Tower. When they reached the outer courtyard, Titus's heart slowed, pulsing noisily in his ears at the sight that greeted him. The little girl with the raven black locks ran forward first, her brown eyes sparkling in the sun, her screech of joy accompanied by a gap-toothed smile.

"Titus!"

He knelt down just in time to catch her, bringing her tiny child's body up against his chest. He buried his nose in his sister's hair, tears springing to his eyes as he inhaled the familiar scent of pine and clean outside air.

"Farrah," he whispered her name, holding her back from him to inspect her. Satisfied that she was all right, Titus stood to embrace his waiting mother. Rashi's face was heavily lined, and Titus felt nothing but guilt at the sight of her red-rimmed eyes. It was no wonder his mother looked so worn and grieved; she'd lost her son to the evil queen's hands and now her husband.

"I'm back. I'm here, Mama," Titus crooned as he held her, letting her spill her grief out onto his shoulder. He had failed her. His father hadn't meant to, but by turning himself over to Eranna, he too had failed her. Titus rubbed her back gently, absorbing every tear she shed into the fabric of his shirt. When she was finished, she pulled away and smiled up at him, stroking his jaw with a trembling hand.

"My son," she whispered. "You have come back to me."

"Yes. Very soon, we will all be together."

"Adrah has told me of her plans for you. Are you ready to do what has to be done?"

"We have already spoken of it. There is to be an assembly tonight."

"I must warn you," Rashi said, her eyes wide, "they will not be receptive at first. Many of them think to hide out the coming war here in Goldun. They think that they will be safe from her here."

Titus frowned. "That is madness! Those are our pack mates out there, our families. We have to save them!"

"I know this, my son, but they do not. You have to tell them; you have to make them understand. Come, you should rest first. You will need every ounce of your strength. Adrah has given us a lovely apartment here in the tower with plenty of room for you."

Titus grasped his mother's hand and lifted Farrah onto his hip. At the prospect of a hot meal and a nap, he was suddenly very drowsy. "That sounds wonderful," he said, allowing Rashi to lead the way.

As they walked, Rashi eyed him curiously out of the corner of her eye. After a while she smiled.

"Oh my. When were you going to tell me that you had found your mate?"

Titus felt a flush coming over his cheeks at the mention of Selena and his mother's perceptiveness. He had never been able to hide anything from her.

"I was going to get to that later."

She squeezed his hand. "Is she of the Awcan pack?"

Titus winced. "Sorry to disappoint you, but no. She is not even a wolf."

Rashi gasped. "Oh dear. You'd better tell me everything that's happened. Mating between our kind and non-shifters is rare. This is truly an odd match."

"You have no idea. Mother, how do you think you'd feel about being related to royalty?"

"CLOSE YOUR EYES. Now, slow your breathing and try to grab on to that feeling you get just before you start to run. I don't mean that rush of adrenaline; I am talking about something which hovers just above that within your senses. That oneness you experience with the very air around you. Do you feel it?"

Selena focused on keeping her eyes closed as every hair on her body seemed to stand on end. Did she feel it? Hell, how could she *not* feel it? She could feel everything around her; the heat she was slowly becoming accustomed to, Thaddeus standing just behind her and Eldalwen circling her, the deep timbre of his voice vibrating through her.

"Yes," she said, her grip on the staff in her hand tight. "I feel it."

"Good," Eldalwen said. "Now, focus on it. Pull it into yourself. The best way for me to explain it, is like a ball of energy coming directly from your center. It will expand and grow as you focus on it, until you can no longer contain it. You will release it from your body in a blast of power. Channel it through the staff. Think of the weapon as an extension of your body. It is now a part of your arm. Use it to direct the wind in the direction you wish it to go. Now open your eyes, without losing your hold on that feeling."

Selena opened her eyes slowly, squinting against the sunlight that blinded her at first. They stood on the balcony of the eastern tower of the palace overlooking the city. Though the air around them was calm, the charge of energy that Selena felt was like the winds of a hurricane. She was glad they'd brought her to this tower. The sensation she experienced was all-too familiar to Selena, and she'd always related it to running. Now, there was nowhere to run and Selena had to do something with her power.

She allowed her thoughts to drift back to the fight with the Minotaurs, with the surge of power she'd felt then. Just when she thought the energy welling in her chest would bring her to her knees, Selena thrust the scepter out in front of her, her lips parted on an uncontainable scream as a the power worked its way out of her chest and down her extended arm. The wind whipped around them powerfully, blasting her hair back from her face and howling noisily. Thaddeus' grin was wide, his own hair flying in the face of the windstorm she'd just conjured up.

"Well done!" he bellowed to be heard over the wind. "You're doing it!"

Eldalwen was silent, but his grin was wide. Selena held on to the scepter and laughed, closing her eyes against the feel of the wind on her face and dancing through her hair. This was it; this was what everyone had been expecting from her when they found out that she was the eldest princess of Damu. *Maybe*, she thought, *just maybe I won't let them down.* The power coming from her was massive, something she would have never thought herself capable of. The realization lifted her spirits, gave her more confidence. At least, until Eldalwen's voice shattered it.

"Now make it stop!" he yelled near her ear, jolting Selena out of her 'I am woman, hear me roar' moment. She frowned, realizing that the wind was still going and she had no idea how to stop it.

This could be a problem.

Selena decided not to let it get the best of her. She kept hold of that feeling, deciding that if focusing it outward caused it to manifest, concentrating it back in on herself should contain it. Selena tried it, and it worked. Within seconds, the air was still again, though her hair was beyond repair. She couldn't suppress a giggle at the sight of Thaddeus' locks standing on end as well. He frowned and worked to put it back to rights as Eldalwen pulled her into a crushing hug.

"That's it! You are learning fast. Much faster than a certain brother of yours."

Thaddeus's frown became a scowl. "Hey!"

Selena smiled. "Sorry, big bro. Daughter of the Red Dawn here. It's kind of pre-programmed."

Thaddeus rested his hands on the hilts of the two curved swords he wore at his hips and grinned smugly. "Oh yeah, little sis? Let's see you take it to the next level then."

Feeling confident after her first achievement, Selena crossed one leg in front of the other and rested her weight on the staff. "Bring it on. What's next?"

"Oh, nothing too taxing for someone as powerful as yourself," he said with a mischievous glance in Eldalwen's direction. "You can handle it."

Selena looked to Eldalwen, who appeared to be enjoying every second of this exchange. "Well, will one of you tell me what it is?"

Eldalwen grinned. "Flight."

Selena's mouth fell open. "Shut up."

Eldalwen shrugged and swept his hand out over the dessert below. "The air will carry you if you let it. You must allow it to happen naturally and not try to force it. Pull on the current around you and allow it to propel you along. It is much like the speed you gain while running and pulling upon the wind."

Selena shook her head. "No way. It is nothing like that. While running, my feet are on the ground. What you're talking about is insane."

Eldalwen laughed. "Insane, maybe; impossible, no."

He slowly backed away from them, keeping his eyes locked on Selena's. With his back braced against the outer wall of the tower, he looked out over the balcony's edge.

"Watch."

The second the word had left his lips, her father launched himself away from the wall at a run. He was nothing more than a blond blur as he disappeared over the side of the balcony. With a gasp, Selena ran to the balcony's rail, gripping it until her knuckles were white as she watched Eldalwen careening toward the desert sand. A cry tore from her mouth as he swooped back upward at the last second, twirling a few times in the air before shooting back up toward them. When he landed on the balcony in front of her, Selena thought for sure her heart was ready to beat right out of her chest. She clutched her chest tightly, both amazed at what she'd just seen, and terrified at the thought of them wanting her to do the same. She shook her head rapidly from side to side.

"No way. I'm not doing that. I can't."

"There's really no way around it, Selena. It is an imperative part of your training," Thaddeus said with a shrug. "The important thing is to remember not to embrace your fear of falling. You have to focus on your power at its height and allow it to do its job. After a while, all of this will become second nature to you."

Selena knew she could trust them after all they had done for her, but she just couldn't get past the part where she was supposed to jump over a balcony railing and possibly fall several stories before flying.

"Is there any way we can do this from the ground?"

Eldalwen sighed. "We could, but it's easier the first time to try it from a high point. Once you've flown the first time, you will recall the feeling and become capable of channeling that while on the ground."

"There's only one problem with that," Selena said. "I'm not jumping."

"Well, that leaves only one option," Thaddeus said, his hands crossed over his chest.

"What's that?"

Suddenly, Thaddeus had lifted her into his arms. Before she had a chance to register what was happening, he'd run across the balcony and tossed her right over the edge.

And then Selena was falling.

❦

TITUS FOUGHT to calm his rapid breath as he stood on the raised platform erected at the center of the courtyard at Osbel Tower. The eyes of over two hundred Werewolves bored into him, many of them filled with suspicion or annoyance. These were the people he had to try to convince. From where Titus was standing, it seemed nearly impossible. Those who were not filled with doubt or anger were obviously afraid. Many of them clung to their children tightly, showing clearly their stance in the protective Goldun. Titus didn't blame them. If it were possible to bring Selena to the land of the Fae and shield her from the ugliness of war forever, he would. Unfortunately, there was only so much the beauty of Goldun could block out, and before long Eranna would bring her fight to the floating city. It was now or never, and a stand had to be made. With that in mind, Titus squared his shoulders and began to speak, hoping that his voice would carry out over the crowd.

"Thank you for coming tonight. I know many of you are only here at the request of Queen Adrah, but I hope that you will hear what I have to say."

"We already know why you are here," bellowed the massive Alpha male of the Beldane wolf pack. He stepped forward from his place at the front of the crowd, crossing his beefy arms over his chest with a deep scowl. "The men of the Beldane pack are not interested in joining your army!"

Many others chimed in, shouting their agreement with raised fists. Titus soldiered on.

"And what of your women and children? Will they be prepared for the firestorm that will descend upon Goldun once Eranna has drawn enough power?"

"Was that a threat?" another voice bellowed from the back of the crowd, stirring up even more anger and fear.

"It has already been seen. All across Fallada, our kings and queens are gazing into their Eyes. They have seen the wasteland

Fallada will become if we do not fight back! Even now, Eranna has possessed your pack mates, your brothers, your sons, your fathers …" Titus trailed off, a lump rising in his throat as he thought of Orem. "…my father," he added softly.

"Going against Eranna is a suicide mission," the Beldane Alpha said. "We have lost too many of our own to her. She fills her ranks with Werewolves and sets them against their own kind!"

"And what will you do? Turn tail and run like a bitch? Are you not the Alpha male leader of the Beldane pack? Where is your outrage? Where is your anger?"

Rage flared in the Beldane Alpha's eyes and fur began to bristle along his spine. Transformation gripped him and before long, he was on all fours, a mass of muscle and black fur, coming at Titus with deadly intent. Before Titus could shift and defend himself, a brownish-red wolf leaped at the Beldane Alpha and pinned him. Titus understood the meaning of his throaty barks.

"Let the boy speak," the wolf growled as he shifted back into his human form.

Titus recognized the man as the Alpha of the Iaser pack, a friend of his father. He nodded to the man and shot the Beldane Alpha a glare as the wolf turned back to a man. He crossed his arms over his chest and huffed angrily, but was otherwise silent.

"Yes, I know that it will not be easy. Many of our brothers are possessed by Eranna, but they can be saved. There are others who have gone to her of their own free will. They think themselves safe on her side and will do whatever they must to survive. I know this for a fact, as I have seen them with my own eyes. Many of them are of your packs, all of them are of our kind. Today, new alliances must be made. We must join together against the evil that rises in Mollac. And if we should find our brothers on the wrong side when the battle lines are drawn, so be it! We are not just talking about the destruction of our own homes, we are talking about the loss of the Elvin forests and the caves of the Dwarves. Where will the Pixies go when Eranna has burned down their trees or trampled their flowers to enlarge her iron citadel? I tell you, we would only be safe here in Goldun for a time. Before long, the fight would come to us. I urge you, do not let the fight come to you. Take your anger and your ferocity to the black-hearted witch queen herself and free your brethren! The Day of the Red Dawn is only six days away. I will lead an army of our kind to join the ranks of the Damunians and the Fae. Who will go with me?"

Silence.

Titus began to fear that his speech had been all for naught. Fear was still present on many faces. Doubt was there, too. Titus felt panic overwhelm him as failure washed over him. He had just lowered his eyes to the platform when a movement brought them back up.

Hope surged in his chest when he realized that the Iaser pack Alpha had stepped forward, as had his two sons. "I am Isaac of the Iaser wolf pack," he said, loudly enough for everyone to hear. "These are my sons, Tor and Gais. We will go with you."

Titus stepped down from the platform and took Isaac's hand, shaking it firmly with a nod of respect and gratitude.

"Thank you," he said.

Another voice rang out from somewhere in the middle of the crowd. "Percy of the Enmos pack. Fifteen of us have come to Goldun to seek refuge. Count us among your number."

"Vorves of the Koiyser wolf pack. Count me in, and my four sons as well."

Titus was surprised to be confronted next by a woman. Her long dark bangs hooded equally dark eyes. The tilt of her chin was superior and the thickness of her body hinted at a seasoned warrior.

"Raykal of the Etxeld wolf pack. My husband, our pack Alpha, was slain as we ran for our lives. Many of our males were lost. I can offer ten female warriors and my son. He is young, but capable and we are mostly women, but strong and capable."

Titus smiled. "Anyone who wishes to fight is welcome."

The cacophony of voices that followed was deafening. Titus felt tears again, and this time he let them come. As the names of the pack leaders and their numbers rang out through the night, Titus looked out over the mass of bodies with hope.

ʁ

"HEY, SIS."

Selena glared at Thaddeus as he dropped to the marble steps of the palace beside her. She brought her knees up to her chest and wrapped her arms around them.

"Leave me alone."

Thaddeus chuckled, leaning back onto his elbows and stretching his long legs out over the stairs. "Come on, you're still not mad about that little tumble off the balcony, are you?" Selena shot Thaddeus a murderous glance but didn't answer. Thaddeus shrugged. "You were never in any real danger, you know. The only thing that was hurt in the end was your pride."

Selena knew he was right. After a few seconds of falling and ear-splitting screams, it had become clear that Selena just wasn't getting the flight thing. Thaddeus had swooped down and rescued her; placing her, red-faced and spitting mad, beside Eldalwen on the balcony. After Selena proceeded to cuss Thaddeus out three ways from Sunday, Eldalwen declared their session over. Selena had retreated to the shaded palace steps to nurse her wounded pride.

"All right," Thaddeus said with a sigh. "I'm sorry. I really thought pushing you would do the trick. Worked for me when I first learned."

Selena peeked at her brother again out of the corner of her eye. "Yeah?"

Thaddeus snorted. "No. I squealed and cried just like you did. You know what?"

"What?"

"I climbed right back up that tower and tried it again."

"Did you get it the second time?"

"No. I climbed to the top of that tower with Father every day for weeks before I finally got it. Just thought you should keep that in mind."

"Why, so I don't feel bad when the day of the battle comes and I still can't fly?"

Thaddeus grinned. "No. So that next week, you can look me in the eye and brag that you beat me. Isn't that what siblings do?"

Selena laughed. "I don't know. I never had any siblings until now."

"Well, neither did I, since both my sisters were kidnapped before I was old enough to get the hang of it. But I think I'm getting it now. Hair pulling, teasing, pushing from terribly frightening heights … oh yes, I think I'm going to make a great elder brother."

Selena nudged him with her elbow. "I think you're doing great. You've already taught me so much. I just hope I'm ready for all of this."

Thaddeus stood, offering her his hand. She took it and allowed him to pull her to her feet.

"A true warrior follows his instincts. You do not realize it yet, Selena, but you've got perfect instincts. You just have to learn to understand what they're trying to tell you."

Selena mulled that over silently for a minute before speaking. "I think I know what you mean," she said. "I believe I'm starting to understand what it's trying to tell me."

Thaddeus raised an eyebrow. "Oh yeah? What's it telling you about a sparring session with me in the war room after dinner? Think you can handle that?"

Selena draped on arm around Thaddeus' shoulders and the two headed toward the dining room.

She smiled. "Absolutely."

Chapter Fifteen

Selena staggered into her bedroom and collapsed onto the bed. With two days left until the Day of the Red Dawn, her weariness was bone deep. She'd been training from sunup to sundown every day without fail. Each day began with wind harnessing before rounds of sparring. Her muscles screamed in agony as they remembered wielding the heavy staff against Thaddeus' blades and Eldalwen's axe. It had been worth it though, she thought with a smile, as she remembered using her golden weapon to sweep Thaddeus' feet from under him before jabbing him in the gut with the staff's end. Her smile widened as Eldalwen's laughter came to mind. He had teased Thaddeus mercilessly over dinner, bringing Selena and Axonia to tears with laughter.

Selena peeled herself off of the soft, downy comforter, deciding that falling asleep in her dusty clothes and cape was not a good idea. She stumbled toward the bathing room—which had quickly become her favorite room in the house—peeling off layers of clothing as she went. She sank into the prepared bathwater with a sigh, mentally reminding herself to thank the girls who tended to her rooms. They always seemed to know when she was coming or going, and ensured one of her two training outfits were clean and laid out every morning, along with her cape, which she was becoming incredibly attached to. They also remembered that she loved the combination of eucalyptus and peppermint oils in her bath and made sure they had the pool filled with steaming water as soon as she returned to her room at night.

Selena dunked her hair into the hot water and allowed it to soothe away her tension. Even though it had only been four days, she felt stronger than she ever had. Axonia had told her it was because she was where she belonged. The hot, spicy air of Damu was like a steroid, enhancing her strength, speed, and agility. She had pretty much mastered wind harnessing. All it had taken was for her to learn how to conjure up that tingling feeling at will. She could even do it now, laying in the tub, but decided against it. With a strong enough gust of wind, Selena was liable to turn a relaxing bath in to a hurricane.

Instead, she allowed her thoughts to drift back to her training. A frown pulled at the corners of her mouth as she recalled days' worth of bungled attempts at flight. At first, she'd been eager to try again, to climb those stairs as many times as it took to get it right. With each failure, the weight of her disappointment became heavier, until walking up those stairs began feeling more and more like a stroll to the gas chamber. Selena had never liked failure—who did?—and knowing she wasn't able to do something that was supposedly hard-wired into her DNA made her feel like an idiot.

Eldalwen had assured her that she was making progress. Now, she was able to get onto the balcony railing and jump without fear. She just couldn't make it back up without her father or brother catching her. Frustration swept through her and Selena left the tub with a sigh.

Two more days to turn into Wonder Woman, she thought as she toweled off and reached for the soft pink, luxurious, silk robe Axonia had given her. She combed through her hair with her fingers as she moved back into the bedroom, deciding to focus on something a little happier than fighting wars and her failures at human flight.

She went to the armoire and pulled out a pair of soft, cotton pajamas, and put them on. Then she went about choosing an ensemble for tomorrow night's celebration. Axonia was planning a huge party right at the center of town; a welcome home bash of sorts, as well as a celebration of the Red Dawn. Everyone in the entire kingdom would be there, many of them would be seeing Selena for the very first time. She wanted to look her best.

After a few minutes of rifling around in the closet, she found a deep red, silk outfit with the signature harem-style pants and jeweled midriff top. A pair of gold slippers matched the gold thread embroidering the top. Sheer sleeves were slit to reveal her arms, so Selena laid out a pair of gold arm cuffs and a beautiful piece of jewelry that looked like a three-roped belly chain with a diamond at the center. Zoe would be green with envy if she could see the getup. Selena topped it off with a ruby-encrusted, gold headband and a pair of gold hoop earrings.

A knock at the door sounded just as she'd laid the entire ensemble out on the window seat. Selena frowned, wondering who could be coming to her room this late. She crossed to it anyway and swung it open, finding Wilhelm Grimm standing on the other side. His hair was windblown as if he'd just stepped off the deck of *The Adrah*, and his wrinkled, weathered face was split by a wide smile.

"Well, look at you. What a difference your time at home as made. Look at you, girl, you're stunning!"

Selena smiled and opened the door wider, motioning him toward the sitting area of her cavernous room.

"I will admit that coming here has worked wonders," she said as she took a seat across from him. "It has been interesting."

"I am certain it has. Jake and I have just returned from seeing your grandmother and friend home. They've sent back letters for you, as well as their love."

Wil removed a few folded sheets of notebook paper from one of his many vest pockets. She clutched them close to her chest and closed her eyes, missing home more now than she ever had. She knew that Damu was her true home, the place where she would live out the rest of her life, and she truly wanted to be here. But the little house in Twin Oaks with the sweetest old lady in Texas and a cat named Freckles would always be *home*. She lowered the papers into her lap, deciding to read them when Wil had gone.

"Thank you," she said, clearing her throat to rid it of the thick, emotional rasp. "I'm surprised to see you. I would have thought you'd be out looking for the other girls."

"And miss the Day of the Red Dawn? Not a chance! There's nothing a Grimm brother likes more than an adventure. Well, really, there's nothing Jake likes more than to write about said adventure, but you know what I mean."

Selena nodded. "It's nice to know there will be familiar faces there."

"Are you ready?"

Selena shrugged. "As ready as I can be, I guess. I've been training a lot with my father and brother. I think I've done pretty well."

Wil nodded, bracing his hands on the arms of his chair to stand. "I know you have, girl, I know you have. I'm going to get out of your hair now. Jake and I will be staying here until after the big day, so I'll see you around. Good night, Princess."

"Good night, old man."

After he had gone, Selena walked over to the bed and spread out Rose and Zoe's letters, deciding to read her grandmother's first. Both letters put a smile on her face, reminded her of what she was fighting for. If staying in Damu and fighting kept the people she loved from being enslaved, then she would do it, even if it meant possibly never seeing them again. Selena dove beneath the blanket, clutching the letters to her chest. She fell asleep with them there.

THE DAY of the celebration came and training passed quickly. Eldalwen decided to keep it light, just a few wind harnessing exercises and some sparring. Selena was relieved that he didn't push her to try flying again. Today was supposed to be about celebration and she hated the thought of letting him down. After training, Axonia sent Selena to her room to dress. She sent one of the handmaidens along to style her hair as well. When Selena emerged from her room, she decided that Zoe had been wrong about redheads wearing red. Not that she was the conceited type, but she had to admit she looked pretty good. Her hairstyle, consisting of a mass of coiled and twisting braids adorned with the jeweled headband, was flattering as well.

She was surprised to find Titus waiting for her in the front steps of the palace. He was stunning in an all black get-up shot through with silver thread. His dark hair was gleaming in what was left of the waning sunlight, and his eyes crinkled at the corners as he smiled. He extended one hand to her and she took it, wondering how just a single touch could make her feel so many things at once. She smiled back as he kissed her forehead.

"You're back," she said.

"I wouldn't miss this. Besides, tomorrow will be our last day together before the Dawn."

"Where did you go?"

"To Goldun. My mother and sister are there, safe and sound."

"That's wonderful! Are they here?"

Titus shook his head. "I left them there. It is safer for them. I did bring over a hundred Werewolf warriors and twice as many Elves and Fae. They are all here to celebrate with you, to fight with you."

Selena eyed the convoy that was gathering within the palace's courtyard. Three massive litters, complete with cushions and velvet curtains, were positioned at the center of the group. The twelve burly men who would carry the litters into the city were stationed at the four poles at the corners of each litter, ready to carry the royal family io the celebration. All around them, entertainers had gathered: dancers, musicians carrying flutes and cymbals, as well as jugglers, fire breathers, and acrobats. Selena couldn't wait to watch them in action as they paraded through the streets of Damu.

At the back of the procession stood the Fae, dressed in their flowing white garments and shining silver, the Elves adorned in their brown and tan leather with leaves and flowers decorating their hair, the Centaurs with their tattooed bodies, feathered hair and gleaming gold armor, and the Werewolf shifters, draped in their deer pelts, furs, and copper jewelry. The Damunians were all at the center of the city, lining the streets and waiting for the procession to come through. Selena knew there would be food, and could already smell the aroma of cinnamon and other spices wafting through the air.

"All of this for little old me?" she joked.

Really, her heart felt as if it were ready to burst inside her chest. While she had always hoped to be something—someone—important someday, she could never have imagined this.

"You deserve it. You are their Princess, their hero."

Titus hooked her arm through his and led her toward the very first litter. Eldalwen and Axonia had already climbed into the second and were reclining against the cushions with smiles on their faces. Thaddeus was just climbing onto the last litter. Titus let her step on before him and then joined her, wrapping one arm around her as they both leaned back against the purple, red, and royal blue cushions.

"This is wild," she said as the four burly men lifted her litter onto their shoulders. Selena gripped the front of Titus' shirt and held on for dear life as the procession began to move, the musicians bringing up the front and the entertainers surrounding them on either side.

"I don't know if I'll ever get used to this," she said as they began to move.

The music had started playing, first the hypnotic flutes and then the pounding drums and tinkling chimes. Guitars joined in, and the horns, with notes ranging from deep and low to very high. The dancers moved along beside them, twirling their sheer scarves around their heads and gyrating their hips, causing the coins dangling from their hips and ankles to tinkle.

Titus rested his chin on top of her head. "Whenever you need a break from being a princess, I'll come and rescue you—take you back to Goldun and our little nook beneath the Pixie trees."

Selena smiled up at him. "That sounds wonderful."

"Did you miss me?"

Selena's smile turned coy. "You tell me."

Titus stared at her a moment, blue eyes flashing as he dove deep into her thoughts. His fingers entwined with hers as stars began dotting the darkening sky. The fire-breathers lit up the night with bursts of flame.

"You missed me almost as much as I missed you."

"I did. I'm glad you're back."

"If I can help it, I won't be leaving you ever again."

Usually that sort of talk had Selena ready to run for the hills, but tonight it felt right. The whole evening was alive with a feeling of rightness and Selena knew she was where she was supposed to be. She leaned against him and watched the dancers and acrobats as they led the way into the city, which was slowly coming alive as they neared its center. People lined the streets, shouting and waving to her wildly. Caught up in the moment, Selena sat up and waved back. Flowers flew at her from people following the procession and Titus sat up to help her gather them all. By the time they reached the city center, he had placed a dozen of the fragrant blossoms in her braided hair.

A feast had been spread out right in the middle of the market-place. Tents and wooden stalls had been replaced by long, wooden banquet tables that stretched on as far as the eye could see. Candle and torchlight kissed the night with a warm glow, and the musicians added to the atmosphere by continuing to play softly along the perimeter of the party area. Food and drink lined each table, so much that some of them seemed to bow in the middle from the weight of it all. Just like in the palace, tons of roasted meat, nuts, fruits, decadent sauces and desserts overflowed, and wine and cider spilled from wooden casks.

The big, beefy men set their litters down and the second Selena's feet hit the ground, she was surrounded by people. They called her name and reached for her hand. They shouted their welcome and their love. Selena tried her best to greet them all, to shake hands, smile, and accept another handful of flowers, but was grateful when the burly men created a ring around her, escorting her, Titus, her parents, and brother to the head table. The table had been erected onto a platform and was draped with silk red and gold tablecloths. Red candlesticks glistened and fine china gleamed. Eldalwen and Axonia took seats at the center, with Thaddeus on their left and Selena on their right. Titus sat beside her and the Grimm brothers took seats on the other side of Thaddeus. Everyone else took that as their cue to sit, and soon the tables were filled with people. All eyes were on the head table as Eldalwen stood, his arms raised.

"People of Damu," he said, his voice carrying out over the circular center of the city. "Tonight, I am pleased and honored to present to you my eldest daughter, Princess Eladria, returned to us from the world of men!" The cheers and screams that went up were thunderous. Eldalwen waited until they had gone quiet before speaking again. "In a few days' time we will mark an occasion that I have only had the privilege of seeing four times within my life. The Red Dawn!"

More cheers. Eldalwen chuckled and waved for silence.

"I know. It is an honor to be alive at such a time. Our people will be blessed with new power, a rejuvenation of our strength. The evil that comes upon us from Mollac will not stand in the face of our power!"

This time Eldalwen encouraged the cheers, raising his hands and working the people into a frenzy as they howled, clapped, and stomped. "But tonight is a happy occasion!" he yelled over the noise.

"Tonight is in honor of my daughter and her return. Eat! Drink! Dance! Tomorrow we prepare to make war!"

Selena felt a chill running down her spine as the people raised their arms and cried out with joy and unity. Her dad sure could get a crowd going. She had a feeling her warrior king father had roused many an army on the battlefield into a bloodthirsty fervor. Selena only hoped such magnetism would manifest in her when she needed it.

All thought of anything but celebration faded as a large goblet filled with wine was set in front of her, and she began heaping her plate with food. While there wasn't a Dorito or Snickers bar in sight, Selena found the food in Damu to be the best she'd ever tasted. The meat was rich, the sauces spicy and flavorful, and the fruit sweet. She was sure she'd even drop a few pounds from her waistline without all the packaged and processed foods she used to indulge in on a regular basis. She eyed Titus out of the corner of her eye, wondering if he had noticed the difference—the glow that kissed her skin, the sinewy muscles popping out along her arms and shoulders, and the deep, red luster of her hair.

I notice everything about you, he said in her mind, smiling at her as he popped a roasted nut into his mouth. He chewed and smiled. *It's taking everything I have not to scoop you up into my arms and run back to the palace so I can have you to myself. Don't even get me started on that getup you're wearing.*

Selena laughed and took a sip of her wine. *Be good, Titus.*

I'll try, but no promises. I can't tell you I won't try to steal a kiss or two.

My father is sitting right on the other side of me.

All the better. Let him see how much I adore you. When the time comes, I want him to accept my proposal.

Hmph. Aren't you supposed to ask me first?

Titus shrugged and reached for the fruit bowl across from them. He held up a deep purple clutzia fruit and grinned, putting a blush in Selena's cheeks. He took a bite and licked his lips, leaning toward her with a devilish grin.

"I already know what you're going to say."

The fragrant sweetness of the clutzia reached out and grabbed her, drawing her toward him. All sound seemed to fade and the world around her was a blur as he leaned in to capture her lips. His kiss was quick, sweet and rated G for her dad's sake. She could feel his eyes burning the back of her head as well as Thaddeus's. Barely one week as their daughter and sister and already they were overprotective. She pulled back and accepted the other half of the clutzia fruit, taking her time and savoring its sweetness in a way she hadn't been able to savor Titus' kiss.

Later, he promised, turning his attention back to his plate.

As soon as most everyone was finished eating, tables were pushed aside and the musicians and dancers took the floor. While people still nibbled on nuts and fruit, or sipped their wine here and there, everyone was focused on the acrobats and jugglers, who had taken center stage with their alarmingly entertaining spectacles. After them came the dancers, who filled the center of the circle of tables with their colorful, swishing scarves. After a while, everyone had joined in, from the oldest man to the youngest child, until the city center was a sea of twisting, jumping bodies. Selena couldn't refuse Titus when he took her hand and pulled her toward them. She was grateful that they were quickly swallowed up in the crowd, as she'd never been the best dancer.

Dancing in Damu was nothing like dancing in a barn at the Twin Oaks County Fair, though. It was way more fun. The movements were free and in no particular order, a series of turns, claps, spins, and jumps made it less threatening and Selena learned the steps quickly, performing them as if she'd been born to dance this way. Then came the belly dancers with their sheer scarves, circling Selena with joyous cries and wide smiles, jingling the coins on their hips and ankles. One of them came forward with a wrap skirt in hand, coins jingling from the hem. The gold material was beautifully etched with black markings much like her father's and brother's tattoos.

Wide smiles never leaving their faces, they wrapped the skirt around Selena's hips and tied it, motioning for her to dance with them without skipping a beat. Selena laughed, hesitant at first. She shook her head at the dark-haired beauty, trying to demonstrate the proper hip and stomach movements.

"Try it!" Titus bellowed over the music, his face a mask of amusement. "Who knows, you might actually be good!"

Selena allowed the dancers to drag her to the center of the crowd, shooting Titus a glare as he followed, his laughter mingling with the rhythm of drum and guitar.

"Come, Princess!" the dark-haired dancer said, hers smile ever-present. "You are a natural, you'll learn fast!"

Selena had her doubts, but decided to try anyway. Within ten minutes, she was amazed at the results. It was as if, like everything else she'd experienced in Damu, the dance was a part of her, leading her in a way that she could not control. She faintly registered the faces of Titus, her parents, and Wil and Jake Grimm as she fell in step with the other dancers, accepting a crimson scarf from one of them and twirling it over head in imitation of their movements. She threw herself into it, enjoying this more than she could have ever enjoyed the Senior Prom. Dancing in a hot gymnasium while wearing an itchy, sequined gown and being felt up by one of the McClendon brothers had nothing on this.

Titus watched her, his eyes hooded and glazed over as he followed the movements of her hips and the jingling coins. Selena smiled at him smugly. That would teach him to laugh at her. He didn't look like he found anything funny about her dancing as he watched her, lips parted, arms folded over his chest. When the music ended and applause rang out around them, Titus swept forward and pulled her up against him.

"You're good at that," he said with a smile, nuzzling her nose playfully with his.

"Yeah?" she asked, wrapping her arms around his neck.

He nodded. "So good, that I want to drag you out of here and go someplace private so I can kiss you without having to stop."

Selena glanced over her shoulder and found her parents dancing. Thaddeus was chatting up a hot Elf girl over by the wine and cider barrels. The perfect opportunity to slip away had just presented itself.

She grabbed Titus' hand and pulled him through the crowd.

"Let's get out of here, then."

Chapter Sixteen

The moon was full and high in the cloudless sky. From their perch on the Eastern tower, Titus and Selena could still see the celebration taking place at the city center. Below them, racing across the open desert were the Centaurs, who had left the celebration early to engage in war games. Apparently the creatures loved to fight, lived for it in fact, and wouldn't waste an ounce of time that could be spent sparring on a party. Titus and Selena leaned against the railing and watched the beautiful beasts, silently talking and sharing a few smooches here and there. The night air was getting cool, but she had her cape and hood and Titus's arms around her to keep her warm.

"I think this might have been one of the best nights of my life," Selena said as they watched the running Centaurs.

"Really?"

Selena nodded. "Mm-hm. I used to think that the highlight of my life would be high school graduation. The day after, I planned to empty my bank account, throw all my stuff in the back of whatever car I could afford, and put as much distance between Twin Oaks and myself as possible." She laughed. "I think I've gone about as far as I could get."

Titus kissed the top of her head and squeezed her in a hug. "And now? Are your expectations any higher?"

"Oh yeah. I mean, nowhere in my world is fruit as sweet as it is here." Selena stole a glance up at Titus and grinned. "The boys are cuter, too."

He laughed, tweaking her nose before kissing her full on the mouth. Seizing a moment she'd been waiting for all day, Selena turned into his body, wrapping her arms around his neck and savoring the flavor of Titus and red wine. It was the best thing she'd ever tasted.

"Gods, I love you so much," Titus whispered, resting his forehead against hers, his breath coming in ragged gasps. "You leave me breathless."

Selena closed her eyes and inhaled his woodsy scent. "You're pretty breathtaking yourself."

Titus's hands gripped her waist, his fingers circling the bare skin over her ribs. Selena quivered as he traced the three-chained belt around her waist and the diamond resting in her belly button. She brought her hands up to his chest, finding bare skin at the open gap at the top of his tunic, running her fingers over his smooth, broad chest. A growl sounded low in Titus' throat as he bent down to kiss her shoulder.

"Selena, I want …" He trailed off, his hands tightening on her sides.

Selena stroked a lock of hair back from his forehead. "I know. Me, too."

"Not here," he said with a smile. "As much as I'd like to put a little sparkle on the best night of your life, I think we should wait. I want a wedding for you, Selena. I want you to have everything a princess should have on her special day. I want our wedding night to be our first time. I'm willing to wait."

Selena sighed. As much as she'd like to lose her virginity to the guy she was practically engaged to—for God's sakes, they could hear each other's thoughts—she knew that he was right. After all, she'd waited almost eighteen years for her first kiss. Oh wait, it had been eighteen years, as of today. She was officially an adult … at least, in the world of men. She had a feeling things worked differently here.

"I didn't forget," Titus said, jerking her out of her wandering thoughts.

"I never even told you today was my eighteenth birthday," Selena said, slack-jawed.

Titus tapped his temple with his index finger. "Hello!"

They laughed together and Selena punched his shoulder playfully. "Well, did you get me anything?"

Titus grinned. "As a matter of fact, I did bring you something. My mother gave it to me when we met in Goldun. When I told her that I was in love and had found my mate, she gave it to me as a gift for you."

Titus reached into his shirt and came out with a necklace—a strand of leather holding what looked like a wolf's tooth.

"It's one of my puppy teeth," Titus said, holding it up between them. The long canine gleamed pearly white in the moonlight. "In my land, a wolf gives a baby tooth to his future mate as a token. The first time I laid eyes on you, I knew that you were the only one I'd ever give it to."

Selena bent her head and allowed Titus to slip the necklace over her head. Tears filled her eyes as she clutched the wolf's tooth tightly. Just that morning her mother had given her a beautiful tiara, and her brother a set of solid gold-handled knives. Her father had given her a chest full of jewelry. All of those gifts were dazzling in their beauty, but none of them could outshine this.

Selena smiled. "I'll never take it off."

"I guess we should make this official then," he said. "I believe in your world, it's customary for the male to kneel."

Selena couldn't move or speak as Titus knelt down in front of her. She hadn't imagined this moment happening for her until she was much older. But who had time to waste with an evil queen lurking nearby with plans of mayhem and destruction? Selena might never get another chance to have the guy she was crazy about ask her to marry him.

"Selena McKinley of Twin Oaks, Texas, will you honor me by becoming my mate?"

Selena smiled down at Titus and nodded. "Yes."

He stood and wrapped her in another tight hug, lifting her feet straight off the ground.

"I'm so happy I could fly," he said once he'd put her down.

Selena scowled. "Don't talk to me about flying, please, it'll only make me mad."

Titus chuckled. "Still having a hard time of it?"

"Unbelievable. I have done everything Thaddeus and my dad told me to do. I just can't do it!"

Titus grabbed her waist and turned her toward the balcony's rail. "Of course you can," he said, gently nudging her toward the edge. "Step up."

Selena shot Titus a puzzled look. "Are you nuts?"

Titus shrugged. "For you. Seriously, get up there, I won't let you fall."

Selena decided to trust Titus and stepped slowly up onto the railing. Titus came up onto the thick ledge behind her, his body glued to hers, his legs spread wide and his feet positioned on the outside of hers. His arms were strong, tight around her waist.

"Keep your eyes open," he said, his lips close to her ear. "You have to look at the horizon, at the desert beyond. I am sure your father and brother are good teachers, and I am obviously not able to fly, but I do know one thing."

"What's that?"

"You are afraid."

"Well, duh."

Titus laughed, his chest vibrating against her back. "You are afraid and relying on the fact that someone will catch you to keep you from taking flight. You have to embrace flight, lean into the wind and let it take you. You control the wind, so stop fighting it. Wrap it around yourself and go."

Selena focused on the horizon, that tiny strip where earth met sky, and spread her arms. The wind was gentle, pulling at her billowy pants and cape, beckoning to her. Selena slid her eyes closed and inhaled, blocking out everything except for Titus and the atmosphere. Warmth infused her and 'the tingle' worked its way through her body. Selena felt herself leaning forward and, surprisingly, her muscles did not clench in fear as they had every other time she leaped from that ledge.

When she opened her eyes, the ground was speeding by beneath her, the sand dunes feet below, and the open sky at her fingertips. Selena gasped and looked behind her, realizing that the palace was growing smaller and smaller in the distance. Titus' form on the balcony ledge was tiny, but his cheers and whoops were loud, carrying out over the desert and trailing behind her in echoes. Selena laughed and spread her arms out, swooping down toward the Centaurs she spotted running across the sand. Their hindquarters gleamed in the moonlight, their tails swishing and their powerful hooves moving swiftly, carrying them over the sand in a spectacular cloud of kicked-up dust. They lifted their swords and spears and cheered as she swooped low, landing in their midst as they came to a stop.

In the distance, she could see Titus' white fur streaking across the desert toward her. The Centaurs surrounded her and she recognized Tinutai and Dargha at the forefront. The female Centaur smiled, extending her hand to Selena's for a handshake.

"Congratulations, Princess. It is an honor to witness your very first flight," Dargha said.

"How did you know it was my first flight?"

Tinutai smiled. "The laughing and cheering coming from the castle clued us in."

"It was pretty epic."

"You've made quite a transformation," Dargha said as Titus approached, quickly donning the pants he'd been carrying in his teeth. He came up beside Selena just as Dargha said, "There's just one thing missing, though."

"What?" Selena asked.

"In Damu," Tinutai said, "it is customary that every accomplishment be commemorated with a tattoo."

Selena's eyes nearly bugged out of her head as she saw the many markings lining the Centaurs' bodies. She gulped noisily and Titus grabbed her arm.

"You don't have to if you don't want to," he said. "It's going to hurt."

Dargha lifted one eyebrow in silent challenge and Tinutai waited silently while Selena eyed the other Centaurs and thought of her father and brother. They were lined with the tattoos, their arms, their chests, their stomachs … each one told a story of a coming of age, an accomplishment. By Selena's count, she needed at least three in order to catch up. She'd learned to harness wind, gotten engaged, and now she had flown for the first time. She squared her shoulders and met Dargha's arched eyebrow head on. She had always planned on getting a tat when she left home. Now was the perfect opportunity.

"Let's do this."

⸙

THE NEXT MORNING, her family sat around the long dining table, their faces grim as they ate silently. The Grimm Brothers were there, along with Titus and Rothatin. The other soldiers were dining in the barracks within the palace's compound and would all gather later that day in the massive war room. Selena had been told she would be required to say something and the prospect left her feeling wrung dry. If anything, she was more nervous about this than she was fighting. Added to that was the tension of everyone's silence.

Selena traced her fingertip over the reddish brown tattoo on the back of her hand. Dargha had done three in a row, starting from the back of her hand and going up over her wrist. The tiny red dots began at her middle finger and went over her knuckle before the first symbol, the Damunian sign that meant 'keeper of the wind' was scrawled onto the back of her hand. With a beautiful scrolling pattern in between, the next two symbols read 'flight' and 'love'. She traced the 'love' symbol right on the back of her wrist and smiled. It had hurt at the time, but didn't anymore and Selena was pleased with the result.

After a while, though, she grew bored at looking at the back of her hand. No one had talked in over twenty minutes and it was driving Selena batty. She wanted Thaddeus's jokes back, Eldalwen's war stories, and Axonia's scolding when he took the bloody details too far. Selena set her fork back onto her plate and fingered the wolf's tooth. It dangled against her chest right next to the Damu ruby, its weight like a heavy stone. Selena had had enough of secrets and silence.

"Titus and I are getting married," she announced, loud enough for everyone to hear.

If anything the silence became more pronounced. The scrape of utensil against plate stopped, as did the sounds of chewing and slurping. Every eye turned toward hers, every expression a mixture of shock, happiness and, in Rothatin's case, annoyance. Selena could tell the Fae still didn't trust Titus, but ignored him. Titus didn't have to prove anything to anybody, and Rothatin was of no relation to her, so it didn't matter. She knew Queen Adrah would be thrilled.

"I'm sorry," she said quickly to Titus. "I know you wanted to wait until after tomorrow to talk about it, but it was just too damn quiet in here and I don't like keeping secrets. I wanted my parents to know, and my brother. I hope you're not mad at me."

Titus's lips softened into a smile and he grasped her hand where it rested on the table. "Of course not."

Eldalwen cleared his throat. "I suppose congratulations are in order. Although, I would have much preferred it if the young fur ball and I had had an opportunity to speak on the matter man to man."

Selena rolled her eyes. "Well, I've already accepted his proposal. I love him, he loves me, and we're getting married. Besides, we're talking about it right now."

Thaddeus rolled his eyes. "Oh, here we go. Quit while you're ahead, Father," he mumbled under his breath.

"Yes, my daughter, but this is not how things are usually done here. You are royalty. These sorts of arrangements shouldn't be taken lightly."

"No one is taking anything lightly," Selena said, squaring her shoulders and clinging to Titus' hand. "The decision has been made, and seeing as how we are both consenting adults—very young adults, but still—I don't see how we need anyone else's opinion in the matter."

"Yes, but—"

"Furthermore," Selena said, her tone sharp, "anyone that has a problem with my fiancé can take it up with me. I would be more than happy to set them straight."

Thaddeus guffawed, trying to hide it behind a bout of coughing as Eldalwen's face turned red. Axonia smiled behind her hand and Jake and Wil Grimm leaned forward silently, seemingly enthralled by the little drama unfolding at the table. Rothatin shook his head, probably in disbelief over her stubbornness.

"Spoken like a true princess," Axonia finally said. She stood and circled the table until she stood directly behind Selena and Titus. She placed a hand on each of their shoulders and squeezed affec-tionately. "I think this is a splendid match. After all, the young Were-wolf played a large part in keeping our daughter safe on her journey. It is obvious that the connection is strong here and, Eldalwen, you and I both know that no Werewolf male is going to let go of his mate once he's found her." Axonia turned her megawatt smile onto them both. "Congratulations. I can't wait until this ugly business of tonight and tomorrow is over so I can throw you a magnificent wedding." Her eyes widened and she clapped her hands together with a gasp. "Oh, there is so much to do! I must begin choosing fabrics for your wedding dress. Oh, and I have to plan a menu ..."

Eyebrows shot up and chuckles rang out as Axonia turned away from the table, mumbling distractedly as she rang for a servant.

Thaddeus nodded at Selena and grinned. "Well done, sis. Very good of you, holding your ground like that and all. Good luck to you both."

"Yes," said Wil with another one of his belly-vibrating laughs. "Let us have a toast to the future Alpha female of the Awcan wolf pack, and this joyous union."

At Selena's wide-eyed expression, Titus laughed. "Don't worry, you won't start sprouting fur," he joked. "Marrying me simply means that one day you will rule by my side as the leader of the Awcan pack. As the Alpha male's son, I will be required to take his place when he dies."

Selena's eyebrows shot up. "Cool. So, I'll be princess of the Centaurs and the Werewolves. I like it."

"Not exactly."

"Hey, let me envision this, don't ruin it for me!"

They shared another laugh as the servants came to take their empty plates away. Once everyone had gone, Eldalwen stood.

"Do not mistake my words earlier by thinking that I am not happy for you both. I am. I will be thrilled to have that talk with you this afternoon, Titus."

Titus nodded, his face suddenly serious. "Of course."

"And now, Selena, you must rest. The next two days will be arduous on you and I want you hale and ready."

"Um, question?"

"Yes, daughter?"

"Why the next *two* days. I thought the Red Dawn isn't until tomorrow."

Jake snorted from his place at the table. "Think, girl. Do you honestly believe Eranna will be so foolish as to wait until tomorrow to attack, when your people will be at their strongest?"

Selena felt a vice-like grip tightening around her throat. It had been different when she thought danger was only a day away. She'd been happy to think she could spend this last day with Titus, with her family, without a care in the world. Things just got serious.

"You mean ..." Selena tried to swallow but barely managed it. "You mean, she could attack today?"

"There is no doubt," Rothatin said, coming to stand beside her father, "my queen has already seen it in the Eye of Goldun. Eranna will attack tonight, when the darkness gives her minions their full power."

"Then what good is this?" Selena asked. "Why all the training and the preparation if she is going to come slaughter us all before the actual Day of the Red Dawn?"

A smile parted her father's lips, gleaming like the cold steel that blazed in his eyes. He laughed. "My dear, Eranna had just better hope that she makes it to sunrise. That's when things will get really interesting."

❧

ACROSS THE WHITE grounds of the wintery land of Mollac, not a soul stirred. Even the wind was still there, as if joining with the rest of the landscape in holding its breath for the coming battle. Within the iron fortress of Queen Eranna, however, the noise was deafening. Eranna's minions chanted as they went about their work, gathering the weapons that they would use against their enemies. Iron swords and knives were sharpened and silver melted down into bullets. Eranna's army would be more than prepared for the Fae and Were shifters. Her possessed wolves waited restlessly in the courtyard, and shifters of other kinds gathered. Eranna especially loved the beautiful white fox shifters and their snowy owl counterparts. They were the crowned jewel in her army, the most beautiful yet lethal fighters she possessed. The Minotaurs sharpened their horns and the Witches and Sorcerers saddled their polar bears in preparation for the day-long trek across Mollac toward Damu. At the place where snow met sand, the battle would commence.

Eranna looked down upon all of this from her tower, wrapped in a raven black dress made of suede, a bustier of shining black leather cinching her tiny waist in. Over this she donned her silver armor and helmet, sheathing an iron sword at her side and taking her enchanted staff in hand. With a satisfied nod at her appearance, she turned toward the unmoving figure of High King Endroth, who sat staring off into space where she'd left him. Eranna laughed, the sound a throaty purr, as she approached the once mighty king.

Gifted with power by her Witches and Sorcerers, Eranna had found it easy to compel King Endroth and place him under her spell. His pain at losing both his wife and daughter had weakened him, and even though he had spurned her offers of marriage, Eranna enjoyed keeping him as her plaything. She ran a hand through his long, graying hair, tugging on his beard with a giggle.

"Look, dear Endroth, my army is nearly ready to march upon Damu. Aren't they splendid? Even the Witches and Sorcerers with their hideousness are of great use to me."

Endroth stared silently ahead, the black pupils of his eyes blotting out the irises. Eranna took her staff and pressed the rounded end of it into his chest. The tip began to glow and vibrate, causing Endroth to groan and writhe in pain. Eranna twisted the scepter, bearing it into his chest with all of her strength in anger.

"You see, Endroth, you have brought all of this on with your stubbornness," she hissed, jabbing him in the chest a second time. "If you had only listened to me when I tried to convince you of the best way to deal with the human trash, I wouldn't have had to go to such lengths to ensure my place in this kingdom. You joined with that insipid Faerie and ruined everything! You could have been my lover and I your High Queen. Together, our kingdom would have spanned two worlds, and all would be as it should."

Eranna pulled the staff away, deciding not to waste anymore of her magic on this useless man. She straightened and closed her glowing red eyes until they had returned to their normal color. After a few deep breaths, she opened them again. King Endroth was slumped over, his hand gripping his burned chest. He was otherwise motionless. Eranna used her power over him to lift his chin until he was meeting her gaze.

"All will be set right very soon. It all begins tonight, Endroth. This time, you and that Faerie will not be in a position to stop me."

Chapter Seventeen

The army leaving Damu's city walls behind was solemn and silent. With Eldalwen and Rothatin leading the way, they marched toward the edge of Damu. Already the air was becoming cooler the closer they got to Mollac. Selena was glad for her cape and hood, mainly because everyone else was wearing red or carrying the red and gold banners of Damu, keeping her from sticking out like a sore thumb. She had a feeling Eranna would be gunning for her, and while the thought made her nervous, Selena felt the warmth of her father and brother on either side of her, as well as Titus behind her. His blue eyes gleamed in the waning sunset, his body a mass of rippling, powerful muscle beneath stark white fur. The other shifters he had brought dotted the crowd, all in their wolf forms. Their fur dotted the sand in shades of black, brown, white, and red, creating a beautiful array of variety.

The Centaurs brought up the left side, their quivers full of arrows and their swords sharpened. Selena realized that Dargha had added a few new tattoos across her stomach. She smiled as she realized that the symbols read 'Red Dawn'. She had to remember to get Dargha to inscribe the same thing on her. The Fae and Elves brought up the left, the Fae decked out in silver armor from head to toe—protection from the enemy's iron weapons, Rothatin had told her. Bringing up the middle, mixed in among the shifters, were the wind-harnessing Damunians, their red dress and waving banners sported proudly.

Her focus snapped back to the borderline of Mollac and Damu. The white snow stretched on for miles in front of them, giving way to jagged purple mountains with white snowcaps and towering green pine trees. Selena's hands began to shake and she stilled them, trying to think of other things so she wouldn't get overtaken by nerves.

The speech she'd given in the war room had gone far better than she'd expected. Selena thought back to the words she'd spoken so honestly to Damu's army and used the words to comfort herself.

"People of Damu, I am told I must give a speech today and, I'll be honest, I'm not sure exactly what I am supposed to say to you. I don't think it would be very wise for me to stand here today and tell you not to be afraid, when I am more frightened of this than I have ever been of anything in my life. Yes, I am afraid! But someone very close to me once told me that being brave does not mean a person doesn't feel fear. Courage is a man or woman's ability to lean into that fear, to embrace it and draw strength from it. Someone I love taught me that very recently, and it gave me what I needed to learn to fly. Do I know how today is going to turn out? Absolutely not. I am told that my being here makes the differ-ence, that it will bring the Red Dawn in the morning and our power will be magnified a hundred times more than what it is now. But, you know something? The Red Dawn does not just need me to appear, it needs you as well. You have believed, you have waited for my return, you have kept your faith and been patiently waiting for this day. And now, I am asking you to stand with me, to hold on until the morning when the sun splits the sky with a red glow. I am telling you that I cannot do this without you. Will you stand with me?"

The cheers and chants had been deafening and Selena had collapsed onto her throne—which had been brought into the war room for the occasion—releasing the breath she'd been holding the entire time. She clutched Titus' wolf tooth tight and closed her eyes, wondering where the words had come from, when her nerves had melted away and a confident woman had emerged. Titus voice had invaded her mind, smooth as silk.

I always knew you had that in you.

Selena lifted her chin now and marched alongside her fiancé, her brother, and her father, new confidence gripping her insides and expanding in her chest. Her fingers tightened on the staff in her hand and her jaw clenched in determination. She was doing this for Titus, for her future in-laws, and for Rose and Zoe. For Adrah, Dargha, and Tinutai, for Rothatin and the beautiful Pixies, the Elves and war-torn Werewolf shifters. She held their faces up in her memory, not losing sight of one for a single moment so that she couldn't lose her nerve.

And then, the enemy appeared on the horizon, approaching them from the other side of the border where sand met snow. As they got closer, Selena could make out Eranna's army. On the backs of saddled polar bears and in chariots pulled by the same beasts, were some of the ugliest creatures Selena had ever seen. They had to be the Witches and Sorcerers she'd heard so much about. Their hooded robes in shades of blue, gray, and black barely concealed twisted, grotesque faces and gnarled limbs. They looked more like walking trees than anything else. They carried curved, iron weapons and heavy burlap satchels hung from their waists.

The Witches and Sorcerers carry explosives, Titus spoke into her mind as they came to rest on the edge of Damu, their feet planted firmly in the sand. *They are much like the grenades carried by human soldiers in your world, but they are filled with enchanted potions. Be sure to watch out for those; they could turn you into dust on contact.*

Magic grenades … dust … got it.

Inwardly, Selena trembled. The shivers were made worse by the chill coming from Mollac and the sight of Minotaurs bringing up the left. Their horns were sharpened to deadly points and so were their long-handled axes. Selena found Ruen at the front, his eyes glowing red, his golden rings shining brightly in his nostrils.

Bringing up the right side were what appeared to be humans. Clothed in deerskin and fur, their angular features and slanted, narrowed eyes reminded her of the red foxes that used to frolic and play in the woods back home.

That's because they are Fox Shifters, Titus said, his ears twitching as he turned his head to scan the approaching army. *Don't let their beauty fool you, they are twice the size of foxes in your world and they are deadly and cunning, incredibly fast in whatever form they decide to take.*

Selena could see the deadly glint in their dark eyes and decided to take Titus' word as truth.

Bringing up the forefront were Eranna's possessed Werewolves, their glowing red eyes a match for the Minotaurs. Selena recognized Orwen instantly. The Awcan Alpha was flanked by at least two hundred other wolves.

Tell your army to leave the wolves to us, Titus said to her, his voice quavering with anger in her mind.

Selena knew he hated to see his father this way, wrapped in Eranna's tentacles like he had been not so long ago. Selena patted his head affectionately and turned to her father.

"Titus asks that the other shifters be left to him and his wolves," she said.

Eldalwen nodded before turning to bellow the message out to the army. Word rippled along the crowd like wildfire until everyone had been made aware of this rule.

"Titus says thank you."

Eldalwen turned and looked the massive wolf in the eye. "You're welcome, son. We will give you what time you need to break the enchantment over your kinsmen. By the time the Red Dawn approaches, if they are still on the wrong side, we will obliterate them."

Selena looked down to Titus and then back to her father. "He says, 'so be it'."

Selena knew Adrah had given him a charm blessed by Fae magic. It would rid the shifters of their possession just she had done for Titus. Depending on how long it took him to get close enough to use it, he would not have much time to convince his father and the others to switch sides. Selena hoped that at least Orwen would listen. She didn't think Titus would ever be the same if he had to kill his own father on the battlefield.

Silence fell over them as the enemy army came to a standstill, facing them on the other side of the border. Humongous, white snow owls circled overhead, barking sounds coming from their mouths as they swooped by. One owl, the largest, carried Eranna. Her black gown fluttered around her, and her matching hair flew behind her head like a banner from beneath her silver helmet. Her glowing red eyes surveyed the battlefield below.

"Coward," Selena hissed.

"Eranna will not get her hands dirty unless she has to," Thaddeus said from her other side. "In the meantime, watch your head. Those owls like to drop stones."

Selena fought the urge to cover her head as one of the owls screeched and dipped; she held on tighter to her staff. Her father took a step forward and raised his sword.

Within the silence, a low roar pulsated in Selena's ears and she realized that it was the sound of her own racing heart. She saw her father's mouth open and knew that a roar had escaped his lips, but she did not hear it or the resounding, answering call that came from the army around her.

"Charge!"

That word was clear, though, and Selena had no choice but to raise her staff and move. Forcing her legs into motion, Selena sprinted alongside her father toward the enemy, who had kicked it into high gear as well. The last thing Selena remembered clearly before the chaos hit, was a gust of wind working its way up her arm.

ALL AROUND TITUS, metal crunched against metal. The bark of

ALICIA MICHAELS

foxes mingled with the growls of wolves. The roars of the Minotaurs mingled with the battle cries of Centaurs and Damunians.
Gusts of wind whipped snow and sand up into sprays of grit and
damp ice that coated his fur. The screech of owls overhead mingled
with the explosive pop and flashes of bright light that accompanied
the Witches' bombs.

Titus dodged the third bomb to fall near him, leaping away in
time to avoid the white flash. Two Elves locked in battle with a Fox
shifter were not so lucky. All three disintegrated into black dust that
was carried away on the wind. Titus barred his teeth with a growl
and lunged at the Sorcerer who had thrown the bomb, tackling the
ugly creature to the ground and tearing his throat out with a single
snap of his jaws. He flung the body aside and pounced onto a
Minotaur who was already fighting off two of his pack mates. With
Titus' help, they brought the massive beast down, horns first, to the
ground.

Titus stood back and searched the sea of fighting bodies, looking
for his father in the fray. The wolves were mixed together, only
distinguishable by the eyes. Titus barked and howled the signal to
his wolves, commanding them to fall into the formation they had
practiced and drive the enemy wolves toward the center of the
battle. His companions obeyed, turning on their possessed enemies
and strategically fighting them back into the center of the battle.
Titus leaped forward to meet his father, who was coming at him
with exposed teeth and a throaty growl. Titus avoided his father's
snapping jaw, protecting his throat as he threw his body at Orwen's,
watching as his white, furry body went skidding across the snow.
Titus didn't even bother to counterattack, realizing that his wolves
were now in a tight circle around the red-eyed ones.

Titus swiftly shifted to his human form and grasped the talisman
blessed by Adrah. He closed his eyes and swiftly chanted the words
given to him by the Fae queen to pull on the charm's power. It
exploded out from his chest in a flash of light, striking the red glow
from the eye of every wolf trapped within his circle. His father

shifted, falling to his knees in the snow, his dark hair glistening in the light of the high, full moon. Without a stitch of clothing on, Titus was freezing. Instinct had him wanting to shift, to protect himself with a layer of white fur, but he was not done yet. Forcing himself to ignore the cold, Titus held his arms up and took a step toward the wolves trapped within his circle.

"Listen to me!" he bellowed, noticing the confusion that crossed his father's face. "You have just been released from the evil queen's possession. You have been turned against your brothers and sons for the good of a kingdom that is sure to fall. Come back to us! Come back to your packs, to your homes, to your mates. We need you to win this fight! We need to stand together against the tyranny of Eranna before she turns our beloved Mollac into a cold wasteland ruled with an iron fist! If you are not for us, then you are against us and we will be forced to kill you."

Some of the wolves howled in acknowledgement, others barked angrily. Orwen stood and faced his son, his hands fisted at his side.

"My son. You are alive."

Titus nodded. "I'm sorry, Father. I thought that working for Eranna would save you, buy me some time. She promised your freedom."

"The dark queen is a liar and an arrogant fiend."

Titus nodded. "Yes. I knew you would never go to her of your own free will."

"When you did not return, I offered my service to Eranna for your mother and sister's freedom. I never would have done it had I known she was turning our people against each other."

Orwen turned to the wolves behind him and added his voice to Titus's. "My friends, we have made a very serious mistake! We have allowed the evil of Eranna to overtake our lands and rip apart our packs. Where we once turned tail and ran, now we must fight! I know that I was one of those in favor of running, and it has taken the courage of my son to show me the error of my ways. The time for running is over!"

"You're right," said another voice as a black and gray wolf shifted into the form of the Joison pack leader, Almred. His silver hair and matching gunmetal eyes combined with dark skin to create a striking appearance. He squared his shoulders and faced Orwen with a scowl. "It is not time to run, it is time for self-preservation. Going against Eranna is suicide. The members of the Joison pack went to her gladly to offer our service. If this means that we must fight against our kind to ensure our pack's survival, then so be it."

"Coward!" Titus spat, crossing to join his father in standing against Almred. "You would allow Eranna to make you her bitch, while killing your sons and brothers?"

Almred bared his canines and growled, saliva dripping from the corners of each one menacingly.

"Watch it, puppy. I could rip your throat out in a second."

"You and your pack have chosen your side," Orwen said, placing a beefy shoulder in front of Titus to block him from Almred. "And we have chosen ours."

With his voice raised, Orwen turned to the other wolves. "Let every man who wishes to be free of Eranna's tyranny join with his brothers in battle. Let all others who stand against us be condemned to death."

In an instant, all three men had shifted back to wolf form, taking their places on their chosen sides. Titus was thrilled to see more wolves coming to their side, abandoning Almred, his pack, and very few others who had chosen the side of evil. Titus braced himself, waiting for his father's signal. Chills rolled up his spine as Orwen's howl rang out over the battlefield. He and the other wolves joined in, springing into a run, teeth bared, their courage soaring as they flashed their sharp teeth at the enemy.

SELENA WAS EXHAUSTED. They moon had been high for hours and the morning had to be near, but it didn't feel that way just now.

She lifted the scepter and pulled on another gust of wind to propel a Minotaur and his sharp axe away from her. She sent the beast crashing into three others, leaving them to the bows and arrows of the Centaurs.

The Centaurs were beautiful in battle, the most magnificent thing Selena had ever seen. They ran together as one, in groups of four and in five, in perfect formation, shooting their arrows with precision and speed. The Fae and the Elves fought together valiantly, the Faeries careful to avoid the iron weapons of the enemy. Selena whipped her staff over her head and swung it like baseball bat, catching a Witch in the middle with it before bringing the rounded end down onto the hag's head. With another swing, she deflected one of the Sorcerer's deadly grenades, sending it flying into the ranks of the white Fox shifters. The explosion took ten of them out at once, disintegrating them into ash on contact.

Selena fought for breath and wiped at the sweat on her forehead. She was rapidly running out of steam. Sunrise couldn't come fast enough for her.

"Well, what do we have here?" The deep, gravelly voice was familiar and Selena turned to find Ruen standing behind her, his axe gripped between his meaty fingers. "I see someone taught you how to fight."

"I see you're still as ugly as sin," Selena taunted with false confidence. "Some things change, others don't."

Ruen growled, his wide nostrils flaring. "I should have killed you when I had the chance. No one will stop me now."

Selena jammed her staff into the snow and left it there. She reached for the two curved knives at her side, her birthday gifts from Thaddeus. Hoping to remember everything he'd taught her about fighting a large opponent with the knives, Selena raised the weapons to meet Ruen's first blow in the air. The larger weapon made Ruen clumsy, allowing him only one swing of his axe for every three or four swipes of Selena's knife. His strength was greater than hers, though, and Selena had to use every ounce of her speed and agility to avoid the crushing blows of his weapon

She ducked to avoid the sweep of his horns as he charged at her, then used the wind to lift her from the ground and over Ruen's bulky body. As he turned to swipe at her with his axe again, Selena pulled her staff from the ground and swung it, deflecting the blow that nearly decapitated her. She followed it up with a blow to Ruen's midsection and one to the head. As Ruen stumbled backward, Selena ran toward him, using the staff like a pole vault to launch toward him, landing a solid kick to the top of his head. With a roar, Ruen went down to his knees, still reaching for Selena with his large hands.

Selena avoided his grasp and grabbed her knives, moving at lightning speed toward the Minotaur. The two blades disappeared into his chest all the way to the hilt and Ruen threw his head back with a roar of agony. Selena planted a kick in his chest, throwing the beast to his back, before jumping onto his torso to retrieve her knives. The red glow faded slowly from the beast's eyes as Selena pulled her blades free. She turned away from the gruesome sight and cleaned her blades in the snow. Selena could hear Eranna's enraged cry from above and she looked up to where the evil queen circled overhead on her owl. She kicked Ruen's corpse and glared up at Eranna.

"You wanna come down here and do something about it, bitch?"

"Do not tempt her," Eldalwen said as he appeared by her side, his sword coated in the black blood of the Minotaurs and the blue gore of the Witches' and Sorcerers' innards. "How are you holding up?"

Selena caught one of the flying witch-bombs in midair before it could land, hurtling it back at the Witch who had thrown it before using a gust of wind to propel him away from her soldiers.

"I'm exhausted," she admitted, swinging her scepter to club a white Fox flying right at her face. "How much longer until the Dawn?"

Eldalwen glanced up at the sky, which had just begun to lighten from midnight to royal blue. "Minutes," he promised. "Just hold on."

Selena nodded and turned back to back with Eldalwen as he had taught her, fighting against the Minotaurs, Werewolves, and Foxes. She dodged the occasional falling rock from the owls above and made sure to avoid their sharp talons; she had seen them swoop down and carry handfuls of Elves and Fae up into the air before dropping their bodies to the cold, hard ground below. She shuddered at the thought of ending life that way.

A blow from a falling rock finally clipped her and caught her off balance, knocking her to the ground. The back of her head struck the cold, snowy ground, sending pain radiating out from her head to other parts of her body. The ringing in her ears drowned out the sounds of her father's concerned voice as he crouched over her, shouting her name and waving his hand in front of her face.

Selena closed her eyes and then opened them, shaking her head to try to clear it of the dizzy sensation that was gripping her. She was reminded of a time she'd sat down in the cellar with her grandmother during one of the worst tornadoes to ever hit Twin Oaks. Just the sound of all that swirling, howling wind had made Selena dizzy. She'd clapped her hands over her ears to block it out, but it had been too powerful. Thankfully, their house had survived, but many others hadn't. It had taken months to rebuild many of the stores and homes that had gone down in the face of the monstrous twister.

Selena flew upright, a wide smile on her face as inspiration struck. She didn't know where the memory had come from, but it had given her the answer to ending this thing once and for all.

"We need a twister!" she shouted to Eldalwen, whose face instantly crinkled in confusion at Selena's declaration.

"I think you've sustained a very serious head injury," he said, helping her to stand.

Selena shook her head. "No, I'm fine."

Really, her head hurt like hell, but she could ignore it.

"I just figured out how we're going to win this thing."

Eldalwen grinned. "Spoken like a true warrior. I'm all ears, daughter."

"Back home we have these big storms called twisters. Long story short, they happen when cold air fights against hot air, creating a funnel of storm clouds that can spin at up to one hundred miles per hour. They'll tear up anything in their path."

Eldalwen's eyes widened and so did his smile. "Yes!" he cried, clapping his hands together. "My daughter is both strong and smart! We stand on the line between Damu and Mollac, with cold winds shifting on one side and hot on the other."

Selena nodded. "Exactly. When the Red Dawn begins, we can take this thing to the air. Fly up and amass all of our power into a twister. Half of us on one side, half on the other. Once that funnel cloud hits the ground, it'll do all the work for us."

"A display of power," Thaddeus said as he grabbed a Minotaur by the horns and slammed it down to the ground. "I like it."

Selena nodded. "All we have to do is hold on until the Red Dawn."

~

TITUS WAS FADING RAPIDLY and he knew it. Holding up the fight throughout the night had been easier said than done. Open scratch wounds from the Foxes lined his ribs and the bite mark of another wolf had taken a chunk out of his thigh. He knew the Fae could heal him when this was all over, but at this point was beginning to doubt he would survive long enough.

As he looked up to find Selena fighting back to back with King Eldalwen, a burst of energy rushed through him. He had to survive, for her. Breaking of a bond as strong as theirs would crush her. Titus would never intentionally do that, so he had no choice but to keep fighting. Hope flared in his chest as he joined his father against three of the enemy wolves. The sky was now light blue, lined with orange and pink along the horizon. A tiny blot of red began to rise against the sand dunes, bringing shouts and cheers from the Damunian army.

Eranna's shrieks of anger could be heard from above. "The Red Dawn approaches!" she bellowed to her flying owls. "Kill her! Kill her now before it's too late!"

Rage exploded through Titus as he wished that he could fly as easily as Selena. He would have ripped the ice queen's heart from her chest hours ago. In a flurry of movement, the white Foxes turned away from fighting the Werewolves and converged onto Selena all at once. The Centaurs picked them off with their bows and arrows one by one, and Selena and Eldalwen whipped the rest away with a burst of wind. Titus took down a Minotaur before it could reach her, and Orwen ripped one of the massive owls right out of the sky as it swooped down toward the princess. Titus turned away as his father tore the owl to shreds in a spray of blood and feathers. The sun continued rising steadily, and the war cry of the Damunians became 'protect the Princess'. They had no chance without her. The sun was almost up … just a few more minutes.

Pain ripped through him as a Witch leaped onto his back, digging her gnarled fingers into his open hip wound. Titus kicked her off and tackled her, avoiding her sharp claws as he went for her throat. By the time he climbed from off of the dead Witch, the sky had come alive with a red glow. All eyes turned toward the horizon as a massive ball of red flame rose into the sky. Even the cheers of the Damunians went silent as the tip of Selena's scepter began to glow. A white light poured from her eyes and a golden shimmer surrounded her, kissing her skin and flaming hair. Titus watched, enthralled, convinced that she had never looked more beautiful as she slowly rose and levitated several feet above the ground. A gust of hot air blew through the crowd, bringing with it the surge of power that the Damunians had been waiting for.

Each and every pair of eyes went white and they all stretched their arms out and ascended to join Selena in the sky. Wordlessly, they careened upward, their figures growing smaller and smaller as they ascended toward the clouds. Anticipation struck him, and even though Titus had no idea what they were about to do, he knew it would be something spectacular. He had heard enough about the previous Red Dawns to know that these events were always awe-inspiring.

The battle commenced below, with Eranna's bellowed commands to her army ringing out overhead. The owls tried to reach Selena, but the other Damunians kept them from her, striking them from the sky with their wind-harnessing weapons and knives. The floating Damunians spread out over the battlefield, half of them moving over to the side of the enemy.

Then, they began to circle each other.

Titus could hear the howling of the wind as they flew in circles, picking up speed and harnessing their wind into a funnel. The clouds above answered with thunder and rain, darkening the sky rapidly as lightning flashed. The wind whipped over them power-fully, and it took everything within him to keep his feet on the ground. The clouds began to fold into the wind, creating a circular formation with thunder and lightning crashing inside. Rain poured from the sky, drenching them all. The cloud began to funnel down-ward, bringing with it more wind and more rain.

"Get back!" Eldalwen bellowed from his height and Titus helped spread the word through the other wolves as the Centaurs, Elves, and Faeries fell back from the battle lines. The enemy, mistaking this for a retreat, cheered and taunted the running army, heedless of the funneled cloud slowly descending upon them. The Damunians dropped to the ground once again, their bright, white eyes turned up to the sky as the cloud continued to drop. The ground shook once it touched down and Selena raised her scepter in unison with the others who lifted their wind-harnessing instruments. A gale of forceful wind propelled the twisting mass of thunder cloud toward the enemy.

"Retreat!" came the cry from Eranna overhead as the storm ripped through her army. The cloud funnel pounded the ground, ripping up snow and chunks of earth, as well as Foxes, Minotaurs, Witches, and owls. Those who were not swept up into the storm ran, mounting their polar bears or the swooping birds. Many took off running on foot, only to be chased down by the swirling storm.

The eyes of the Damunians faded back to their normal colors and the shimmering glow surrounding Selena burned out. The sun cried out in a sonic blast, swiftly obliterating the red color from the sky and squashing the uncontrolled storm in the blink of an eye.

Cheers went up from the crowd as the wind quieted and the swirling sand and snow settled back to the ground. The shifters all went back to their human forms, hastily donning the clothing provided by the Elves from carts stationed at the edge of the battle-field. The Healer Fae were already moving about among the wounded, tending to those who had been hurt. After Titus pulled on a pair of leather pants, one of the Healers swiftly saw to his injuries. Breathing a sigh of relief as the wounds on his hips and ribs closed up, he accepted a drink of water from the Faerie's wineskin grate-fully before donning a tunic, vest, and boots. Then he went in search of Selena.

He found her hoisted onto the shoulders of her people, a bright smile on her face. Her hair was windblown around her face, which was streaked with grime, but Titus was looking into heaven. Her brown eyes twinkled as she found him in the crowd and reached out to him.

"Titus!" she screamed, motioning for the men to put her back on her feet. They did, reluctantly, and the crowd parted to allow her through. She ran to him, throwing her arms around his neck and her legs around his waist. Titus laughed and held on, fighting to keep his balance as she mashed her lips against his.

"We did it!" she cried, tears mingling with laughter. "We won!"

Titus smiled and set her on her feet. "Yes, we did, my princess. Damu's peace has been restored for now."

She kissed him again, gripping the lapels of his vest in her fists.

"Now what?" he asked after she'd left him breathless. The celebration continued around them but Titus heard none of it with Selena in his arms.

Her smile was bright as she laughed. "Haven't you ever read a fairytale, Titus?" she asked with a giggle. "Don't you know how they always end?"

Titus caught Jake Grimm's eye as he walked past, a double-barreled rifle over his shoulder. He winked at Titus.

"And they lived happily ever after," the Grimm brother said with a smile, disappearing back into the crowd.

Epilogue

Yes, my friend, that is how we won the battle on the Day of the Red Dawn. I have watched these events through the Eye of Goldun and could not be more pleased. Our Selena has certainly come into her own, hasn't she? I am sure you'd like to know all about the wedding ceremony. Yes, I attended, and it was a beautiful night. Queen Axonia did a splendid job planning it, and was gracious enough to allow Selena to choose the location; the sweet, little Pixie glen just outside of Osbel tower. Selena and Titus married beneath the Pixie tree, sharing their first kiss as man and wife in a cloud of golden fairy dust and dancing Sprites. The Brothers Grimm returned to the world of men with their ship to invite Rose and Zoe to the ceremony. The two of them spent two days here in comfort and luxury, with tears in their eyes as we prepared Selena for her day. I sent them back reluctantly, with promises of allowing them to return soon. It is not safe for them to be here too long. While the battle of the Red Dawn was a victory, we still have a long way to go on our journey toward peace.

I'm sure you'd like to know that Selena's gown was made from the most delicate of Goldun's white and silver lace and her hair was worn in loose waves, dotted with fresh white blossoms. Titus' tooth never left her neck.

And so, my friend, if you are ever in Mollac or Goldun, and you happen to see a blur of red and a wisp of white fur, know that you are in the presence of Princess Eladria and her chosen prince, the future rulers of the Awcan wolf pack. Young Titus has proven his strength, and I am confident that he will lead them well with Selena at his side.

Oh, there is a knock at the door. It is Wilhelm Grimm, how delightful! I am excited about the latest development. One of the lost princesses of Mollac has been found. Yes, my friend, I speak of Eranna's own daughter. Of all the lost princesses, besides the daughter of King Endroth, this girl might be the most at risk. I fear for her, but am also confident in her ability to speak to the earth. It should prove to be an interesting fulfillment of prophecy.

But, that is another story altogether.

Child of the Sacred Earth

THE LOST KINGDOM OF FALLADA BOOK 2

Now Available!

Get a degree, get a job, save adorable foster siblings from the clutches of the evil foster mom ... These are Jocylene Sanders' top priorities as she enters her sophomore year of college. The last thing she expects is to find herself the champion of an entire kingdom. However, that is just what happens when the mysterious Faerie, Rothatin Longspear, appears to her, tasking her with saving a parallel world full of creatures from her wildest dreams.

Jocylene journeys with him into the world of Fallada, hoping for answers about her birth parents and background. What she finds is a mystifying past, and an even more uncertain future, as her heart becomes entangled with the stoic, battle-hardened Rothatin, as well as Eli, the untroubled Panther Shifter with no loyalties and no home. With her heart and soul pulled in so many directions, can Jocylene find the strength needed to become the savior one nation so desperately needs?

The Lost Kingdom of Fallada Series

IN READING ORDER

Fallada's Faerie Tales (A Prequel Novella)
Beyond the Iron Gate (A Prequel Novella)

Book 1: Daughter of the Red Dawn
Book 2: Child of the Sacred Earth
Book 3: Rise of the Tide
Book 4: Tempest's Fury
Book 5: Flight of the Phoenix
Book 6: Dragonheart

Book 7, Dreamwalker, is coming soon!

About the Author

Ever since she first read books like *Chronicles of Narnia* or *Goosebumps*, Alicia has been a lover of mind-bending fiction. Wherever imagination takes her, she is more than happy to call that place her home. With several Fantasy and Science Fiction titles under her belt, Alicia strives to write multicultural characters and stories that touch the heart.

The mother of three and wife to an Army sergeant, she loves chocolate, coffee, and of course good books. When not writing, you can usually find her with her nose in a book, shopping for shoes and fabulous jewelry, or spending time with her loving family.

Made in the USA
Coppell, TX
09 July 2022

79759255R00142